HUNGER HILL

To Emma,
who does what she "really
wants to do" and whom
I love dearly
Jim Ohmann

HUNGER HILL

Lisa Ammerman

iUniverse, Inc.
New York Lincoln Shanghai

Hunger Hill

iUniverse, Inc.

For information address:
iUniverse, Inc.
2021 Pine Lake Road, Suite 100
Lincoln, NE 68512
www.iuniverse.com

This book is a work of fiction. Names, characters and places are products of the author's imagination. Any resemblance to actual persons is entirely coincidental.

Cover picture by Julia Turk: 'Page of Wands' (*Navigators Tarot of the Mystic Sea*); design by Terry Henderson.

ISBN: 0-595-29881-8

Printed in the United States of America

For Terry

There is guidance for each of us,
and by lowly listening we shall hear the right words.

—Ralph Waldo Emerson

Contents

❀

Prologue: The Cab 1

Chapter 1   The Train 3

Chapter 2   The Arrival 10

Chapter 3   The Meeting 17

Chapter 4   The Ride 32

Chapter 5   The Voice 41

Chapter 6   The River. 53

Chapter 7   The Idea 63

Chapter 8   The Beach and the Farm 74

Chapter 9   Hunger Hill. 86

Chapter 10   The Rival. 104

Chapter 11   The Airport. 111

Chapter 12   The Chase 127

Chapter 13   The Silence 146

Chapter 14   The Build-up 151

Chapter 15   The Awakening. 156

Chapter 16   The Reunion. 163

Chapter 17   The Church. 173

Chapter 18   The Reckoning 183

Chapter 19   The Smuggle. 192

Chapter 20   The Pie Contest 202

Chapter 21   The Code. 211

Chapter 22   The Return 216
Epilogue: The Dream 221

Prologue

The Cab

As the fool thinks, so the bell clinks.

Or so they say. The trouble is, you can't fool yourself all the time.

I'm reminded of this whenever I get in a cab and tell the driver where I want to go, which is usually a pub called *The Swan*. The driver either chuckles or smirks to himself before he inevitably asks, "So, then, where are you from?"

My first response is impatience. I frown, then sigh. This question is always forthcoming and has nothing to do with my destination.

"Lichfield," I reply, trying even harder to disguise the American accent.

"No, no, what I mean is, where in the USA? Or is it Canada?"

"Southern California."

He'll be looking at me through his rear view mirror. Not that my appearance would give it away: a middle-aged brunette, with pale, sun-starved skin, wrapped in a crinkly black raincoat. Nothing unusual underneath. Your typical Marks and Spencer soft-ribbed gray marl jumper, with loose black trousers and black leather boots. Any fool in Britain knows black is forever in fashion.

I always sit up at this point, and lean closer to the driver so he hears me loud and clear. "I'm from Rhode Island, Wisconsin, Virginia and Florida as well as Southern California—to be precise. But I've lived *here* for the past ten years."

"Thought so." The driver always ignores this latter local distinction and is quick to latch on to the former. "You being American, that is. Never traveled as far as California myself, but—"

At this point I drift off into my own thoughts while the driver inevitably wonders (out loud) why on earth I ever gave up the palm trees and celebrities for Britain—and the Midlands to boot.

"—Though me and the wife went to Florida, once, in 95, with the kids to see Disneyland—"

Meanwhile, I'm wondering for the hundredth time why I haven't picked up the slightest hint of a British accent. Perhaps I should fake it.

"—So—what brought you here?"

"Sorry?"

"Why England?"

"Oh." I turn my attention back to the driver. "You mean—for the past ten years?" I remind him. But I can't help but wonder it's really been ten. Could I be lying? Though in my heart I've been here—true—for at least as long as that.

"Yeah, why Lichfield?"

"Guess."

The cabby shrugs. "Business?"

"No. That only leaves one other thing."

"Pleasure?"

"You got it," I reply.

"Pleasure," the driver repeats. And every cab driver I've ever met—male, female, white, black, brown, old or young—is struck speechless at the thought.

At which point I pay my fare, mumble a thanks, and fail to remind us both how the bell clinks, and the cost of pleasure is high.

The meter turns over: the driver fumbles for change and I'm tossing my life like a coin, as high as a decade. I watch it fall to here and now and the flip side isn't heads. 'It's tails, mate,' I'd like to say but I never do. 'It's an equal amount of pain.'

CHAPTER 1

The Train

The first time I came to Lichfield was back in 1979. It was late September, I'd just turned twenty-one, and the trip was my grandma's idea. I suppose my grandmother considered the trip purely business, in an obligatory "visit the relatives" sense, but for me the prospect was all pleasure.

To this day, I can remember it perfectly. Starting with the train. For some reason the train was the beginning, and from that point every detail, every sensation, sits inside my mind as fresh and vivid as the moment when it all began.

Something strange was bound to happen. The signs were obvious. And it didn't start on the plane, or at Heathrow Airport. I know that because I can't recall a thing about the flight, or how I got to the place where everything just stayed like this, perpetually crystal clear. Believe me—I've got a muddled, worn-out brain, fairly common for someone my age, and most of my youth is a blur. But get my mind back to the train and presto: out from a baffling pocket in time pops a glossy, well-focused picture.

It's strange I can remember it so well, and I knew—even at the time—that something strange was about to happen, because although I'd traveled a lot before, I'd never experienced such a twirling cloud of butterflies in my stomach; a tingling hot prickle in my skin. My heart kept pounding faster and faster as if it might burst.

We were pulling out of Platform 4, Victoria Station.

It started slowly: clack-clack…clack-clack…clack-clack…like a disgruntled beast tethered to a rusty, cumbersome harness, groaning and rattling.

We inched past the platform, gradually gaining momentum: clk-clk, clk-clk, clk-clk-clk-clk while my heart pumped even faster, racing to keep pace with the engine. I'd better calm down, I kept thinking, take a deep breath, get a hold of myself...

Clik-clik, clk-clk, clk-clk well past the station and full speed ahead, I was positively giddy. Taking a few deep breaths—inhaling the damp, dusty air—made me smile even more. An incongruous mixture of codger-and-chanel wafted through the carriage. Even the elbow smudges on the battered walls, the sticky coffee stains on the floor, the burnt pinholes on the faded velvet cushions pleased me.

Still smiling like crazy, I stared out the window in a fixation of catching and absorbing every detail flashing past: red brick houses, blackened chimneys bunched in tight narrow rows, moss-speckled stone, patches of green lawn, pink rose bushes, white panties on clothes-lines, smoking dustbins, red toy buses, miniature sized trucks, enormous baby carriages; a stream of bouncing umbrellas, dark dreary clothes, inexpressive faces. Crowds crossing the streets and parading the shops—disappearing into buildings which looked more to me like the protracted slits of a row of dominoes.

This was England: my first impressions taken through the streaming, soot-spattered window of an English train, heading west through London. In the rain.

Clack-clack, click-click, row after row, the same view repeating. Straining my eyes to take it all in—mesmerized—aware of the British people quite close to me inside the carriage: nameless, half-asleep, bored, reading, vacantly gazing at the neutral space in front of them.

The other passengers, Jesus, they all looked so calm...while I...on the jittery brink of euphoria, had to cling to the edge of my seat, grinning ear-to-ear like a real dipstick hoping if I held my breath it just might keep my heartbeat from careening right off the tracks.

During all this (*all this* being too much for me to absorb) there was no talking, only a few composed coughs as the train swept out of the city; plowed through fields and country. Not a word past landscapes of green: deep rich, lush green, neatly mapped out in borders of hedge and stone, dotted with sheep, sprinkled with cows; no litter, billboards, or ugly debris in sight. Not a speck of modern rubbish—not until the momentum slowed again and the long brick wall of another station rolled past.

I stared at everything. I mean everything, including the graffiti of objects trimming the approaching platforms; purple Cadbury wrappers, greasy fish-

and-chips paper, news pages plastered in bold ink headlines, unfamiliar brands of cigarette packs…then a jolt, grinding to a halt, bang-bang-bang slamming doors of the train, passengers rushing aboard and clack-clack, clack-clack, off it carried me again.

By the time we'd reached the outer suburbs of Oxford, I was thinking: funny, really. Why did everything outside look so strange? Then it hit me—the brick. Everything seemed to be made of brick.

Yet how lovely and perfect, brick! Perhaps it was crazy, but that was the feeling. All because—bam—sitting on that train I'd come alive again; struck by that rare affliction some people call the 'joy of life.' True: the signs were obvious. I couldn't stop smiling, I didn't really believe I deserved it—but suddenly there I was, in England, and every fibre of my being was grinning ecstatically.

I had to thank something. Whatever it was that made it possible…*thank-you God, thank-you God, thank-you God*…chanting to myself in rhythm with the train, not daring to look at the pale, prim British faces around me. Faces reeking of indifference or maybe even disdain. I wanted to look, but I know I shouldn't stare.

Then I imagined myself in *their* shoes, facing the obnoxious open gaze of a tourist, an outwardly timid, brown-haired girl. And look at her: slouched like a rag doll in a knobbly knit sweater (granny's favorite popcorn weave), the color much too bright. What would you call it, a vivid violet? Add that chewing gum, faded denim jeans, a tatty green knapsack in place of a purse, and she's got to be an American. Tut tut. Taking the liberty of dissecting our every intimate detail. Oh my. How impolite.

'But I'm different!' I wanted to protest.

Yet what difference would it make, that my grandfather was born and bred English? Regardless, I was not one of them.

So I stared discreetly. Out of the corners of my eyes.

Across the seat: a brown tweed suit, a beige trenchcoat draped and folded over a rigid pair of knees, a mahogany-handled umbrella and matching briefcase wedged tight between two legs and well anchored by a set of buffed leather loafers.

Moving upwards: a ginger-red moustache chiseled like a pencil, a thin-and-grim set mouth, busy brows well furrowed, puffy lids for eyes, right arm adjusting a pipe in the left shirt pocket.

Across the aisle: a pair of black stiletto pumps, sleek ivory stockings, tailored black suit not a spec of lint, starched poly pink collar. Soft milk-white face, glossy pink lipstick, dash of rouge—half obscured behind a paperback.

So neat; so tidy; so British. And then quite suddenly, all that grandeur of propriety was shattered.

BRRRUUUUT! Jesus!

A fart, a really loud one, and who else but my own grandmother?

"What's that?" Harriet exclaimed, her voice sounding, as it always did, as loud as a newly fired cannon. Having just nodded off, she looked around in confusion.

I stared back in disbelief. I wasn't sure what was worse, the fart or her amplified voice. Though she, of course, was not about to admit the bottom honk might have been her own.

"Are you watching for our station?" she shouted. (Honestly, she bellowed whenever she spoke and God forbid if she ever got hard of hearing.)

In the rather bizarre, hushed atmosphere that followed, I couldn't help but feel amazed at the thunderous power (both ends!) generated by such a petite, eighty-year-old woman. Changing the subject didn't help. Heads turned, ears cocked in our direction.

"Yes, I'm watching," I finally managed to whisper back, hoping (against all odds) my grandma would take the cue.

"Well it can't be much longer, and it's a good thing too because I'm just about ready to collapse!" she bellowed. And just in case she hadn't made quite enough noise, out came her handkerchief, followed by one of those infamous Henshaw nose blows.

Jesus!

In the nick of time, the high-pitched whine of wheels grinding to a halt intervened: passengers leapt up and swayed against the doors, as if eager to get away from us.

"Where are we?" barked Grandma. "Does the sign say Lichfield?"

I shook my head. "No, the last station was Banbury. I'm afraid we've got a way to go yet."

She settled down and said nothing more as the train moved on again, leaving the nearest seats empty. Within a few minutes the rocking had soothed her back to sleep.

The sun set. It was getting dark. I couldn't really see much out the window.

Restless and using the pretext of stretching my legs, I ventured out of my seat. I hadn't gone very far; in fact I was standing in an open space at the end of the third carriage when I encountered a young man about my age, a can of beer in his hand.

"Would you like one?" he asked.

"Beer?"

"This one's bitter, actually. Though I do have some lager and stout too, in my bag over there."

"Okay. Thanks. I guess I am pretty thirsty."

"Which will it be?"

"Just a beer, any beer."

His expression changed as soon as I opened my mouth. A bigger grin and more hopeful, perhaps. He raised his hand to smooth a wayward strand of slicked back hair, and then—motioning for me to wait—turned to retrieve another can.

"Here you are, one lukewarm Worthington's finest bitter. Is it true, that Americans prefer their beer ice cold?"

He popped the can before handing it over.

"Sorry, I'm assuming you're American, and Canadians hate being—"

"I'm American," I replied rather curtly, hoping to discourage him. Not that I'd ever been asked this sort of question before. In fact it was quite nice, being in a strange land where my accent stood out, and having someone start a conversation because of it. But something about his self-satisfied grin put me off.

He certainly wasn't a dashing prince set to whisk me away to a twelve-turret castle in Camelot.

"I'm Nigel."

I was thinking that maybe he wasn't so bad looking either, with jet-black hair and skin as soft and spotless as a baby's. But the weird thing was, he wore a proper suit. A double-breasted jacket, white shirt, decent tie. Such armour at his age—in my view—was a gallant climb up the social ladder.

Ignoring my abrupt snip, Nigel winked and leaned even closer. "American. So. Where are you from?"

I raised the can to my lips and took a good swig before answering. "I never know how to reply to that question," I muttered.

"It's just a simple question."

"Is it? I could say Newport, Rhode Island because I was born there. But I left Newport when I was three."

"Fair enough. Where did you grow up then?"

"Several different places in several different states." I sighed, and offered a weak smile. "I suppose on average I lived in California more than anywhere else."

"Ah...so you're a California Girl!"

"No I'm not," I retorted.

Inevitable, what was coming next. Yet I'd always liked that Beach Boys song; suddenly now on the train I hated it. Shaking my head, I edged further away from him.

Nigel simply waved his can at me, and started humming the tune.

"I don't have a tan, I don't have bleached blonde hair, and I don't wear bikinis or sandals," I cut in.

He stopped. Then, after a short pause, proved equally proficient at improvising: *"and the nowhere girls, with their long brown hair…and the bell-bottom jeans…they all do wear…"* which floated down the isle and ruined any possibility of true camaraderie between us.

I stood there scowling. I just couldn't help it. But the young squire of Worthington's was far from bitter. He wasn't about to give up so easily.

"East Coast, West Coast, Southern, who gives a stuff. Wherever you come from, you're a lovely lass," he drooled. After a brief pause.

"My dad's a captain in the Navy," I quickly changed the subject, trying not to blush. "Which is why our family moved so often. My two brothers were all born in different states—Wisconsin, Virginia and Florida."

"Are they here with you?"

"No. But my grandmother is…we're on our way to Lichfield, to visit her—and my—relatives."

"Ahhh…" With his hands carefully smoothing his slicked-back hair, Nigel seemed sufficiently deterred—or at least momentarily lost for words. "Well, a pleasure meeting you, and good luck."

"Same to you," I said, feeling guilty for being so rude. No matter, for he was already retreating back to his seat, and for the first time that day I was truly relieved to be traveling with my half-senile grandmother. Farts and all.

Obediently returning back to my charge, I found her oblivious and snoring as before; wrinkled cheeks twitching as she dreamed, safe and sound just where I'd left her. Fine and good! For there wouldn't have been this trip to England—not without my Grandma Harriet. Unfortunately, age eighty-one, she had certain habits which made the long journey from Boston to Lichfield a challenge—but at least we'd managed so far. From plane to bus to train, I was only just beginning to realise just how muddled and boisterous she could get, over just about anything.

Yet despite all this, or perhaps because of it, the excitement kept mounting. I was getting to know my grandma again, after all these years. Eight years to be exact—while Harriet (who refused to budge from Boston) watched the rest of the family roam around the country like farm migrants, or to be more precise—a pack of Navy brats. Not until 1975 did Harriet finally relent and fly to California for a visit. By then I was in the middle of exams and couldn't leave college.

So why she had chosen me, of all people, to accompany her to England—I hadn't the faintest idea. Whether it was fate, or luck, or simply the passage of time that brought us closer together, I certainly appreciated the opportunity. And I was keen to make up for the years I hadn't given her much more than a second thought.

Exhausted from all the staring, I closed my eyes. Though I couldn't sleep. Not when I knew Harriet's outbursts, the re-awakened excitement, the September rain, the train and bricks and British faces were only the beginning. We'd just passed Birmingham and Lichfield beckoned: the heart of England; the West Midlands; the home of Harriet's husband's family. What would these British relatives be like?

But I already knew I'd remember my journey to Lichfield for years to come. A particular smell. An umbrella with a mahogany handle. A lad called Nigel. Even a can of bitter. And all because of a feeling; a strange sense that something momentous was about to happen. How could I describe it? A kind of clumsy, whimsical motion, making my heart race with anticipation.

Clack-clack, click-click, click-click…Wheels rumbling over rails, moving closer and closer into the spell of a mystery.

Because when you're a girl and you're just twenty-one, there's no final destination. There's no stopping. It's all around, in extremes. If up to now I had learned nothing else, at least I had learned that.

CHAPTER 2

The Arrival

"Is this it? Can you read the signs?" Grandma suddenly yelled in alarm, arms waving frantically at her purse and coat.

I opened my eyes and nodded.

Extremes. Is that how it worked? I wondered. Is it all extremes when you're young and then again when you're old? I knew all the symptoms and I knew what my dad would say, too. He'd be shaking his head and muttering: "Lauren, what's the big deal? Calm down. Stop it. Why do you have to be so serious, so intense all the time?"

Which was why, I was thinking now, my encounter with Nigel and any future prospects here or anywhere else were simply doomed to fail. Even in High School, I scared all the boys away. That's how my dad put it, and he was probably right. I never did manage to keep a boyfriend for very long. They all dumped me, like a hot potato, using the same old lame excuse. "I just don't think this is going to work," or, "You're a really nice girl, but—" It was like that, this "but" kept cropping up and my dad was the only one who ever had the guts to finish the sentence.

In college I tried to smarten up and take his advice. Yet no matter how flippant and superficial I played the game, the college boys sensed it underneath (whatever 'it' was), the minute they got close. Being too serious and intense was proving hard to disguise. Then again, maybe I never really tried to hide it. Maybe for a while, I secretly believed that sometime, somewhere—there wouldn't be a "but."

But I was wrong.

So eventually I woke up. I accepted the reality of romance to be a very brief and fleeting phase in the greater scheme of things. True romance, I decided, was basically deluded stuff, and the wonder and magic and passion of love is something you make up. You make it up, in your head, to keep life interesting.

Even in England, on the train, with my eyes open and head resting against the cool, hard glass of the windowpane—I was already convinced.

And neither my dad, nor anyone else, had to remind me.

"Hey! Is this it?" shouted Grandma.

Jolted out of my reverie, I realized the train was indeed preparing to stop.

"Is this it?" she repeated, tugging my arm. "Lichfield City Station? Oh! Grab our luggage, these trains don't wait around, you know!"

In a panic, Harriet ignored my nod and tugged the arm of the nearest person. "Is this the Lichfield Station?"

The nearest person, a gray-whiskered man holding a rolled-up newspaper, released his arm. "It is," he affirmed, politely.

Despite an awkward struggle and a completely useless fight against blushing, I managed to endure the scene. I did this by gingerly stepping off the train and heaving—in one gigantic stroke—three suitcases out the door and thus out of everyone's way. (A feat instantly undermined by Grandma, who, with a moaning wail, threw herself on top of the pile and collapsed. Me thinking: Go on, people, pause and look. Some of them did, using my corners-of-the-eyes trick.)

The air was damp, smelling of grease and wet leaves; the platform hushed and lonely, once the echoing parade of clicks and clops vanished down a cement stairwell.

All we had to do now was wait for someone to fetch us. At precisely five-thirty in the afternoon, according to my watch, we'd arrived on time. And the rain had stopped.

I looked up, distracted by the intricate wooden arches—painted a viridian green—supporting the station roof. The sight was enough to send a shiver down my spine: as if in another life, I might have stood here before, waiting, pacing. A real Victorian lady, skirts sweeping the pavement and brushing the spiralled posts as I moved between the glorious arching curves.

Suddenly I could see myself as this other me, a perfect picture of confidence and grace, adjusting my feathered bonnet with gloved hands; wearing a velvet burgundy gown with ribbons of green satin.

I looked down, admired my own cleavage—snuggled inside a bodice trimmed in delicate lace—the corset pulled so tight at the waist it cradled my breasts like a hammock. How easy it was—right here—to slip back in time. A mere change of clothes and whom did I meet but a creature called dear Lady Lauren, draped in the finest cloth, tailored to hug and enhance every noble, sensuous curve.

It might have been two, or twenty minutes later, when I was forced back to reality by the sudden appearance of a man and woman who emerged from the station lobby. The pair pointed to our stationary pile of luggage. They smiled and waved, though they looked a bit worried too.

The couple were probably around my parents' age, in their mid forties; the man with white hair and a reddish beard, short in stature, eyes squinting and jolly like a leprechaun. He wore jeans and a heavy pair of work boots. His wife, slightly taller and rounder, had short dark hair (probably a tomboy in younger days) and stern, practical eyes. She wore an olive green nylon padded vest-warmer and brown trousers, flat rubbery shoes, no make-up. Her eyes weren't jolly, but they weren't unfriendly either: merely scrutinizing behind a pair of glasses.

"We made it!" Grandma exclaimed, throwing up her arms and scrambling out from the pile of suitcases.

"Sorry we're late, the car park was full," the leprechaun muttered, already loading himself up with half of the luggage. His wife swept up the remaining bags in similar swift, efficient motion.

I glanced at my watch. Indeed. They were a whole four minutes late.

"This is my grand-daughter Lauren," Harriet (now breathless) explained, forgetting to finish the introduction.

But I already knew their names. And being the tag-along youngster, I said nothing. No one seemed to mind. We were ushered into a tiny white car; all suitcases miraculously disappeared inside the trunk. Or rather the boot, as they called it.

The leprechaun was Chester Henshaw—my grandfather's nephew. His wife was Elizabeth. Technically, this meant they were my first cousins once removed. Chester was driving us straight to his parents' house—where we were to stay. Harriet told me to call Chester's mother 'Aunt Bea' and his father, 'Uncle Henry', since he was my grandfather's brother. Very confusing.

None of this family tree business had ever mattered to me before. My grandfather, who'd left England when he was sixteen, hardly ever spoke about his British past, or his relatives. Sixty years later Grandma (a blue-blood Puritan from Massachusetts) suddenly decided it was time to visit, before she died too. A kind of reconciliation, one would suppose.

Luckily, fresh out of college, I was free to provide a helping hand. I'd instantly accepted the all expenses paid offer—though I hadn't anticipated the drawbacks: the fussing, the confusion, the panic attacks, and the elderly limitations. But there was another side too, and that was worth it.

Sitting in the car, the narrow streets of Lichfield raced past in the post-rain evening mist. As the jetlag finally gave way to drooping eyelids, the details merged into a jumbled mass of more brick upon brick, running neighborhood terraces in twos, stained-glass windows and cut-glass doors, lace net curtains, fancy stone driveways and pots of chrysanthemums adorning front walks.

Suddenly above us, the majestic spires of a Cathedral.

And everywhere, the smell of burning coal.

Aunt Bea opened the front door. Hands clutching her apron, hair half-falling out of a nylon net, black pump shoes—she reminded me of a housewife straight out of the thirties.

And she lived in a Georgian town house.

"Oh hello, come in, come in," she said. "Oh Harriet, I hope the train wasn't too awful for you, but you're here now, and this must be Lauren, come in, come in, Lauren—Chester, just put the luggage down in the hall. We must have some tea at once."

Ears still trying to decipher the strange sound of Aunt Bea's accent, I floated into the parlor, a small room with flowered curtains and matching wallpaper, a gas flame heater glowing in the fireplace. On a couch in front of this fire, with a woolen blanket tossed over his legs, sat Uncle Henry.

A bit odd, I was thinking, how Uncle Henry completely ignored us. He just sat there and stared, but not like I did. This was a vacant stare, at nothing. Or was he staring at something that looked like nothing ahead of him?

I wasn't sure. All I could really see was a frail skinny body with hollowed facial features vaguely reminiscent of my grandpa.

"Don't mind Henry," Aunt Bea whispered before I approached him, "It's his head, bless him, a softening of the brain. He can't help it, and can't speak or do things for himself any more, poor thing…nothing to be done."

Nothing to be done, I repeated to myself, as I savored my first English tea: a great clatter of china tea cups and saucers, silver spoons, sugar cubes and cream; a passing-round of carefully arranged assortments, all sandwiches and biscuits, built atop delicately flowered serving dishes.

Aunt Bea was a constant fusser. No guests of hers dare refuse a second helping. "Have more, have more, my dears." She fluttered, she flustered, she giggled, she warbled on and on, like a happy chickadee. Even I, with heart pounding and no real hunger for food, consumed what was left on the plates. I couldn't bear to disappoint Aunt Bea. It seemed such a crime to destroy the illusion that all Americans had appetites as big as Texan ranch hands.

Meanwhile, the conversation switched to the journey itself, which inevitably sounded rather pointless and boring. Really. Why did it matter—now? Luckily, with my mouth full, I wasn't obliged to answer. Grandma, on the other hand, was only too willing to comply.

"So the flight was on time?"

"They're *never* on time these days."

"But you had a good flight?"

"It was *terrible*. Too stuffy and hot. I forgot my *earplugs* and *two* babies didn't stop *screaming* for the first two hours!"

"Poor things. The altitude hurts their ears, you know."

"I *never* thought we'd *ever* get out of Heathrow. It's a long hike to customs, and *none* of my suitcases have wheels. I forgot how *these* days the terminals can be *three miles long*."

"Heathrow isn't too bad, though, is it?"

"Not like *Houston* or *Chicago*," boomed Grandma, her American accent putting emphasis on every other word which I suddenly noticed and found rather annoying. "You need a *golf cart* in *some* airports," she went on, "just to *get* to your *connections* on time."

"What do you think of Britain so far?"

"The train fare was *rather* expensive. I'm *sure* the bus driver *overcharged* us, too."

"It's a shame about the weather."

Grandma paused, giving our hosts the opportunity to steer her complaints in a weatherly direction. Bea and Chester obliged by debating the forecast, with no interruptions. I listened, fascinated by the odd-sounding British accent and the rapid, unbroken strain of half-murmured sentences. I had to really concentrate to catch what they were saying.

Eventually I gave up altogether, and focused my attention on Henry, who said nothing at all. Maybe his brain was soft, but his eyes looked as sharp as a hawk's. I don't know why but I felt this sudden urge to test him.

I'm sure nobody else noticed. I waited until I thought I'd caught Henry's gaze, or rather blank line of fire, bulls-eye. Then I stuck out my tongue.

His eyes narrowed. Just a fraction. Other than that, he remained oblivious. Sure, his mouth opened, but only for a few seconds to take a sip of tea. And only after Aunt Bea had raised his cup and pressed it firmly to his lips.

I felt pretty silly. And it wasn't long before I swallowed and noticed a lump in my throat. The lump grew even bigger when Aunt Bea, with the greatest loving care, took out her handkerchief and tenderly wiped the dribble from Henry's chin—even though she'd probably done it a million times.

Henry probably wasn't counting, nor from what I could see, did he give a damn about Aunt Bea. But something was going on. Why such beady eyes? Mind rigidly fixed—yes—but blindly hunting. Prey nonexistent. How sad. He had no purpose but he hardly looked defeated to me.

Of course I felt drawn towards the old man because we could have been mutual spies. Just the two of us. Wordless cohorts present at the scene, but observing from another world. Another realm.

At some point Chester and Elizabeth stood up to leave. This entailed a long-winded session of good-byes in the hall, which Grandma obviously considered quite unnecessary and therefore her prerogative to cut short.

"I'm *pooped*! That's it! I'm going *straight* to bed," she announced, grabbing Aunt Bea's arm and nudging both Chester and Elizabeth out the door.

"Good night,"

"Good night."

Without protest, I followed Grandma and we both staggered upstairs. No wonder—it was around one in the morning, our time. Bea had prepared separate rooms, so I kissed Grandma before disappearing into mine and crawled between starched white sheets, crisp and smelling of soap and mildew, in a box-shaped bedroom with one tiny window. Still in a dream, I listened for the faint rumbling, the last vestige of clack-clacking—from a distant train.

But all I could hear was the muffled swish of a few passing cars. Wheels splashing in the rain.

Road traffic: a sound which actually struck me as being very odd—coming as it did from midget-sized vehicles that drove to the left, ran on petrol and stored luggage in boots—hardly more than a few feet from the front door.

Even stranger, too: lying in a bed in the very city where my aloof, tight-lipped grandfather had grown up as a boy; sleeping under the same sky that rained on Shakespeare; listening to the water patter gently against a Georgian sill; relishing each impression which makes up a memorable time, perhaps with a growing sense of English pride.

And perhaps, too, I couldn't help mulling over the thought. Just a thought that maybe, after all, the magic isn't *always* something...

You make up.

CHAPTER 3

The Meeting

"Lauren, time to wake up!"

The morning began with the trill of a high-strung songbird—the voice of Aunt Bea.

I opened my eyes and waited. Would my warbling host let me sleep? No. And sure enough, after a brief tap of warning, the door opened and a tray with steaming teacup materialized—firmly suspended—in front of my nose. Quickly, I sat upright before it shot down on my lap.

"Do you like your milk scalded? I always heat my milk first, but it's a funny habit to most, they say use cold milk, never hot, oh fiddle-sticks, who says it ruins the taste?" chirped Aunt Bea. "I can't say I agree. Keeps the tea nice and hot, all right? If not, I'll bring you another one."

"No, this is fine," I mumbled, trying to sound more pleased at being awake. But Aunt Bea looked so delighted at having provided an American guest with tea in bed, I felt I had to sip it quite happily and smile back in return.

Convinced the strength of the brew was to my taste and just the right temperature, Aunt Bea disappeared. I decided I might even begin to like tea. And what did the English have for breakfast? Aunt Bea's melodic voice was singing away in the kitchen as she prepared it.

Another knock: this time Grandma's face (obstinate wrinkles set in a stern expression) poked around the door.

"And how do *you* feel this morning?"

"Wonderful, grandma!"

"Well, I'm *not* surprised—I see Bea's *already* spoiling you with tea in bed."

I was thinking how to compare the sound. My Aunt Bea's voice, definitely a chickadee, and Grandma's, more like a magpie…

"But Grandma, tell me, what does she mean by scalded milk?"

"It's milk heated until it's *just* about to boil. Didn't Bea explain? She likes her tea really *hot.*"

"Good grief," I replied, "I can't imagine going to all that trouble."

"Well," Grandma stated, with a hint of nostalgic pride, "When *Alfred* and I were *first* married, a *maid* used to bring us tea in bed! Though I'm sure the custom of scalded milk is just one of Bea's idiosyncrasies."

Half-smiling to herself over such memories, she slowly closed the door and left me to dress.

Squeezing into my favorite bell-bottom jeans and red long-sleeved body suit, I went to the little window and opened the frilly violet-flowered curtains. Aunt Bea's back garden extended, like a long green finger, straight down toward the brick wall of another house. Neatly cropped grass trimmed each side with a patchwork border of flowerbeds—all perfectly maintained.

I'd always assumed the postcards and travel brochures were misleading, but here was the proof. Floriculture was a mass religion. Bea's life-long piety had produced an amazing pattern of color and variety of bloom—including two rows of carefully pruned roses, stems drooping like grapevines under their own juicy weight. Ripened bunches of yellow, white and deep pink petals; tender bursting young hearts.

The gardens on either side of Bea's, divided by a short wooden fence, were just as perfect.

On my left, a boy who looked about six was trotting up and down his garden with a small bucket. He carefully searched, stopped, and picked up every stray leaf, twig, or flower petal he could find. He appeared very intent and dedicated to his task: well trained by his mother, no doubt, to remove every blemish from the lawn.

I couldn't believe it. I kept thinking, was that little boy the norm, or an aberration? I was still glued to the window when Grandma shouted through the door to come down for breakfast.

In the dining room, giggling and fussing, Aunt Bea waved me to a chair; threw an assortment of egg, mushroom, bacon, baked beans and sausage on the table; stuffed a clean napkin under Henry's collar.

The thought suddenly crossed my mind then: no, don't do it. Don't even mention the little boy.

"That's something I've never seen before," I exclaimed, fairly certain there'd be no offence in discussing the toast. A dozen slices, all evenly spaced, stood on end in a tidy row.

"Keeps the toast nice and crisp. Don't you have these at home?" answered Bea. Then "Henry, dear, mind your manners now we've got company," she said, adjusting his bib to catch a drop of egg yolk.

"A toast rack? No, I had no idea they even…"

"Now Henry, keep your mouth closed when you chew and try to say something won't you, dear, to your relatives come all the way from America!"

Bea, smiling sympathetically at me, turned to kiss her husband's cheek. She ignored his blank expression and wrapped her arms tight across his sagging shoulders.

Jesus, how many years had gone by, I wondered, with Henry 'softened?' And yet Bea still acted as if he was completely normal. She seemed so genuine about it, too. If the thought crossed my mind that love did exist—on rare occasions—I instantly passed it off as an old-fashioned notion stubbornly kept alive by old couples like Bea and Henry. Or was it simply a habit, grown effortless through repetition?

I wanted to know how she managed it. And why. It seemed quite pointless giving a virtual zombie such selfless devotion—even if he was your husband. Could I carry on like that? Without any kind of acknowledgement in return?

Yet another example, I was thinking, of using love to explain what we're making up in our heads to keep life interesting. Of course Bea still felt a connection with Henry. She had to—if not in body, at least in her mind's eye.

As for me, I had no excuse for sticking out my tongue.

"What shall we do now?" asked Aunt Bea, clearing the table after breakfast.

"*I'm* not moving an *inch* today," said Grandma.

"I don't blame you." Bea nevertheless marched to her desk and rummaged through a stack of papers. "But what about Lauren?"

"She can go out if she likes," Grandma admitted.

"It's only a ten minute's walk to the center of town," cooed Bea. A map plopped on the table. Aunt Bea winked.

"You can't get lost with this," she said, arms fluttering rapidly across the table to clear away the crumbs and make some space.

I unfolded the map. "I would like to take a stroll and check it out," I said.

"Fine. The rest of us can stay right here and catch up on the family, which would bore you to death anyway," exclaimed Bea. "Well good, that's settled."

"I guess so," muttered Grandma.

"You could stop at the Cathedral on the way," Bea suggested. "You can't miss it, and it's well worth a visit."

"Those beautiful pointed spires I saw last night, were they—?"

"Oh yes my dear, that's our Cathedral. There's only one, and no other Cathedral like it in England, I'm told, not one or two but three spires. We call them the Ladies of the Vale." She paused, then added, "That's v-a-l-e—vale."

"What's a vale?"

Both Bea and my grandmother laughed.

"You'll be wanting to know what a Green is next," Bea giggled. "Don't you have vales in your country? Gracious, and what about fells? Coppices? Dales? Heaths?"

"I know what a moor is," I said. "But only from reading *Wuthering Heights*."

She was an *English* major in college, you know," Grandma added.

"A vale is a valley," explained Bea.

"Oh. That makes sense. A dale isn't a dalley, though, is it?"

Bea didn't see the humor. "Dale is another word for valley. It's used more up north, in Yorkshire."

I wasn't too bothered one way or the other. All I wanted to do was get out there, and hopefully find the cause and cure of my creepy excitement: the niggling butterflies and tingling skin.

Following Bea's advice, I left the house wearing my quilted down jacket and carrying her spare umbrella. The overhead clouds, a moving bed of white fluffy pillows, could easily switch to a stormy blanket of grey. Or so I was told. So turning left on Beacon Street and ready for anything, I headed toward the spires.

This time I was free to walk as fast or as slow as I wished; no shrieks, shouts, flatulence or other such Henshaw assaults threatened to deflate my composure.

Though I still stood out. I knew that, with my overly long, mismanaged hair, jeans full of worn spots, shoes raised on rubber soles, and goose-feathers poking through my puffy jacket. Not that I had ever considered myself a sloppy, rebellious youth—or even a half-hearted hippy—but everyone else who walked past were dressed in jackets, ties, and suits. Boys, girls, men, women. The entire population, it seemed, were properly attired to social convention. All marching past, heads high, to the appropriate corporate or scholarly institution.

An exaggeration? Could be, but I felt completely out of context. And then, having reached the entrance to the Cathedral, I found myself bombarded by an army of high heels. Petrified, I stood aside and took cover; cowered behind the nearest post as the hurried barrage of clicking and clopping raced past and echoed up the steps. Next, a few anxious shouts followed by a few stragglers. And, much to my relief, I discovered these particular ladies had just been off-loaded from a departing coach.

Once the coast was clear I continued on, moving in the wake of the clicking stream, head thrown back, gawking up the blackened mosaic of carvings running over every inch of the Cathedral. High above me, under each successive vault, stood a line of ancient Kings. I suddenly felt awkward being alone, and followed close behind the handy native crowd.

Once inside, we all weaved through the vestibule.

I stopped to read some of the tourist blurb and detached myself from the group. Then, for the first time in my life, I faced my heritage—not just in print, but in marble and stone; no longer just a dream, or a piece of information gleaned from a book, or an image inside my head.

Inconceivable that I was standing inside this church, which stood on the same site for nearly 1300 years. I crept to a row of seats at the back and sat, as still and silent as the solemn pillars of sandstone—to absorb. To simply *be*. That's when it really came back, everything I'd felt on the train: pulsating, thick, teeming with emotion. Centuries of it, layer upon layer, and all for some purpose. As if to prove something.

At that moment, completely undisturbed, I could practically touch it: a hushed undercurrent, a kind of ghostly whispering inside a soundless space that's so dense, you have to strain your ears and calm your mind to notice it. Something strange and eerie floated all around me.

In this Cathedral. Over a thousand years. Men, women and children. All living and dying. A constant procession of flesh, pink and pulsating with life; a mounting departure of dust and rotting earth to support the whole charade.

But no apparent end.

Was that it? A feeling, a vibrating echo—running right through my bones. Of dead people praying, invisible choristers singing. A dizzy scramble of whispers, moans, laughs, looks, hopes, desires: you name it. Nothing and everything all mixed together. Alive and kicking.

Perhaps such things were all in my head, for my head kept trying to tell me so.

But in my heart, I was sure I could also hear the murmur of my own hungry soul—building up inside the carved stone walls, drifting amongst the damp semi-darkness, hovering above the altar, and finally reaching into the inner depths of my being in the hope of finding some semblance of a God.

No them and me, then and now. *Just this.*

Here, of all places. A feeling like I'd finally come home.

"Marge! Marge! Hey honey, wow, come take a look at this crypt!"

Jesus. Not now!

"Hey Marge, honey, I'm over here—"

It was bound to happen. A jolt, a halt, an end to the promise of heaven: a true reminder of home. That grating drawl was unmistakable. Another American.

I could hardly contain my disgust. But turning around to glare wouldn't make any difference. The guy would simply carry on gawking out loud and, besides, he'd already broken the spell.

Then I remembered Leo. I often thought about Leo, my last boyfriend—who I'd rather reluctantly left behind in Santa Barbara. My lank and stalwart Leo! Right now I wished he was by my side, saying "Hey Lauren, come look at this"—but in a softer, more soothing tone of voice. He'd wince and mutter "Honey, my ass" before telling the arrogant bastard to shut up.

Still. Leo was an atheist. And I, learning from him, had aborted my search for the Holy Grail—though I still took solace in ancient, improbable things. I liked to think of us both as reformed romantics. Never again too intense and extreme.

Marge found her husband, looked at the 'crypt' for a moment, and groaned out loud as even more wows and gollys swept past the crypt, then down the aisle, unceasing and unrelenting, all the way to the altar.

Though I could hardly hold it against them. What else could one actually say, to describe the breadth and depth of Lichfield Cathedral?

Leaving the spires behind, I walked through narrow, medieval lanes: the passers-by impatiently bumping my shoulders every time I stopped to study the map.

Bird, Dam, Bore. And this street…

Nudge, bump.

"Sorry."

Wade, Frog.

Nudge, bump.

"Sorry."

Breadmarket.

Whew.

I weaved to Breadbasket. Or was it Breadmarket? Better stop and check.

Brush, bump.

"Sorry."

"That's okay," I said. But I wasn't convinced any of the sorry's were very sorry. How come they all looked so annoyed? Was it a crime to stop abruptly on a sidewalk? Was it my fault they were tailgating?

At any rate, the street I wanted was Breadmarket. Aside from the lure of a probable bakery, a blue square marked out the definite birthplace of Samuel Johnson. So I turned left.

Museums weren't my thing but in this case I had to make an exception and go inside. Having just graduated with a B.A. in English, I knew darn well who Samuel Johnson was, and what he'd written, besides a dictionary. It seemed a sacrilege not to pay a visit.

And how easy—here—putting myself in the 1700s. Holding my breath I creaked slowly up the steep, polished wooden stairs. Prints, manuscripts, books. Warped ceiling beams. Candles. Ink-pots. Powdered wigs and port. Snuff. Pewter plates and heavy woolen waistcoats. The earthy smells of humble sweat and scrapings; of leather, wax and wood.

I was alone. The unexpected solitude made me turn, smile, and clear my throat.

I checked and turned again, as if the ghostly presence—this time—was actually me. Snooping around from yet another lost century gone by.

In the bookshop corner, I opened a pamphlet, and chuckled as I read my favorite Johnson quote: 'The whole endeavor of both parties during the time of courtship is to hinder themselves from being known.'

Once, when I'd recited this very quote to Leo, he'd inserted the word 'cun-thunt' in place of the word 'courtship,' and we both had a good laugh. Cun-thunting in place of courting. And why not? Though for better or worse, these days the wooing had only the fucking—not a marriage—in mind.

Lost in my thoughts, I flipped through a copy of *Rambler*.

"Can I help you find something?" asked a gray suited lady wearing pearls, who'd been surveying me from behind her desk.

"I'm not sure what I want to find," I replied. "Have you ever found anything that makes any sense—outside of books?"

No answer. Just a blink.

"Does anyone know who you really are, and even so, won't try to change you?"

"Sorry?" the lady quipped, after a pause.

"Forget it. Anyway, I don't read much any more. I'm just browsing, if that's permitted."

It wasn't normal, speaking my mind like that to a stranger, but in England I was finding the temptation hard to resist. Odd. And it wasn't coming across as very friendly.

I vowed to hold my tongue in future, and quickly left Dr. Johnson's shrine in search of food. Finding my bakery, I went inside and purchased two meat pastries, or rather pasties. Then, sitting on a bench along Minster Pool Walk, I devoured them.

The pool was wind-rippled, and the clouds dropped a sheen of gray over the surface, making it look like a restless vat of liquid aluminum. A few ducks quacked as they paddled beneath a willow. I brushed the flaky crumbs from my lap and watched the birds dip slowly out of sight. Samuel Johnson was still on my mind when an old man ambled along with a walking stick.

His hair was as white as chalk, tucked under a checkered wool cap. His long black coat might have been fashionable in its day. He looked confused, but that still didn't prevent him stopping—and pointing his stick at me.

"Hello, young lady. Would you awfully mind?"

"What?"

"I'm afraid you don't belong here."

"I don't?"

"Oh no. My dear, everyone in town knows I use this bench to sit on in the afternoons."

"It doesn't have your name on it."

The stick, still wavering in the air, began to tremble. Yet he continued to point. "Look behind you, and you'll see it says dedicated to Mrs. L. B. Lewis who spent many a happy hour here, nineteen fifty to nineteen seventy six."

"Oh." I looked. And he was right.

"I'm Mister L.B. Lewis, as it happens," he retorted.

"Excuse me," I replied. "I guess I better move then. I'm sure Mrs. Lewis would rather sit with you."

"Thank you," he answered, not seeming at all surprised by my remark.

"There's another bench down a bit further that's vacant." His eyes were moist with memories.

I nodded.

Leaving him to it, I marched over to the bit further bench and sat down, wiping the tears from my own eyes. Who knows why. If the people in Lichfield were still so civil and nostalgic…perhaps it was rubbing off.

Staring hard at the distant ducks, I felt guilty for even thinking the c-word. And talking like that to the lady in the museum. It was no excuse, reading hundreds of books and being an English Major. Although it explained, in part, my keen desire to accompany Harriet to England.

"No, you don't belong here either…you're a no-where girl," I mumbled to myself.

Although it wasn't completely true either, I thought, remembering the 'I'm not a California girl' remark I'd made to the young man on the train. In many ways I was a typical West Coast babe. To start, I felt like a fish out of water if I wasn't near the sea.

But Navy-brats were like that. So even when it came to choosing a college, I'd picked the University of Santa Barbara for its lovely beaches; perched on the point of ocean meeting land, gently sloping upwards to those beautiful half-barren hills stretching along the coast.

My major was English because I loved books, and reading more of them seemed to be an easy and pleasurable way to obtain a diploma. But what was I going to do now? What did all those books accomplish, except help me become even more of a hopeless, embittered ex-romantic?

The man with his stick stared straight ahead as he sat on his bench. If he had any inkling of his wife's presence he didn't show it.

I finished my second pastry and decided to call it a day.

Walking over the bridge, I must admit I was convinced already that some sort of life-saving encounter was hardly likely to happen. And yet that was what I'd sensed in the air—ready to strike—as soon as I'd set foot in England.

Well. Nothing quite like that had happened so far, aside from my pounding heart…and a sense of pilgrimage.

"Come to Lichfield," said the brochure, tucked away in my rucksack. I pulled it out and checked again. The message was perfectly clear.

> *Come to Lichfield.*
> *A beguiling mix of past and present.*
> *A hidden gem, deep in the heart of England.*
> *A haven for pilgrims.*

It made me want to laugh, this reference to pilgrims—as if they still might exist. And yet it seemed to explain what I was feeling. Either that, or once again the bell was clinking...and so the fool was thinking.

I couldn't really blame Litchfield, of course, for turning me into a pilgrim. Not at that point. For a long time afterwards I blamed Elizabeth and Chester for insisting we go round for dinner.

I wasn't happy about having to go there for dinner.

Grandma certainly didn't understand my reluctance. "It's only a simple meal," she said. "Why can't you manage *that?*"

"I'm just not that keen to be put on show," I answered.

"Oh, and what's so *hard* about *eating*?" she grumbled. "Come on, as a courtesy to us *older* folks," she added. "You should *at least* be *introduced* to their sons."

"Are they around my age?" I asked.

"I think so, but I'd better *warn* you. They're no-good ruffians, *those* two. They ride *motorbikes* and hang out in *pubs*. I doubt you'll have much in common."

It was hard not to laugh. "They sound all right to me," I replied. Well, after all, Grandma was right. I could manage a simple meal.

But first, we had to accompany Aunt Bea on her twice-a-week food shopping ritual. I offered to stay behind and keep an eye on Uncle Henry, but Bea wouldn't have it.

"Elizabeth's coming to collect him," she insisted.

Henry sat with his blanket in front of the gas-powered flame, and that's where he stayed most of the time. Aunt Bea grabbed her list, Elizabeth rang the bell, and Grandma couldn't find her purse.

Before long we were ushered out.

I'd have called it a very brisk pace, all the way to the centre of town. Fortunately Grandma kept up, but she didn't look pleased. Bea didn't notice: she was too preoccupied getting from A to D before the shops ran out.

Shopping for food—aside from a supermarket—was a whole new adventure for me: I loved watching Bea carefully pick out the best bargains and purchase (in a state of constant twitter) what was to become the focal point of our future meals.

Apparently the regimen was always the same: first the butcher's, then the baker's, then the greengrocer's, then the sweet shop, finally the flower stall.

For special occasions like this: rack of lamb, roast beef, and fresh sausages; several baker's loaves, nutty wholemeal buns, cream cakes; asparagus, leeks; Thornton's chocolates and a big bouquet of blue-eyed chrysanthemums.

I argued that since we were guests for dinner that night, we should pay a visit to the Off-license.

"Wouldn't it be nice to bring some wine with us?" I said to Grandma.

"*That's* a good idea, Lauren, now *why* didn't I think of it?"

"Aunt Bea, where can we get some wine?"

"Oh my yes, how thoughtless of me, you should have wine of course while you're here, though I never know what to choose, I guess something French, you know we're not known for our wine in Britain, should we have white or red?"

"Lauren will find something," cut in Grandma.

"But I haven't the faintest notion, if it's Market Square or not, selling wine at a discount—" twittered Bea, turning around in circles. She clearly couldn't cope with unplanned detours.

"My *feet* are *killing* me, so let's settle for the *closest* shop," Grandma moaned.

Happily for me, an Off-License was just around the corner. I picked out several bottles of both white and red. After a long debate, Grandma paid for the lot and I had to admit it was obvious I'd be the only one drinking any of it.

The day progressed quickly and soon we were getting dressed for dinner.

I opened a bottle of wine to test it, you might say. After three glasses I decided it was fine and there was no point in getting nervous about meeting a couple of very British second cousins.

Aunt Bea kept insisting there was a possibility I'd never meet the boys: Ian, 20, and Seth, 19. Boys being boys, maybe they had other plans that evening, or didn't understand the importance of greeting visiting relatives, as Bea put it.

I kept insisting I really didn't mind if I missed seeing them. The introduction would be awkward, to say the least; my shyness was bound to make things even worse. But of course I was a little bit curious.

Chester arrived in his car to pick us up.

Clutching the paper bag concealing the wine, I followed Bea, Henry and Harriet as they marched behind Chester. We all got into the car, sat through the eight minutes it took to get to his house, then piled out again to march up the driveway.

A few more steps, and wobbling from too much wine, I took Grandma's arm just as we reached the front walk.

Unlike most of its kind on the street, I noticed the Henshaw's 1930s semi-detached house looked slightly unkept. Or rather 'kept' in a sort of higgledee, piggledee way.

A kaleidoscope of spreading plants (and weeds) in the front entrance greeted us haphazardly, like an overgrown jungle. I thought to myself, "Good, I like the feel of this place already."

Past the front door, I was led into a rather small room, overcrowded with comfy chairs (well-worn but practical), large cushions, and miniature laminated coffee tables. Nothing matched. The surrounding walls were covered in utility shelves crammed full of books.

A young cousin sat waiting, looking very smug in a long-sleeve white shirt and black leather vest. A fair-freckled face beamed back at me, red-brown hair cropped neatly at the shoulder.

He stood up and spoke with a crisp, curt voice, "Well hello Lauren, I'm Ian, and how have you been enjoying England?"

His savvy smile curled like a cat's in the middle of a rather fetching, well kept beard.

I gulped. "Oh, it's been fantastic."

"And how long are you here for?"

"Two weeks."

"Ah, well, Seth and I will have to take you around to some of our favorite spots before you leave. You can't spend all your time puttering around with the old folk."

"That would be nice."

The rest of the conversation dwindled into a dismal failure—on my part anyway. It seemed as if Ian asked all the questions to get things going, only to have me thwart all his efforts with feeble three-second replies.

"Did you have a nice flight?"

"Yes."

"Did you get a chance to see anything of London?"

"No."

"How long have you been here?"

"This is our second day."

"Have you been to the Cathedral?"

"Yes."

He attempted a few witty remarks, then threw me a few jokes, but I found it hard to follow his kind of humor. Meanwhile I kept looking at him and thinking, twenty? He definitely seemed more sophisticated—at his age—than anyone I'd ever encountered before. In my eyes, Ian could have passed for thirty. Keenly aware of this difference, I went into culture shock and clammed up.

The old folk had left us to it, and poor Ian, beginning to wilt from these one-way questions, decided to excuse himself and offer his assistance in the kitchen.

I felt powerless to salvage the situation. And for the first time during the trip, I resented being a pawn in the grip of my grandmother's plans. So what's the big deal, I was thinking, if I embarrassed *her* for a change?

Suddenly the front door slammed. Grandma and Bea abruptly broke off their conversation and the second son entered the room: a rush of air, a helmet dropping to the floor, a ripping open of zips. We all watched as Seth, encased from neck to foot in leather, assessed the scene; and after a quick double take, appeared to acknowledge the fact we'd all been waiting for him to appear.

Seth, like his brother, had a mop of wispy reddish-brown hair. He also sported a beard. But his face was sprinkled with freckles and his physique rested on a much thinner, lankier frame.

He flung himself in a chair and looked at the gob-smacked group, retorting, "Well what's everybody looking at?"

"Seth," Chester yelled, "Get up and properly greet your relatives!"

Seth rose, and two strides later was bending over to hug Grandma: "Oh yes you've *grown up* now, do you *realize* the last time I saw a picture of you, you were only *nine* years old?"

And then my turn; he leaned over, leathers creaking, to touch my hand. Briefly. He muttered something under his breath but I didn't hear what he said.

That was the moment it happened.

And what did Seth say to me? Probably something proper and polite. I think I went straight into shock the minute I gazed into those piercing hazel-green eyes. A light, a wave of sparkling energy or whatever it was—swimming in his eyes—hit me with a sudden jolt.

I fell back into my chair as if he'd smacked me on the forehead with his fist. And yet the blow was invisible. To describe it was like catching dead center the bright, electric charge of a lightning rod. The hairs of my face, my body, all seemed to stand on end; my fingers prickled and trembled not so much from his touch, but from the look in his eyes.

Had anyone else noticed my reaction? I looked around, thinking of course not. Come back to earth, you silly girl. Nobody else sees a halo. Then I cursed to myself—stop it, damn it: calm down. He's human, he's run-of-the-mill, he's your second cousin. He coughs, sneezes, burps like the rest of us; he rides a motorcycle and drinks beer in the pubs.

And he wasn't even what I'd call handsome. Then what was it? Ian was better looking. Eyes included. Sitting wordlessly in my chair, I couldn't figure it out. I couldn't imagine why I'd be making it up. My imagination might be deep—but not that deep.

Maybe Seth was a paradox, and mysteries intrigued me. The first impression: body, defensive and rebellious; face, seeking and poetic. A strange alliance.

Chester interrupted: "Seth, go change your clothes, you ruffian, tea's going cold because of you!"

Seth scowled. "Yeah, yeah, all right."

He stomped upstairs. I heard him mutter under his breath: "How was I supposed to know? I don't understand all the fuss. I didn't ask you to wait just for me!"

We were seated at the table when he returned, having changed into a black Genesis T-shirt with a hole growing just below the left armpit. The sagging tear exposed an open patch of freckled skin. Below that, the shirt tucked into a pair of blue jeans, with the seams all smeared in grease.

Chester glared at his son's chosen attire but said nothing more.

Seth glanced my way and caught me catching his dad's reaction.

I couldn't help but smile back and sympathize with him.

We ate. I wondered, chewing without tasting much, if Seth and Ian wished we hadn't come at all. Grandma and I were now a pressing duty, an inconvenience, to the younger generation—both boys being skeptical and reasonably selfish, if you asked me. We'd probably never meet again, so what was the point?

Only now, I knew for sure I'd be wishing I'd never met one particular cousin: the one the parents had named Seth. I'd always assumed Seth was a Jewish name. But Seth wasn't Jewish, nor did he seem very Christian. What else but the black sheep of the family? A pagan devil. Determined to snap my defenses.

Spellbound, I was his unwilling pawn.

Meanwhile, Ian attempted a few more stabs at polite conversation, Chester argued with Elizabeth over which places tourists should visit, Grandma's booming voice rose through the din like a sporadic clap of thunder, and I tried even harder not to say anything.

I didn't dare direct my line of vision, but I knew the lightning bolt eyes were as real as ever—waiting and biding their time—from the far end of the table.

Then, over pudding, I gulped and collected what was left of my wits. And looked.

Blatantly, no bones about it. No, not at anyone else. I looked at Seth, just Seth.

Busy pouring a good dollop of custard from a plastic jug, he seemed intent on his second helping.

I waited, forcing myself to hold my aim, and sure enough as soon as he looked up, he looked right at me.

Just a brief meeting of eyes. And as if to test my own feeble efforts to squelch such an attraction—possibly suggesting a million things.

Defiantly anti-social during the entire evening, he still managed to put me in a position of utter panic. Again. I was consumed with fear and dread: an overwhelming, undeserved, disempowering sense of impending doom.

It happened just as I caught Seth's eyes traveling down from my face to my chest, where I suppose most male glances, despite themselves, sort of end up.

And despite myself, I secretly hoped that devilish smile of his meant…

He approved.

CHAPTER 4

The Ride

The next morning Aunt Bea noticed I wasn't feeling so good. Although she didn't mention last night's wine-testing and subsequent re-sampling all through dinner, I suspect she assumed the cause to be a hangover.

"Come with me, dear," she said, holding my hand and leading me to the bathroom. "I've prepared just the thing to make you feel better. A proper ladies bath."

The tub was an old-fashioned affair, filled to the brim with steaming bubbles and smelling as sweet as a florist's shop.

I never took baths at home, so taking my time, I stripped down and stepped slowly into the fizzy foam, starting with my big toe. The water was scorching—but I'd expected as much, considering the way Bea liked her tea.

Gritting my teeth, I eventually took the plunge and discovered the initial torture was worth it. Completely submerged, only the tips of my breasts drifted in and out between the lilac valleys; the rest of me soothed under mountains of fluffy white sponge.

I watched my breasts—my own tits—bob around in the bath and wondered why I hadn't really appreciated them before. The headache was beginning to clear and I was thinking, what a terrific pair of boobs. I'd never really considered them an asset—more like a curse. How many boys, after all, had been attracted to me simply because of my breasts?

Every one of them, surely. But that hadn't stopped me from wearing the tight-fitting, low-cut tops. You shouldn't try to disguise the truth. Was that my excuse?

Bullshit. If big melons brought some male attention my way, then what else could I hope for? Not much. Not with bland brown hair, ruddy skin and a square-shaped face. Pretty brown eyes? Only in an earthy, robust kind of way, and entirely wasted on a big-boned, lumpy body.

It was important to admit all this so I could put my feelings into perspective, and shrug off Seth. Settle for a few seconds of sexual attraction.

As for me, the allure was much harder to accept, or explain. The magnetic pull of a lightning bolt wasn't quite in the same league. I'd fallen in love before. But *this* was frightening.

"Forget it," I murmured to the rising steam. "There's nothing to forget," I reminded myself, determined to soak in the bath until I felt completely cured. All because—perhaps—my breasts had, if nothing else, caught his interest. And that, right now, seemed to matter more than anything else in the world.

After forty minutes, the bubbles finally disappeared. I kept thinking I'd better get out, but the phone rang and then Bea rushed up the stairs.

I sat up. The bath sighed, in one big whoosh. No, it couldn't…

"Lauren, there's a phone call for you!"

I could hear Bea breathing heavily behind the door, eagerly awaiting my answer.

"For me?"

"Yes, yes, it's Seth!"

"I'm still in the bath, can you tell him I'll call him right back?"

Three minutes later Bea returned, exclaiming, "Lauren, Seth wants to know if you would like to go on a country walk—with some friends—around Gentleshaw Common—at one o'clock!"

"Okay. Fine, tell him I'd love to go."

Drying myself, I kept mulling it over. Seth called. Not Ian, but Seth. That little fact seemed to make all the difference in the world.

When I opened the door, Chester's red face beamed back at me.

"Hello," he said.

"Hello," I said.

"I've come to pick you up," he announced, in case I wasn't sure. Huffing and puffing, he'd obviously driven over in a rush. And now he was peering anxiously over my shoulder to see if anyone else was around.

"No, I won't come in."

No sign of Bea or Harriet. He relaxed a bit, and smiled. Until he looked down at my feet.

"This won't do," he hurriedly whispered. "Do you have any boots you could put on?"

"Oh...sneakers would be more comfortable for me, if we're hiking," I explained, confused.

"Yes, yes, of course, but you'll see...you must have boots, all right?"

"Chester, what are you doing here?" Aunt Bea was behind me now, clutching a brown bag which I assumed to be my picnic lunch.

"I'm the taxi service, as usual," grumbled Chester, kissing his mum's cheek, "and I have strict orders to bring Lauren back immediately."

"Well go on, then." Aunt Bea waved her arm.

"Just *one* sec, I'll be right back," I interjected, rushing up the stairs to grab my boots.

And forgetting every vow of a bath's resolve, I allowed my heart to pound like mad in the car, all the way from Beacon Street to Seth's front door.

Outside the house stood a long line of parked motorcycles. Suddenly I understood why Chester wanted the boots.

"Bea and Harriet wouldn't like the idea of your riding a motorcycle," Chester explained, maneuvering the car between the entourage of gleaming steel. "But what they don't know won't cause a fuss, right?" He winked and patted my knee.

A gangling leather feature emerged from the jungle, carrying a helmet and extra set of jacket and pants. I knew who it was before I got out of the car.

"Seth, thanks for inviting me."

"Lor-en," with a lovely sound to it—the British version—he said my name, "Are you ready for this?"

"Oh yes!" (What was I saying? Doing? No! I wasn't ready for this!)

"Well then, get this gear on and we'll see if it fits."

He handed me the kit, which dropped heavily in my arms. While struggling to pull the leather and zippers over my trembling limbs, I met the rest of the gang. They piled out of the house and shook my hand before donning their own helmets: three guys and one couple—Ian falling in behind.

"It will do," Seth eyed me over. Explaining how to use the visor on the helmet, he bent close and I could see the deep hazel green of his eyes, the sprinkle of light freckle on his fair complexion, framed by a soft, youthful moustache and half-beard.

So up close I think I stopped breathing.

On went his helmet and that wispy brown hair sticking out beneath.

I tried to smile, but my lips felt anchorless and the effort was more like a spoon fumbling to serve jelly.

He adjusted his gloves, the engines of the other bikes revving up to a kind of roar, and kicking down on his starter, Seth motioned for me to sit behind him.

"Where do I hold on?" I shouted.

"Me—or, at the back."

Chester waved, smiling and thoroughly enjoying my novice excitement. Seth's bike took off, throwing me backwards. I let out a surprised squeal and instantly grabbed for Seth's waist.

I was reviving.

The first few minutes of the ride were a lesson on oscillation—thrusting both forward and backward: hands gripped white-knuckled on the bar behind, or arms flung ahead in a death-grip around the driver. Followed by a continuous sequence of stifled screams, and an uncontrollable visor clapping up and down.

Nevertheless, we weaved and leaned and flew. While the road raced a few inches under my feet, the wind threw Seth's hair in front of my face.

Cushioned so tight behind him, I couldn't help but feel his thighs pressed against mine, or my chest resting along his back.

Beyond Seth, I could see the crowded streets give way to countryside; we raced on past tiny villages, squeezed between traffic, until finally at a stop-light Seth turned around and asked, "Are you all right?"

"How do you secure this visor again?" I meekly enquired, at the same time wondering if I'd died and gone to heaven.

"Here." He snapped the snap once again. "Oh, and try to lean into the curves," he added. "Don't resist the gravity—go with it."

"Sorry I'm holding on to you so tight."

"Don't worry about it."

Don't worry if you die and go to heaven. Amen. The light changed, I'd finally secured my visor, and this was definitely the way to experience England: out for a Sunday ride through hills and fields, bouncing on an open-aired two-wheeler...and clinging fast to a lightning rod.

The road narrowed; we glided between thick hedges so tall you couldn't see above them—beyond lay green fields, stone farms, sporadic patches of forest.

So serene, so picturesque, in fact so perfectly like a storybook fairytale I couldn't believe it all still existed. Smiling like an addict whose blood courses after a long awaited fix, I lifted the visor to wipe away the moisture from my eyes.

The riders ahead raised arms to signal a stop and we pulled up next to a pub. Streaked with moss and ivy, the pub's post-and-beam walls caved inwards; the roof sagged like the spine on back of a farm-horse. Its windows were so tiny I wondered if my forebears were midgets.

"King Charles II used to come here," Seth announced, correctly assuming I would find this information of great interest. Then throwing off his gloves and lighting a cigarette he added, "We'll have a pint or two before heading out, and on to Gentleshaw Common."

In a trance, I stepped inside the pub.

"How do you like it so far?" Ian asked, balancing four bitters in his hands and handing one of them to me.

"It's fantastic!"

"Do you feel safe riding with Seth, or would you rather ride with me?"

"No, that's okay, I'll stick with Seth," I said. I studied my beer and hoped he'd change the subject.

"Hah, you see? She knows the best rider of the bunch," laughed Seth, raising his glass to his lips. He might have thrust a subtle wink at me, but I couldn't be sure.

"Bloody heck, it's only fair to take turns," one of them cut in, grinning right back at Seth. "We don't often get a tasty American bird to show around."

"So next time you'll just have to be the first one who asks her," Seth replied.

"Where's the bathroom?" I cut in, getting very uncomfortable.

"No time for a bath!" Ian answered, laughing at my use of words. "You mean toilet, don't you?"

Which prompted a whole new direction for the jokes to head…much to my relief.

A few pints later we left the pub and whizzed through country lanes: the view getting even better as we wound our way up to Gentleshaw Common. Stopping at the top of the hill, I followed the rest of the group as they ambled along a path leading through the heath.

Was heath short for heather? I wondered. Dare I even ask?

At the highest point, I gazed across the lush green sloping fields unfolding in the distance, bathed in wistful silence. The land seemed to sense the final strokes of harvest. A combine tractor could be heard in the distance. Several trees had already begun to shed their coats...

And the woods were splashed with hints: rusty copper and golden orange, mixing an occasional patchwork into the green. In open areas, gorse and heather wove living color through the yellow clumps of dry hair-grass; the tips of wilted bracken poking out like spears of curled bronze.

Unfortunately it was already turning to dusk, so we wouldn't be able to stay for very long.

"Where shall we head?" asked Ian, as the trail forked. "Further down, or turn left?"

At the same time, we both spotted a small herd of deer grazing near the edge of the woods below.

"Let's go down there and see the deer," said Ian, kicking a pile of leaves at his feet.

"Let's throw Philip down the hill," Seth suggested, grabbing one of Philip's legs. Ian took hold of the other leg and Philip went flying—straight into a clump of fern.

He scrambled out and chased them, but laughing and joking, his buddies escaped by rolling down the hill in somersaults.

"Come on, Lauren, it's how we Brits get down hills!"

"No, I can't."

Yes, you can!"

"Nah..."

"Yeah...if you don't then we'll come get you..."

So I did.

I probably laughed more—as I did it—than I'd laughed over the past six months.

Ian and Seth's friends, it turned out, had a knack for turning any venue into a hilarious atmosphere of play and fun.

I envied them, and realized that being British included a wide variety of attitudes. Prim and proper was only the tip of the iceberg. Take a couple of bikers, and go one better than rough and rude.

Just look at them now, I was thinking: stalking the deer like Monty Python's circus, all silly walks and serious clowning. Props—two wheels and chrome, costumes—studs and leather.

In contrast, I felt completely inferior, but as nobody appeared to care, I didn't worry about it. Besides, being a stranger as well as an American—put me outside their realm of judgment.

Later, however, they all joined me—wordlessly rooting themselves in the grass, to watch the grazing deer.

"So, is America as wonderful as what you see on TV?" Philip eventually asked. "Is everyone stinking rich, living like the cast of Dallas all over the country?"

"No, of course not. And I think it's much nicer here," I replied. "Maybe a bit behind the times, but in America we don't have the 'oldness,' the unspoilt beauty of your villages, for example. All we have are slipshod shanty towns of chrome and billboards, sprawling junk..."

I didn't dare look at Seth as I said it, though I hoped he was listening.

"But it's cheaper to live there, right? You have more, your standard of living is higher."

"Cheap, yes—cheap, ugly and transient." I knew my description was somewhat unfair, but so far, compared to England....

Philip shook his head. "I wouldn't mind cheap petrol...."

I knew Philip or even Seth probably wouldn't understand, not until they'd actually gone to America themselves.

"We'll all come over and visit you some day," Ian volunteered, "and you can show us the States."

"Fine," I said. "Just one condition: you'll have to bring your bikes with you!"

"A bunch of West Midlands hoodlums—bet you're already sick of us," Seth mumbled.

"No, not at all..."

As we walked back to the bikes, I noticed Seth seemed unusually quiet.

I fought the urge to speak, but it seemed oddly crucial at that moment to break the ice.

"Seth?"

"Yes? Is something wrong, Lor-en?"

"No, no. I just wanted to ask you...I've noticed these little wooden signs all along the roads, and I wonder what they're for."

"Oh, you mean the footpaths."

"That's right. They all say footpath."

Seth seemed pleased by this question, and explained in detail how footpaths were a British tradition since Medieval times: walk-ways trod by people on their way to the villages and farms, paths for sheep and cattle runs, at one time the only roads to get from one place to another.

"They're still here," he boasted, giving me a peculiar look, and a rather infuriating grin. "From centuries ago and up to the present day—our public right-of-ways stretch all over the country. Through farms, fields, forest, moorland, private property, anywhere. They're properly marked and maintained, all over Britain. Access for any walker willing to explore!"

"Really?"

"If you want, I could show you more of these footpaths," he went on, "if you like walking in the country…"

"Oh yes!"

I wasn't thinking, of course. Not about how time was running out and in less than two weeks I'd be escorting Grandma back home. I was only conscious of how badly I wanted to see Seth again.

"It's a shame you're not staying longer."

It was Seth's last comment as he casually rummaged through his jacket in search of his keys. We'd reached the car park. It was time to leave. Then it hit me.

God, what a mistake. And all in the name of a footpath.

I tried to reason it out. The heat and excitement of a stranger, a foreign accent, a motorcycle ride…blown out of proportion, the mystery of a British male, a nice muscular body that looked very sexy in tight leather…piercing and contemplative green eyes…a reflection of my own thoughts?

Probably. How could I feel like this so soon? We'd hardly spoken to each other, really. *The perfect recipe for romantic delusion.*

I waited for Seth's signal to mount. My whole body tingling with the thrill of another ride, I swung my leg over the seat, snuggled in place, placed my hands behind me on the back bar—and braced.

As we rode down the hill, I could see the fields begin to change color, reflecting the oranges and pinks of the setting sun. Misty vapors hung across the horizon, shrouding the scattered clumps of trees in an enchanting veil, a scene so simple and peaceful…it reminded me of…grace! I almost laughed out loud. Grace! A pilgrim's word. A spiritual place in the heart, impossible to describe….

And suddenly the bike slowed. We pulled over.

Turning around in the seat, Seth flipped up his visor. His steady gaze flashed at me, revealing a shyness, a sliver of tenderness. "Do you mind if we get off the bike and stand here a minute? To watch the sun go down?"

"—I was just wishing we could myself."

"Good."

The other bikers had simply carried on—then disappeared. We were alone. A couple of crows cawed in the tree nearby, the only sound as we silently stood and gazed across those gentle fields, bathed in fading color; the sun slowly dipping it's mellowed hue down, then down, and into the distance. Motionless, in the silence, we watched it completely disappear.

Two statues, taking it all in: the surrounding wonder, every last detail and impression, as if by osmosis.

When it turned completely dark, we finally moved, our leathers creaking in unison.

We looked at each other.

"Guess it's time to go," Seth finally whispered.

I nodded.

Thinking yes, probably enough worshipping for one day.

❦   ❦   ❦

And that evening the bathtub changed: no longer a bath, but a vessel of leaning, rushing, careening, whirling, bumping, flying motion; the water's surface reflecting a road, a pavement ever-on-the move; the rising steam encircling a stretch of fields bidding hazy goodnight to the day.

I submerged my body until only the top of my head remained; I closed my eyes but I could still see his swaggering confident stride; wispy auburn hair blowing out from under his helmet; eyes turning to face me in a sagacious lightning-bolt grin.

"Are you ever going to get out of the bath?" asked Bea from behind the door. "It's Henry's bedtime, dear, and he needs to have a wash."

"In that case I'll be right out," I said. But I was thinking, no, if I had it my way I'd never get out of the bath.

I climbed into bed and buried my head under the covers. I closed my eyes but I could still see the beauty of Seth's face and hear the crows cawing in a country lane in Staffordshire....

Fool, fool, fool!

Spending all night tossing and turning between the sheets, trying in vain to put a simple sunset behind me.

CHAPTER 5

The Voice

I was awake. But I kept my eyes closed, which made sense, as it was much too early to wake up.

Going back to sleep was impossible: my mind kept reeling this way and that, thrusting all sorts of thoughts into my head. And one thought kept niggling me in particular: How did I get here?

Assuming there wasn't really any proof for the existence of a personal destiny or fate—I tried, nevertheless, to follow the twists and turns of the path that led me to Lichfield.

True: I'd always dreamed of visiting England, but left to my own devices, I doubt I'd ever have managed it on my own. Something suspiciously similar to fate lent a helping hand. Was it a stroke of luck, being in the right place at the right time? Or did luck take the guise of my grandma?

In fact, I was quite certain I'd never have come on my own, because the whole idea was just a dream. Normally my dreams stay as dreams. It's safer that way—no chance of disappointment.

But so far, the fantasy-world of England had remained intact. I'd not been disappointed. Yes, that was it. The real England could have been a terrible disappointment. And *disappointment* was the dreaded bane of my life. Really love something, or someone, and such a dream is bound to turn to worms and die. This had been a bitter lesson for me, but I'd learned it: a lesson I called Lauren's Law.

Lauren's Law was a proven fact, a cause-and-effect personal rule of thumb I'd grown to accept. So there weren't many heartthrobs left that hadn't already been slapped to sobriety by the cold, heavy hand of reality. Really love something and it's bound to turn to worms. The bubble will always burst—Lauren's Law. The easiest solution is to stop dreaming, stop loving, and avoid the bursting altogether.

But the handiwork of so-called fate entered the scene and led me astray. I couldn't get this out of my mind. When had it started? Did this twist of luck or fate actually start with Grandma? No, that wasn't the beginning. And the more I thought about it, the further back I had to go. If I hadn't left Santa Barbara for Rhode Island—I wouldn't have been Grandma's choice of a chaperon in the first place. I had to be handy—near Boston—for that to happen.

Then I remembered how I'd left Santa Barbara for no good reason, other than a little voice inside that told me I should go. Could a hunch be the same thing as fate, or a sense or destiny?

"How about taking the trip across country with me?" my father's voice had boomed over the phone. "How about taking this opportunity to finally visit your true birthplace? You know, Lauren, New England is an area you should visit. It has a charm all of its own."

Santa Barbara, the 4th of July: my dad had called from L.A. to tell me the news. He'd just been transferred back East, to the War College at Newport, Rhode Island—the place where I was born.

"Well...dad...I don't know..."

"You won't have to worry about money. Consider it as my final graduation present. This can be your last fling before you settle down in the real world. I'm sure your mother would have wanted..." he trailed off.

My mom died of breast cancer when I was fifteen.

"It sounds tempting," I confessed. But how could he possibly know the wants of a cremated mother?

"You haven't found a job yet, have you?"

"No..."

"Then what's holding you back?"

"I don't know..."

"Your father too square for you to hang around with any more?"

"Come on dad, that's not it!"

"That boyfriend of yours won't like it, eh? I thought that's why nobody gets married these days—so you have the freedom to do what you damn well please."

"His name is Leo, dad. Why do you always have to refer to him as that boyfriend?"

"Well, do you have to ask him first?"

"No. But look—give me a few days to think about it."

A few days went by—then I announced the invitation to Leo. I don't know why I waited so long to tell him. Maybe my dad was right and I needed some time to rehearse my lines.

"So, Leo, I think I should go, don't you?" I'd braced myself for the inevitable debate.

Leo had been staring at a crack in the floor throughout my speech—which wasn't his usual pose. Over six feet tall, thin as a rail and deceptively energetic, he normally stood like a fixated pole in a gale. His eyes would bore through my mind. Utterly forthright and unbending, he had an unbeatable will.

Annoyed by his apparent lapse of attention, I leaned over and touched his knee.

Leo, will you look at me?"

"I am."

"No you're not. What's the matter?"

"Well…how do you expect me to feel?"

"Interested enough to say something, or at least look as if you're happy for me."

"Why?"

"I thought you liked living with me."

"Well, it's obvious now, that's not enough."

"What do you mean by that? It's only a visit!"

"It is?"

"So you think I'll go and won't come back again?"

Leo didn't answer. His toe traced along the edge of the crack in the floor.

"Why do you think that?"

He didn't have to name why, we both knew. There just might be something that would come up, turning a leave of absence into a permanent end.

I removed my hand from Leo's knee. I hadn't expected such an evasive reaction. But then I suddenly remembered Leo's nightmare: a few weeks ago I'd woken up in the middle of the night to discover he was wide awake and holding me tight. He was holding me so tight he was shaking.

I'd pleaded with him several times to tell me the dream—finally he admitted he'd dreamed he'd woken up in the morning and I wasn't there: in the dream I had simply disappeared.

"I know it's bound to happen some day and yet I can't imagine living without you," he confessed. "What a shock—I've never felt like such a sucker before—but I'm scared to death it's about to happen."

My assurances seemed to calm him and the dream was never mentioned again. Besides, it seemed impossible that he and I would split—we'd been living together for over a year, and there were no signs of trouble or unhappiness in the relationship.

Of course I had no reason for wanting to go away. For the first time in my life, I felt safe. I was mutually part of an intellectually stimulating, sexually satisfying love affair. I wasn't 'in love' with Leo, but I liked him in a way that was better than love. Which, under Lauren's Law, meant it would last. I'd be crazy to let it go.

"Leo, it's just an opportunity to travel and spend some time with my dad. Who knows when I'll be able to see him again?"

"I understand."

"Now is the time to do something like this, before I start looking for a job."

"Yes, go, and do what you have to do."

"Two months will fly by. I'll write every week."

Leo raised his eyes to mine and smiled. But I could see that smile hiding a sadness, a resignation. I suspected he knew all along—no matter how much I loved him in return, it just wasn't quite the genuine, passionate, true-love 'it.'

I wanted to explain. But how? How could I convince him that the 'it' was a feeling I no longer sought or desired? What was 'it,' anyway, except a destructive yearning for an impossible ideal? What we had was still special and sacred; I would definitely come back to him.

I started to explain. But nothing came out of my mouth. I guess it's virtually impossible to speak when your throat gets so choked up you can't even swallow.

So the news provoked our first big disagreement. This made me very unhappy; knowing Leo wasn't backing my decision to go. In fact, I wasn't looking forward to the prospect of being away from him either. Yet why was a little voice inside insisting I should do it?

Leo cleared his throat. "Well, let's start again and discuss this reasonably," he began, making a point of looking me straight in the eyes. "If it's good for you personally, then you shouldn't think twice."

"Right," I agreed.

"Now I don't want you to get mad, but have you thought about how your dad has made his offer pretty impossible to refuse? Lauren, think about it.... don't you realize what he's trying to do?"

"Give me the chance to see New England?"

"Disguised bait to get you out of Santa Barbara."

"But only for a few weeks!"

"—Time to talk and wheedle you into your senses."

"But I'll do what I want to, not what he thinks is best for me! How can you think I'd let him influence me against my will?"

"You wait: he'll lure you back into the comfortable folds of the upper-middle-class flock. He'll convince you that your life here is a rut, where you wallow with pigs like me..."

He stopped, leaving it as he usually did, hot under the collar. For Leo could be as passionate as his Greek father when it came to being a socialist. Always philosophical and bent on politics, he'd majored in Political Sci...

"Leo, come on now, don't you trust me?"

"I don't trust life. You can't help it—but your parents raised you on a conventional social creed. Let me ask you something—think about it. Aren't you partly ashamed, deep down, of living like this with me?"

I glared at him, furious.

"And do you really want to travel with your dad, to live with him again for a few months? Or are you just doing it to make him happy?"

"No, I really want—I do—to see New England!"

"And what if I promised to take you there next year?"

I didn't answer. Leo stopped looking at me again. Having exhausted all interest in the crack on the floor, he got up from his chair and strode restlessly across the room.

Jesus! Wasn't Leo, after all, only trying to encourage me to make a decision that was mine alone, for reasons I would make clear to myself? Wasn't that what I found so special about him? Damn it. No shams, no evasions.

But despite all Leo's suggestions, which were probably right to some degree, I nevertheless went ahead and did it anyway. Something inside said 'Go,' something quite apart from all those other reasons.

That's right. Just go.

Thinking back on it, a very secret, inexplicable voice softly tugged at my conscious mind. Maybe some people call it intuition.

At any rate, not really knowing why, and despite myself—I simply followed it.

And now, falling back to sleep in Aunt Bea's extra bedroom in Lichfield—I was beginning to understand why.

❦   ❦   ❦

The next time I saw Seth, a whole week had gone by. Grandma and Bea kept me busy. I could tick off Roman ruins, castles, chapels, locks, and gardens from my list. Lots of sightseeing from buses and trains. I loved every eye-opener minute of it, though I was getting pretty tired of hanging around—night and day—with the old folk.

It was Ian who phoned this time. I accepted his invitation to join the entire gang, who were meeting at a pub that evening in town. I insisted I'd take a cab. God knows why. If I did know, I certainly wasn't about to admit it.

The pub was called the Earl of Lichfield. Philip and John were watching out for me, and waved to establish their exact position in the crowd.

Ian politely handed me a pint, waiting and ready. I'd almost finished it when Seth appeared—out of nowhere.

"Cheers, Lauren!"

"Cheers."

"Are you sampling a real ale?"

"Yes."

"Which one?"

"Can't remember, Ian told me, but…it had a funny name."

"Oh, then it must be Scrutter's Old Foreskin," Seth cut in. "Here, I'll just take a sip…yep."

"And how do you know for sure it's that one?" I asked.

"I can taste the cheese!"

We both laughed, and Seth winked. I had barely caught my breath before he was off again. One sip from my glass and he was pulled away by an unknown arm in the crowd.

The pub was really packed that evening, the air thick with smoke. Here it was easy to forget I was an American, as long as I kept my mouth shut: gulping down the hearty real ale, and sharing 'jollies' with the mates. By the time I'd finished my second pint I was smoking their hand-rolled fags and playing darts.

When I spotted Seth again, he was standing at the bar. He looked my way…and without hesitation, quickly moved to stop me on my way to the toilet.

"Are you happy?" he asked, eyes piercing through mine.

Suddenly I wondered what he meant, after all, by asking such a question. But coming from him—it sounded different. The intent was dead sincere.

"Oh yes," I replied.

The first time he'd asked me 'Are you happy?' was after that sunset, and my 'yes' felt like a special signal between us, a kind of code. Just to check that we understood each other. Or so I thought.

But tonight his special question had lost its spark.

And my yes was a lie. Did I say yes?

"Just checking," he said, tilting his head and looking a bit dismayed.

I quickly turned and rushed toward the loo. I thought I could handle it, but oh no. Shrug it off as a harmless fancy? A friendly rapport between cousins? Oh, no. I wasn't about to be let off so easily. Lauren's Law still applied in England, and I was breaking it lock, stock, and barrel.

Jesus! I was jealous. That's how I knew. *Seth had a girlfriend.*

I hadn't even considered the possibility, yet there she was—a proven fact—popping out of the corner like a surprise jack-in-the-box. A colorful blur, at first, jumping in and out of my peripheral vision but definitely attached to every inch of Seth…and why not? How stupid of me not to imagine the likelihood. And what a fool, to think Seth might…

"Why can't I be happy for him?" I asked myself, emerging from the toilet.

Humble as a mongrel who'd just been kicked, I began to watch her every move, furtively, from a safe distance; fascinated and devastated because this particular female embodied the sum total of everything I envied about…*pure English girls.*

In my opinion (from what I'd seen so far), a *pure English* female had a flawless, ivory-chiseled face, high cheekbones, full rosy lips with an impish twitch, and flashing eyes adorned with dark lashes scorning any need for mascara. This type of female was the spitting image of pure, classic, ethereal European girl-beauty.

And now here she was, in the flesh, in all her glory, to justify every drool of delectation. Seth's girlfriend was petite, small-breasted and firm. Her impulsive, provocative movements made me wonder if she was always so restless. Chatting away, she pranced around like a dainty thoroughbred filly, not quite sure what to do with herself but confident she was eliciting attention.

I noticed how abruptly she turned, how her silky chestnut page-boy hair would fall across one of her eyes; how her mini dress, made of a wispy flowered material, flounced in and out—constantly—between her thighs.

I hated how she sat down and crossed her shapely legs—swinging down to a pair of beige short-topped boots, which looked so enticing I winced each time she leaned over to speak to Seth—waiting for them to touch, hoping to witness a sign of utter defeat. But it never happened. In fact, much to my astonishment, Seth appeared to take his lovely little creature quite casually.

"If I was him," I kept thinking, "I wouldn't be able to keep my hands off her!"

And her name? Of course: Naomi.

"Lauren, let me introduce you to Naomi," said Seth.

"Hi," I offered, dreading this moment, face to face.

"Hi."

The gorgeous Naomi smiled, but had more important things on her mind. She made no attempt to prolong the conversation and neither did I. Not that she had any cause for worry. As she pranced away again, I was thinking: she knows there's no competition.

Rivalry? No need for Naomi to worry. As for me, I'd already acknowledged defeat—looking so undeniably ugly and unfeminine standing next to an English filly. What else was there? Just a clumsy big-boned American donkey, trudging along in a baggy T-shirt and jeans.

I almost felt relieved the bubble had burst so soon. So despite the terrible revelation, I tried to make the best of it. I accepted Naomi's rightful position on top of Seth's knee. I even cast aside my seething inner jealously and feigned feeling happy.

It took four pints.

"Stop talking constant bikes, can't you find anything else inside your burnt-out brains to discuss?" Seth shouted above the music.

Someone handed me a joint. We were back at Seth and Ian's house, squeezed into the dining room, attempting to carry on where we left off at the Earl. (Due to some unexplained stroke of luck Naomi had gone straight home after the pub.)

I cheered up considerably. In fact, I began to regret two of the previous four pints.

Seth was sitting on my left, reaching out as I passed him the joint. In slow motion, the tips of our thumbs carefully came together. We smiled at each other as we touched.

"Bikes, bikes, bikes," Seth muttered, taking a long suck and inhaling the drag.

"I don't mind it, as all this bike stuff is new to me," I confessed, trying not to slur (and failing).

"Well I'm sick of it," Seth complained, "the same old crash stories, mechanical problems, engine rebuilds, performance analysis—I insist we stop talking motorbikes now."

"All right mate," a guy called Andy conceded, "No bike talk for as long as we can manage it."

The rest of the gang nodded in unison and there was a long period of silence.

"What do you think of Steve Hillage's latest album?" Andy asked Ian, to revive the conversation.

"Motivation Radio? Great."

"Hank, when are you going to score some more blow?"

"Yeah, I need some stash too."

"Wednesday I'm taking my wheels to the shop, so I thought on my way I'd stop at Ape's flat to score, so—"

"What's wrong with your piece? Bearings?"

"I'm not sure, but like I said, if you want some stuff give me the dosh now—"

"Don't take that bike to the sodding shop yet! I'll have a look at those bearings for you."

"Stuff the bearings! You're talking bike again," Seth sneered.

I was so high by then I didn't mind if they spat gobble-de-gook across the room, all night long. I hardly noticed when the last stragglers sauntered out the door.

Ian had phoned Bea and Harriet earlier to let them know I'd be staying over for the night. So everything was fine. I only had to move toward the stairs to my allocated sleeping quarters, a tiny closet-room with a cot squeezed into it.

At the top of the landing I could hear Chester and Elizabeth snoring. They obviously didn't mind their sons having a party now and then...

Ian had disappeared.

"Could I have a glass of water?" I asked Seth, who was turning off the stereo.

"Sure."

He led me into the kitchen.

At four A.M. we were still in the kitchen, sitting on stools with a bottle of whiskey between us. The glass of water had inadvertently led to more drinking. The whiskey led to more conversation. Hours lapsed without notice: we were wide-awake passing the bottle back and forth.

Something weird happened. We sobered up the more we drank. The lightning bolt settled into a lucid glow of shifting lines, a dancing whisper between us. The words we spoke hardly mattered. It was just like watching the sunset again, I was thinking, watching part of the unsaid mystery unfold in front of our eyes. For whenever Seth looked at me and spoke, it seemed as if he already knew my secrets. He instantly recognized the hurt and betrayal, the pain of love, the loss of passion. He didn't have to spell it out, or mention the cynical shell left in its place; he simply argued against Lauren's Law. And that side of me certainly didn't want to be recognized so easily.

So in the back of my mind, I kept thinking: why would I make all this up?

"You're always so quiet," he said.

"I know."

"That's what I like about you."

"You're joking."

"No, I'm not. You don't have to talk."

"I don't?"

"No."

"And why not?"

"Because behind all that," he insisted, "I know there's a person who's saying a lot...and most of it's wild...impulsive, outrageous...and..."

"Go on...and what?"

"What a censor might consider X-rated."

His telltale smile brought back all my extremes, and I could feel my lips begin to quiver. "No, I used to be like that when I was younger," I replied, "but not any more."

"Not any more? Are you sure?"

"I'm sure. And I'm glad I stopped it, too, because back then I was such a stupid idiot, a silly, misguided..."

"Lauren?"

"What?"

"Listen to what you're saying."

"It's the truth."

"You just said you stopped it."

"Okay, I suppose I can't stop it completely, but—"

"Let's assume you have. But what's left? Can you honestly feel true to yourself now?"

On the verge of tears, I simply muttered, "No. But I can't be that person."

"Lauren, what do you really, really want?"

"I can't have what I really, really, want," I said.

"You're giving in already?" Seth exclaimed. "Like a corked volcano? All the adventures and magic lost, just to avoid what you think is silly? A bit of embarrassment and pain?"

"—I still suffer, I'm not that cautious."

"I don't know, but it seems to me you might be suffering from selling yourself short…pretending you're happier that way…"

"Meaning?" (I knew what he meant.)

"Living a life that isn't as you would have it, really. And remember, it takes one to know one."

Seth paused. Gazing into his eyes was like flitting past a two-way mirror. I could tell he was mulling something over. Would he say it?

Finally, almost reluctantly, Seth lowered his head and muttered, "All right, I'm a touch junkie. A love addict. A misfire. A gushing needle—" and just as abruptly, raised his head and looked at me eye to eye. "But shit, Lauren," he whispered. "Hell. I'm going to moan, kick, fall, float, curse, or fly toward what I believe in, despite what anybody else thinks."

With that he splashed more whiskey into his empty glass.

"And what if," I cut in, "you find out your addiction is all just a bunch of junkie bullshit?"

"Of course I won't—not all of it—but whatever happens it's a hell of a lot better than creeping around inwardly hiding and regretting yourself. How boring! Ultimately the world around you becomes the same way."

I nodded.

Seth leaned across the table. "So. Promise me. When you get back home?"

"I'm going to be more assertive and outgoing for what I really want."

"Good!"

The tears were streaming down my face at this point, but I felt so relieved I didn't bother to hide them.

"The mystery of you, of this earth, is out there waiting," Seth insisted, "If you have the guts to seek it out. You know you've got to find it again, don't you Lauren?"

"Yes." I felt an overwhelming rush of grateful joy and hope as I said it.

That's all it took. A bolt of light, a bottle of whiskey, and a smile from Seth…to tempt me right back.

CHAPTER 6

The River

"Did you *have* a *nice* time last night, Lauren?" asked Grandma.

"Yes," I replied, bleary-eyed from lack of sleep.

We were sitting at the table, getting ready to eat one of Aunt Bea's best efforts (bar Christmas) at a Sunday lunch. She called it dinner. It was one-o'clock in the afternoon, for god's sake, and a bit too early for me, still hung over and barely able to stomach the thought of swallowing anything.

Steaming platters were passed hand to hand in a line: buttered carrots, parsnips and beans, a mountainous bowl of mashed potatoes, plump Yorkshire puddings, sautéed leeks, steamed brussels and hunks of roast beef.

"Aren't you hungry?" Aunt Bea inquired, shaking her head in disbelief.

Henry sat across from me, staring.

"These puddings are *delicious,*" my grandma insisted, with her mouth full.

"Here, put some more gravy over them." Bea passed a dripping ladle over Grandma's plate.

Gingerly chewing a bit of potato, I could only pray it would stay down.

Henry continued to stare. I began to wonder if a large boil had suddenly erupted on my chin. Either that or my entire head had gone missing. I shifted uncomfortably in my chair; on top of the hangover, the sensation was doubly unpalatable.

Meanwhile my knife and fork stood suspended over my plate, as if I really intended to tackle the beef. But I couldn't move any further and Henry seemed to take an annoying interest in my plight.

This wasn't Henry's usual vacant eagle-eye gaze: he was definitely focused. I wondered what was so intriguing, all of a sudden, about a pair of piss-colored, bloodshot eyes.

"What's the matter, Henry?" Aunt Bea finally asked. "Do you want some salt? Lauren, could you please pass me the salt?"

As Bea busily went about her business sprinkling the salt, Henry turned his eyes away from me and frowned. He spit whatever food he hadn't swallowed onto his plate. And before anyone had time to even marvel over this half-human response, he started to shake all over.

Astounded, nobody moved. The saltshaker slipped from Aunt Bea's hand. Henry kept shaking. Slowly, shaking and trembling, he managed to raise his right hand. A bouncing index finger pointed straight at me.

We all watched Henry pointing, and then, lips sucking in and out, he managed to blurt "Awwwhhh."

Then "Awwwhh!" again, quite loudly.

"Well my goodness!" exclaimed Bea. "He's never made a noise like that before…Henry, what is the matter?"

My first reaction was to wince—a rather weak defense. But already Henry's mouth had closed; his hand dropped to his lap. A few seconds later he was back to normal. Not a clue remained as to what might have caused the outburst, except for a slight upturn of his lips—a quirk of nerves, perhaps, or a crooked echo of a smile.

"What was *that* all about?" exclaimed Grandma.

"Who knows?" said Aunt Bea. "He might have gas, poor thing. Though it did look like he was pointing at you, Lauren. Could be he's quite taken with you, my dear!"

"Maybe he'll try to speak again," I said.

"It's possible…" muttered Bea, but she didn't sound very hopeful.

Strange, I was thinking, and what next? A strange morning after a very strange night, and now even Henry was beginning to act strange.

So after we finished the washing up, I volunteered to stay home while the grandmas went for a walk. I was looking forward to catching up on my sleep—in peace and quiet—and spending some time alone with Henry. I'm not sure what I hoped to gain, because the two of us behaved like a pair of mental patients, once we'd been comfortably anchored and left to our own devices in the parlor.

Henry sat with his blanket on the chair, and I lay with my blanket on the couch. Together we shared a full two hours of mutual zombiedom in silence.

After that, I tried a different stance. But no matter how hard I focused my concentration on Henry, nothing happened.

"You know, don't you?" I suddenly blurted out, unable to keep my patience any longer.

No answer, not a sound.

"You can tell, can't you?"

No answer.

"All right, I know darn well you've been keeping tabs on me, Uncle Henry. Your little baby tricks don't fool me."

Did he slightly raise his head? Ever so slightly?

"That's right. If you're still tuned in, why don't you ever own up and say something?"

Were his lips moving? Just a hair?

"I think you should know, as you seem to be somewhat interested—that it's true. I spent the whole night talking with him! Yes I did, with your grandson, Seth. Is he your favorite?"

No answer.

"We talked, that's all. But I have to admit I do fancy him, to put it your way. I fancy every inch of him. Especially his ass."

Henry still didn't respond. My outburst hadn't changed a thing. Not a thing. He was stubborn, I decided. Determined not to give in, at least yet.

"I bet Seth's your favorite," I repeated, until the eyelids lowered, veiling those persistently vacant orbs, and I realized he must have drifted into sleep.

I finally sighed and let it go. But I'd never forget that "Awwwhhh" or shrug it off like Aunt Bea did. Something must have broken through—to make him want to speak. There must have been a reason for it.

And why did Henry point at *me*, of all people? I had this feeling we both knew—awwwwhhh—that I was nursing a lot more than just a hangover. How frustrating! I'd almost discovered a Henry who was 'still there.' If only he could talk! I had so many questions I wanted to ask him, rather than Aunt Bea. Now I could only listen wistfully to a cryptic pattern of grunts and snores.

Such things never cross one's mind until it's too late. I never wondered why my grandfather refused to speak of his life as a young boy in England. I never bothered to ask him when he was alive. Now I was dying to learn all I could about my British half; about my grandfather as a youth; about his only brother. I wanted a connection, closeness, with Henry, despite the physical barriers. That's what I wanted.

Unconsciously, I was imploring him to come back to the present.

So maybe he almost did. Maybe, sensing this, he had tried to respond. I might have reached him—there—in the silent limbo land.

Pulling the blanket up to my chin, I lay there on the couch and smiled. At least thinking such thoughts meant the 'old' Lauren had really come back. Trying to rouse Henry was as good as believing in ghosts and miracles—without any proof.

I knew Seth was right: I hadn't felt truly 'alive' or inspired for a very long time. And why not? I had abandoned the very core of my nature—the spiritual, intuitive side—in favor of a new, somewhat bitter and cynical Lauren. The 'old' had been tossed aside like a winter coat too tattered and torn to keep out the cold.

And how did Seth see what was repressed and hidden—so clearly? In such a short time? In no time at all? Even Leo (intelligent, attentive Leo) had no idea of this other Lauren, hiding deep inside. Living with Leo, I could understand why. No doubt part of it was due to my own lazy inclination. It had been easier resting in the shadow of Leo's actions; letting him make all the decisions. It was safer keeping in the background: a silent, shy supporter behind the stage. The dramatics were all Leo's, and he'd probably been too preoccupied with his own life-theories to really delve into mine. In the end, hadn't he always tried to convince me to be myself—his way?

"Damn you Seth," I whispered, shutting my eyes tight and rolling over on the couch. "You've done it now. All right, you've got a talent for spotting people like me. Then you say I'm just like you. But why should I believe it? No better than falling for a psychiatrist."

Henry's snores grew louder, to boot.

"But you're not my psychiatrist, you're a long-lost cousin who sets the likes of me on fire, using a god-knows-what kind of method. Damn you Seth, and your lightning bolt."

But despite the grim realities of Lauren's Law, I was determined to keep my promise. Breathe deep. Stay truly alive: not only in England, but when I returned back home as well. Thanks to Seth and a Self that possibly knows.

No bounds.

❦   ❦   ❦

So the bell clinks.

This time it was really ringing: I'd fallen asleep and when I woke up I realized the bell was the telephone.

Wide-awake, I listened as it kept on ringing. Should I answer it?

The persistency had a certain hair-raising effect.

I thought, damn, could it be?

"Hello?"

"Hello Lauren. I didn't expect you to answer…"

"Nobody else is here—except Henry."

"Are you all right?"

"Fine—just a bit hung over." Of all people, it had to be Seth. Skin prickling and heart pounding, I clutched the receiver.

"I'm sorry. We didn't need that whiskey last night, on top of everything else. Guess we got a bit carried away."

"Well, it was worth it…"

"I'm glad you think so too. You know, I rarely get to talk like that with my friends…they get bored and tell me to shut up after fifteen minutes."

I assume you haven't plied them with whiskey first?" I replied. Then I quickly added, "Seriously though, I know what you mean. And I do want to thank you for your…your…helpful advice last night."

"Oh, good then, I actually made some sense to you? You aren't just being polite? Humoring a silly toad of a second cousin?"

"Of course not!"

"In that case, would you be up for another bike trip tomorrow, to King's Bromley? Some of my favorite footpaths are in that area—along the River Trent or Crawley Brook—which we could check out while we're there."

"I'd love to go, Seth, but tomorrow is my last day and I'll have to see if Grandma has something planned…"

"Blimy! Your last day? I didn't realize that." Seth's tone dropped into what seemed a genuine tone of acute disappointment. "Can't you just tell her you've made your own plans?"

"I guess so…"

In the pause that followed, I gulped and swallowed. Down went my last line of defense.

"Okay, Seth. Besides, I expect Grandma will probably need the entire day to pack."

"Good."

"Is…anyone else going?"

"No, I haven't even bothered to ask. It's a weekday, remember. But I'm on flexi hours at the electronic firm where I work. Ian's at college tomorrow. The rest of the gang usually aren't free till the weekends."

"Oh, right. And you don't think Naomi will mind?"

I had to ask. All that talking last night and I never got the chance (or didn't I dare?) to ask him about his girlfriend.

"She probably will mind," Seth muttered, "but it can't be helped."

"Wait, I don't want to cause any trouble," I insisted (and I sincerely meant it).

"Lauren, don't worry about it," Seth's answered. "Naomi and I are on the brink of a split anyway." His voice sounded quite off-hand as he added, "She'll probably be relieved to have an excuse to cut it off."

Even so, I hesitated.

"Lauren?"

"Yes?"

"Hey, Naomi is cute, but she's *fifteen*..."

"Fifteen!"

"Yeah, fifteen, and if she doesn't look like it, she certainly acts and speaks like it. In some ways she's still a child, and I can't really relate—except by hanging out and, well, you know—making out together." Seth's voice dropped to a low murmur. "I'd have to wait a few more years before she could even attempt to understand me."

"Oh."

Seth waited, of course, but for the life of me I couldn't think of what to say next.

"So, then, Lauren. Shall I ask my mum to pick you up around ten? My parents, you see, would rather your Grandma—and mine—don't worry too much, as they'd probably refuse to let you do it."

"Do what?"

"Get on the back of a bike."

"Oh yes...I should have guessed as much." God, do what? A dumb thing to ask. "Ten o'clock tomorrow then. Fine by me!"

When I put the phone down I felt this great chasm of hope open up my heart like the parting of the Red Sea. It swelled up and poured out in a rush of joy too overwhelming to believe: Seth wasn't in love with Naomi!

How could that be? I rushed back to the parlor and gleefully thanked Henry (who was awake again) by grabbing his hands and kissing his cheek.

He didn't notice; or if he did, at least now there'd be no further question as to how I felt.

❦   ❦   ❦

The morning was hazy and wet, but the clouds—a staid blanket of solemn gray—didn't look as if they were ready to dump any rain again for a couple of hours.

The now-familiar pattern of Midland country life followed our course as we headed north: narrow wedged-in lanes turning and twisting through gold and green-grassed fields. Here the land was level, lined out in squares, the fences all shrub and hawthorn. Plots of cropped wheat and autumn vegetables neatly mapped the valley—broken only by the occasional swerve of a canal or brook. An autumn chill seeped through my borrowed leathers.

Bed-sized puddles and dung-sodden mud sprayed in our wake; my warm breath clouded the visor. Beyond the hedges, the chimneys of farms and cottages spun ribbons of smoke into the damp and motionless air.

Seth had chosen a longer, circular route, and we rode through Alrewas, a village of black and white thatched cottages, moss-covered walls, cobbles and shops. When we finally passed through King's Bromley, the church spire rose above us like the mast of ship surveying its domain—a humble sea of bobbing rooftops.

I could have repeated that circle over and over again: riding in the open air, admiring the gentle pastures, villages, earth-dwellings, standing stones, farms, churches, castles, pubs, and footpaths—from the back of a motorcycle.

While Seth (who no doubt took it all for granted) turned off the main road onto a dirt track, slowing to near-stop at one point to avoid some stray sheep. At the end of this track I could see a long row of sleepy trees following the banks of a narrow, serene river.

"The Trent?"

Seth laughed. "Not quite. I've changed my mind. This one's even better. It's prettier, not polluted, and it's called the River Blythe."

We dismounted and walked to a grassy section near the bank, throwing our jackets down to sit on. Suddenly the sun came out. The bright glow drenched the trees in ripened color and, still blushing, spread through the opposite pasture. The temperature changed; the air felt warm; I threw off my sweater.

"Thank goodness," Seth exclaimed. "A break in the clouds, and we might get some decent weather."

The radiant leaves reflected their doubles in the river, a mirror of deep royal blue. The spot was so peaceful and calm, you could hear every tiny ripple pass with the current. To our left, the river bubbled as the current cornered a bend, and past a protruding bush, two swans appeared. They gently paddled toward us, arching their necks and picking up speed.

"Of course there would be swans here too," I mumbled, glaring at Seth as if it were his fault.

"They seem to assume we're the suckers who'll share our lunch…" (articulated American-style)

He smiled back at me, his face infuriatingly soft and glowing from the morning ride, his eyes piously gleaming like a guru's.

"Oh yes!"

No doubt about it, then: Seth shared my reverence for nature. Sauntering along the banks of the river, he often stopped, like me, to inspect the variety of plants thriving in the margins.

"Purple loosestrife," he stated, waving a stem under my nose. "I like learning their names. Here, this one with the narrow grooved leaves is toadrush."

I smiled. "There's even water lilies! They must be lovely, blooming in the summer."

"And the water cress, that stuff growing right into the water, that's yellow cress. I make a point of coming here in July—when the cress turns into a yellow carpet and the river's teeming with life. Not to mention all the rest…"

He stopped talking.

I must have looked rather amused.

"So what's so funny?"

"I don't know…on the outside you look like the kind of guy who'd be coming here to smoke dope and throw beer cans in the water," I confessed.

"Don't be fooled," Seth admitted. "I'm still a complete bastard."

"I expect so."

"Yep, and to prove my point, I've just put my foot in a nice big clump of cow shit," he muttered, gazing down at his boot, and shaking it in disgust.

When he bent down to remove it, I watched his every move: how he rolled up his sleeves, crouched in the grass, balanced both elbows on his thighs. Every gesture filled me with desire. I had this sudden urge to fling myself into his arms, feel his fingers caress my skin. So smoothly. So carefully. The same way he was washing that boot.

Instead I walked away and went in search of something I could easily grab hold of. And keep. I was looking for a tangible memento, such as a sprig of forget-me-not. That would do.

Plowing through a minefield of dung to catch up, Seth, now breathless, held up a dripping wet—but clean—left boot. Then he handed me a water bottle.

"Want a drink?"

"Thanks."

"Are you happy?" he asked, and this time the timing was all-wrong…or just right.

"Oh yes."

"But?"

I nodded. "But…can we stay here all day? I'd just as soon stay here, if Shugborough Estate is going to be crowded with tourists."

"Sure—we can take a quick look at the Church of St. Michael, instead, if you prefer. It's not far from here—we just get back on the footpath where it crosses the river."

After we'd eaten Aunt Bea's cheese and pickle sandwiches, we lay side by side in a rare patch of grass completely free of nettles. Looking up and watching the slow moving clouds overhead, Seth spoke of other places—moors, locks and mountains, bogs and lakes—all to be found on the Isle of Britain.

And once again, I struggled against the urge to touch him. If only he knew how hard it was, resisting. It crossed my mind he was bound to sense it, but if he did, he certainly wasn't offering any encouragement. In fact, it seemed more likely that he hadn't even considered the possibility of taking my hand, let alone anything else.

Nevertheless I prayed for something like that to happen; prayed like a pilgrim prays in the face of death. Completely preposterous. I might as well be living in the Dark Ages, asking for deliverance from the Plague. And besides, what was the point? I'd probably never get another chance to come back to England.

Of course I tried to convince myself if we did touch, it would be even harder to leave. I'd have to say goodbye to Seth and then what? I couldn't imagine how I'd cope. Did I really want to carry the memory of that back with me to America as well?

No.

"Are you comfortable?" Seth asked, during a lapse in the conversation. "Why not put your head on my lap for a pillow?"

"All right," I conceded, despite the 'no' which seemed so dependable just a few seconds ago.

I moved closer, and suddenly Seth's hands were cushioning my head. Then it was all over. Maybe a few minutes: an eternity of space, suspending our physical connection through a long battlefield of mental nerve and courage against fear and uncertainty.

He sat up, holding me down so I didn't move, and began to stroke my hair. I closed my eyes, the back of my head feeling every bulge below his belt.

He sighed. And something inside that sigh made me wonder, only now, if Seth had struggled even harder than I.

Not daring to open my eyes, I knew in the end I'd let it happen, because the old Lauren was back again; that one sign from Seth would be worth a million pangs of aching memory.

His hands kept stoking my hair. I could feel him bending down. Then his mouth lightly brushed the fringe on my forehead.

Nearby the swans, with dipping beaks and wagging tails, fished beneath the willow tree. Oblivious, Seth's lips meandered slowly over both my cheeks, until they couldn't stop, and we lay tangled together in the grass…

Lost in a kiss.

CHAPTER 7

The Idea

"It sounds odd, calling me—'matey'—" I said, trying to answer. Though even odder was the sound of my rigid, well-controlled speech.

"You're my matey now," Seth repeated, putting his hands on my shoulders. "In this country, we call our closest friends 'mate' or 'matey'—or at least I do."

"Even to girls?"

"Well no, not very often, but you, Lauren, you're different than most girls I've known. You and I, even though we've spent such a short time together…we're good mates now. Aren't we?"

"Yes…"

I stepped back and Seth's heavy hands fell from my shoulders. That was it: a dreadful end to the outing, rushing into Chester's car to get back to Aunt Bea's for dinner. That was my goodbye to Seth.

I gave him one last look, fighting the urge to scream and cry out it wasn't fair; shit, the very next morning flying back to the States and Seth standing there acting so damn cool and resigned in front of his father.

Damn him.

Chester sensed something was wrong, and for the first time I noticed he wasn't smiling. Grim-faced, he pulled the emergency brake and started the engine. As we pulled away Seth suddenly lunged forward; with a loud thump he banged my side of the door with his fist.

My final glimpse, as I turned around, caught him standing on the front walk—fiercely hugging my leather jacket.

In a state of shock, I felt myself teetering on the brink of an abyss, threatening once again to take control and destroy all my self-composure.

"It's a shame you're leaving tomorrow," Chester finally announced, weaving in and out between traffic.

I didn't attempt to speak.

"But then, I guess two weeks is about as long as a holiday lasts. Though it's not enough time, is it?"

"I guess not," I squeaked, forcing myself to pretend I was still alive and conscious.

"So you'd like to stay longer if you could?"

"Oh….(stifled choke)…I would like to…."

"Well good, because Elizabeth and I were talking about it last night, and we think you should stay a bit longer. You could spend some time with us, at our house. Shall we ask Harriet?"

"What?"

"If you can stay longer, you're welcome to stay with us."

"That's very kind of you," I assented, slowly taking it all in. As Chester's offer registered more clearly in my mind, I wondered why on earth Chester and Elizabeth would suggest such a thing. After all, why should they care?

Seth's parents were sharp and liberal-minded, obviously. But I hadn't expected this last minute invitation. Perhaps it was merely relative-driven: a move to extend my impressions of the family a bit further than Henry and Bea.

"We haven't managed to see you much, since you've been here," Chester added.

I nodded, and the conversation ended. Chester whizzed through the traffic and left me to my own thoughts, which struggled to move ahead.

Why didn't it make sense? Chester and Elizabeth wanted me to spend more time with them, and take part in their world. Yes, Chester I could believe: perceptive, easy-going and cheerful, he'd probably been the one to suggest it. But Elizabeth actually scared me a little, as her fast-tongued, sarcastic manner seemed critical of those who were different. And Americans, related or not, were no exception. I had the impression Grandma and I amused her, but she didn't particularly like us. If Elizabeth found out, I was thinking, she most certainly wouldn't approve of her son kissing his American cousin.

So I didn't take Chester's conversation too seriously. Nothing more was said, and in the evening I started packing my suitcase. It must have been close to nine-o'clock when I heard the phone ring.

Muffled conversation drifted up the stairs from the hall, with Grandma's booming voice often exclaiming, "Oh I don't KNOW.... WHAT ABOUT...travel ALONE..." and then Aunt Bea rushed up the stairs.

Panting, she swung open the door.

"Lauren, dear, please come down, Elizabeth's on the phone, she wants to speak to you."

"Elizabeth?" I was still amazed.

"Yes, dear, please hurry!"

"Hello, Elizabeth?" I thought I must be dreaming, but here I was talking to Seth's mother, who was speaking in her usual matter-of-fact tone.

"Seems I've caused a bit of a row, Lauren. I suppose you've gathered that we intend to keep you for another few weeks?"

"Yes but—"

"It's done." She chuckled, and added, "I merely used my firm, persuasive manner on your grandmother, same as I do with my boys. Nobody crosses me when I make up my mind."

"But Grandma...how will she manage?"

"A stubborn woman, your Grandma—but—she's as fit to travel as the rest of us. She's capable of doing it on her own, with a bit of help from the airline staff."

I glanced over at Harriet, who looked a bit dismayed, but resigned.

"She's agreed?"

Elizabeth ignored my misgivings. "She had no choice. And as you will be staying with us, Bea will have no say in the matter either."

"That's very nice of you, Elizabeth, but I've spent all my money...I'll lose the plane ticket back..."

"Not to worry—we'll loan you the money and your father has agreed to pay us back if you can't."

"My dad?"

"Well, I decided it was time your father and I had a chat anyway, and he's agreed that it would be a shame for you to end your visit when you haven't spent much time with us."

For a minute, I was speechless. Then I thanked Elizabeth many times until Elizabeth interrupted with, "It's done, we're happy to have you stay or I wouldn't have stuck my nose in your Grandma's plans. We'll take you back to our house after we've seen her off at the airport—is that all right with you?"

"Yes, that's fine."

Fine by me, thank-you-god.

✳   ✳   ✳

"But I just can't figure out your mom and dad," I confessed to Seth as soon as I got the chance.

"What do you mean?"

"What did you *say* to them?"

"Nothing," Seth insisted. "Honestly, the thought didn't occur to me that you might be able to stay longer. Anyway, it would have seemed strange if I'd pestered them with…you know…how much I wished you didn't have to go."

"Well then, I really don't understand it now," I muttered.

We gazed at each other awkwardly, refusing to speak of it further, yet regretting the heavy silence.

Blushing slightly, I nevertheless refused to let it go. "It seems strange," I went on, "because I don't think your mother likes me very much. And yet she went to all that trouble to find a way for me to stay longer. What made her do it?" I wanted an answer. "Did your dad talk her into it?"

"My dad doesn't force her into anything," Seth replied. "They always make decisions on equal footing, as a mutual team."

"That's good," I said. "You're lucky to have them as parents. They don't even seem to mind your parties or smoking pot in the house!"

"They say it's better in the long run if we do it at home," Seth explained. "At least they're around to keep an eye and prevent us from getting arrested."

"Man, I'm looking forward to getting to know them better," I answered. "Though I'll never understand why they did it."

"Did what?"

"Arranged it so I could stay! Seth, how did they know I couldn't bear the thought of leaving so soon?"

"They probably didn't know," Seth replied, unabashed. "But don't be fooled—it was enough to be polite and ask."

"I don't see why they even bothered," I argued, "and besides, I never said a word about *us*, either."

Of course Seth then tilted his head at me, surprised, and retorted, "What makes you think you had to *say* anything?"

I thought about it for a moment. I thought about Henry.

❈ ❈ ❈

"The forecast is rain, wind and gales," Chester grumbled, throwing up his hands in despair. "But if you must go, then what do I care—do what you want."

"Well, are you sure you won't mind the wet and cold?" Seth asked me, for the third time.

"No, not when this is the only chance to see Cornwall!"

The bike gang had planned a trip to the Cornwall coast for the weekend. They were going to camp out in tents on a farm pasture, but the West Coast in October wasn't the best time for either motorcycling or camping. Seth and Ian had just broken the news to their parents during supper.

"I take it Lauren realizes that a five hour ride will make her bottom feel like raw meat," Elizabeth cut in. "Have you boys taken into account the fact that she's not used to long rides?"

"We can take a few extra rest stops," Ian replied. "We'll have to anyway, in order to thaw out."

Elizabeth shook her head, mouth full of shepherd's pie and half mumbled, "Don't think it's prudent, but then again I can't say I was very prudent at your age…"

Three weeks had flown by. Nothing could be more spectacular than spending the last weekend in Cornwall. Let it blizzard! I'd wear an Eskimo suit if necessary.

Ian and Seth excused themselves from the table to start sorting out the gear. I stayed in the kitchen, helping Chester wash the dishes. After a few weeks in their household, I felt like one of the family.

Even so, Seth and I managed to keep our little secret a secret. Unfortunately it wasn't difficult to accomplish, since nothing happened—physically—between us, since that first kiss.

On one hand, it wasn't surprising with a host of other distractions to keep us apart. Seth worked during the day at an electronics firm, Ian went to a local college, and Elizabeth and Chester ran a small engineering business of their own—so I spent the day-time hours hanging out in Lichfield. I became quite fond of the town and never tired of finding some new area to explore each day; but in the evenings I was filled with anxiety and longing, waiting and hoping for a chance to be with Seth. My emotions were completely out of control: the desire to explore more of England had grown into an obsession which included Seth, making it sadder day by day as I faced the inevitable outcome of having to leave it all behind.

Neither Seth nor I seemed capable of acknowledging what happened at the river. I dared—occasionally—to believe he felt the same way; I remembered the scary sensation of his heart beating hard and fast like it would burst against my breast; I sometimes caught his hands trembling, his face imploring me to see his desire hidden behind a cool disguise; I imagined a thousand different ways and means of having that kiss again.

But what actually happened? I'd spend the daylight hours more or less killing time, and in the evenings I'd wait impatiently for the moment Seth came home. Inevitably he'd arrive, I'd hear him come through the door—and grabbing a handy book—I'd pretend to be reading. He'd walk into the room, say hello, and I'd nonchalantly look up as if I'd be quite happy to resume my reading if he didn't fancy a conversation. Just in case.

Then Seth would go up to his room as if he didn't really care if we had time alone together or not. I'd hate myself for feeling so silly and being such a success at faking nonchalance. After several encounters like this, I didn't know what to do. Repeatedly we kept apart as the remaining days quickly dwindled away.

But now, the trip to Cornwall beckoned and I was too excited to sleep. Still awake past midnight, I crept to the toilet and paused as I went past Seth's bedroom. The door was cracked open and I had to listen. He was softly strumming his guitar.

Everyone else had gone to bed.

He looked up, winked, and muttered, "Come in and sit down, if you like such punishment."

I pushed through the door and sat down. Having crossed the invisible barrier, I perched on the corner of his bed—right next to him. Seth leaned over. Out came the bottle of whiskey.

I accepted the whiskey; Seth rose, closed the door, and back to his guitar. I was impressed (though not surprised) by his playing; by the soft, gentle sounds as they gradually transformed into restless tumultuous strains of melodies he made up as he went along. At the same time I kept drinking most of the whiskey, still sitting on his bed, keenly aware every one else had gone to sleep.

I felt sixteen again, shy and nervously waiting for the guy to make the first move. But Seth wasn't about to make a move—other than striking a few steel strings with his plectrum. It began to dawn on me that either Seth's interest had waned, or he didn't see the point. What was the point? Physical closeness would only make my leaving harder to swallow. Whatever the real reason was, Seth abstained. I could see it written all over his face: "Don't touch."

No touching, except when we passed the whiskey bottle between us, hand lingering blatantly over hand.

"Are you happy?"

"Yes."

"Good."

"Lauren…"

"What?"

"Never mind."

"No, what?"

"Shall I stop playing?"

"No."

Stop confusing Seth's passion for life as something else, I kept telling myself. Why couldn't I accept that? Why did I feel he was somehow trying to convince me that we shared something stronger than lust? But I lusted. Despite everything, my lustful thoughts grew into X-rated proportions: hot and wild, aching to touch not just his hand, but his arm; clutch his face, bite his lips, bury my tongue in his chest, feel him pulsating inside me—I wanted every inch of his body, badly. I pressed all my desires against the neck of a whiskey bottle, and the session in Seth's bedroom ended in a hazy, drunken sense of wordless frustration.

And so our relationship progressed.

🍁   🍁   🍁

"Seth," I managed to ask, "Why isn't Naomi coming on the Cornwall trip?"

"She wasn't invited."

"Wouldn't she like to come?"

"Probably, but we broke up last Saturday."

"Oh, I see."

"We're still friends, or so she says."

Silence.

"I've been meaning to do it for weeks," Seth muttered, "but now it's finally settled."

"You don't sound very glad."

"I'm not sure exactly how I feel, now that it's done."

"I see." I struggled to zip the cuffs of my jacket up tight, and over the ends of my gloves. We were just about to take off for Cornwall.

"Ready?"

"Yep."

The conversation ended in a roar of engines.

And the journey itself proved a long, cold, rainy, monotonous slog on a boring motorway. Six hours later, we snaked our way along the farmhouse track (final destination), having arrived safely. Seven bikes and everyone dismounting stood around them in bad humor—even the veterans were frozen and saddle sore.

As for me—the trip was a dream. Behind Seth once more, I could hold his body and feel nothing but the tight, warm curve of his torso and thighs. My hands were frostbitten but I didn't care—I gladly paid the price. My seat felt like an object of torture wedged between my legs; yet I felt no pain, leaning my head on Seth's shoulder and adjusting my legs against his.

It was after midnight when we reached the farm. Being too dark to see anything, the tents were erected hurriedly in the middle of a great unending patch of cow manure. Exhausted (everyone except me complaining), we piled into our sleeping bags. Ian and Philip flopped on either side of me in one tent, leaving Seth in the second tent with Andy, Andy's girlfriend, and Mark.

Then it hit me. I felt terrible. Really awful. Not only extremely tired, but also freezing cold. The ride itself finished, I hated all the rest of it: the wet weather, my sore bum, the uncomfortable and unhappy end to the journey. The next minute I was lying there almost crying in bitter disappointment because—I had to admit—my sleeping bag was positioned completely wrong...

If it wasn't next to Seth's.

What time was it? Possibly three in the morning or almost dawn? It felt as if I'd buried my head—in despair—beneath the blackness of that sleeping bag for several hours. I tried lulling myself to sleep, using various monotonous chants, but that didn't work. Still on the verge of tears (which seemed utterly absurd and silly), I cursed my irrational self. It was easy imagining what a psychiatrist would say.

"So tell me, Dr. Shrink, why am I so unhappy?"

Perhaps you made the crucial mistake of setting up a false assumption. Have you created an expectation that hasn't happened according to your plan? You wouldn't be feeling so bad at all—now would you?—if an expectation wasn't there...

"All right, I expected to be sleeping next to Seth. I assumed he'd be as anxious as me to take advantage of this opportunity...to get close...but he doesn't seem to care one way or the other."

Remember, you're the one who's decided it's a big deal—this sleeping arrangement. But why get upset about that, when all his mates are there too? After all, there won't be any real chance of getting physically close—not without the others knowing.

"True, and I don't want them to know! I suppose Seth did the right thing by not making it obvious..."

So why feel so miserable?

"I guess I'm angry, too—for being in love with him—so much that it really hurts. I'm suddenly realizing how much and I'd rather not face it...."

Oh yes, I see. And we've still got your other problem, the one you call Lauren's Law.

"You said it, Doctor. Couldn't I be mistaken? Maybe Seth doesn't give a stuff about whether he sleeps next to me in a tent or anywhere else, for that matter. I'm just giving myself a convenient set of excuses to protect my illusion, just like I did—you know..."

Like you did in Santa Barbara, with Darren?

"God, I was such a mess with Darren! Haven't I learned my lesson? What if I'm making the same mistake again? Thinking he cares for me, making a mountain out of mole-hill..."

Watch out: you'll be doing it again.

"No I won't."

Why not? If the old Lauren is back...

The last time I'd let myself fall in love was during my freshman year at college, with Darren. I had to admit: I'd made most of it up. All made up in my head, not his...What good did it do? Except turn me into a blubbering, useless wreck.

And it was freezing cold in that sleeping bag. I snuggled deeper inside; the blackness suddenly melted away into a vivid scene on the beach at Santa Barbara.

Darren. He seemed so sincere, so convincing. He said he loved me, but it wasn't just the words. Such was the power of love, and loving blindly. Then the bubble burst.

Darren had arranged to meet me on the dunes, one day, at dusk. I'd suspected nothing, and suddenly without warning it was over. We were finished.

And now, in the darkness, I was envisioning that spot on the dunes, sitting next to Darren at the beach; I kept watching his face, which had changed. He looked nothing like the Darren I knew. His expression had turned all stiff, like a wooden mask with a double mouth: was it an averted frown, or a macabre, makeshift grin? Could this be Death? I wondered. Could this be why he's wearing a death mask?

"Sorry Lauren."

The paradox fell and his weird grin changed to a clenched frown.

"What's wrong, Darren?"

"I can't go on. I'm attracted to you, but it's not enough…. it's unfair to you…This just isn't going to work," mumbled the voice behind the mask.

"Why not?" (Were those my words? It didn't matter; this couldn't be Darren, we couldn't be having this conversation.)

"Why not…?" While considering an answer, a hand (looking like Darren's) plucked a substantial wad of dune-grass from the sand and carefully twisted it into a large knot.

"I can't explain…I'm sorry…but it's over. I mean, I feel it's best to end it now—rather than later."

"I see."

That's what I said but I didn't see. I didn't see any of it. So he wasn't in love with me: the reality was so shocking I didn't feel anything. In fact, I calmly and coolly watched him get up and shuffle across the sand, into oblivion.

I waited. Surely I was about to feel something; I sat there staring at the smooth peaks of the sand dunes, the tumbling waves, the occasional seagull fighting against the wind. I watched the sun gradually turn into a dull orange ball, slowing sinking, sinking, into the sea—until it had vanished completely.

In a trance, I let my heart go. And how quickly it fled, like a pining spirit which after a brief, impetuous dance, split in mid-air and scattered across the beach. Then turned. Then changed into the foam flung by the peak of a wave. To disappear completely, across the dunes and stars mocking sharply in the night.

Even so, I waited for it to come back. All night, but still I found nothing—only emptiness. I thought: "Is this what it feels like, to grow up? To wake up to the real world?"

I had no choice but to let that part of me go: the cheerful, loving, enthusiastic young Lauren. I actually felt my old self, my naive innocence, leaving for good. It was an awful feeling—like a physical entity leaving my body—draining out until nothing remained but a dry, dead shell.

Rolling over inside my sleeping bag, I tried to blot out the picture. But I could still see myself lying prostrate on that beach, praying "Please don't go away!" because never, ever did I want to be bitter, disillusioned and empty. Yet it happened: the time when, moaning and writhing in the sand, I had felt the loss, and everything changed.

After Darren. And vowing never again to fall head over heels in love, a new Lauren emerged from the dunes and made her way back to the dorm.

Yes—it was dark and freezing on those dunes, just like this very night. I remembered how I couldn't get warm; how I spent hours shivering and shivering underneath a goose-down jacket.

CHAPTER 8

The Beach and the Farm

When I awoke the next morning it was still raining. Looking out through the tent flap, all I could see was a clumpy, overgrown field disappearing into the mist and dripping wet. Beyond, just discernible through the fog, stood an old gray farmhouse partly shielded by a hedge and one tilted, scraggly old tree.

The air smelt of the sea. Cows mooed in a barn somewhere and in the background some kind of machinery was making a grinding noise. All else was hidden by freezing fog and rain. I crawled back into my damp sleeping bag.

"Hey you lazy gits, get up," shouted a voice, forcing me awake again.

A chorus of moaning joined in as each sleeping bag was kicked in rapid succession.

"Did you sleep well?" Seth whispered in my ear, giving me a gentle nudge.

"Come on, there's no good reason to get up," Philip grumbled. "I can still hear the rain pounding on the tent!"

"We're in Cornwall, you idiot! A little rain better not stop you—or the inside of this tent will be the only sight you see on this trip," Seth replied.

"So be it. Get stoned and stay in the tent, fine with me."

"Great for Lauren. Why did we bother bringing her all the way to Cornwall?"

"Oh, I could entertain her just fine, right here."

"You're disgusting."

"No I'm not."

"Then get up and make us some breakfast."

Philip rolled himself away from the warmth of my side and tried to trip up Seth with his bundle of sleeping bag. After a playful scuffle he muttered "All right" and got up.

"I'm going out for a piss."

"Get the food bag from Ian's bike and bring it back with you."

"Seth," I asked him, sitting up and pulling down my crumpled T-shirt, "Whose idea was it, to come all the way to Cornwall?"

"Mine."

"Just as I thought. But in this weather—?"

Seth's eyes gleamed with mischief. He was stretched out, half over my bag, and I hated him for looking so good.

"We wouldn't have done it, except you're here," he said. "And I wanted to show you—" he paused, gazing at my long, disheveled hair, "a beach."

So despite the rain, which had at least settled down to a fine drizzle, we all set out for the coast in the afternoon. The destination was a secluded beach Seth had discovered some years before—called Sandymouth.

Cornwall seemed an eerie, desolate land in the gray rain and mist, blown by relentless wind and sparsely inhabited by a few isolated farms—no people to be seen. Life must be hard here, I thought, but just the place where romantic spirits might roam

We traveled on—westward—until without warning, the sloped fields abruptly fell into the sea: walls of rock and erosion tumbling sharply down to a shore of sand and polished rubble.

Our procession of bikes turned left onto a dirt track which was often obstructed by a crowd of sheep, until the track ended at the edge of a cliff and a narrow trail led further down to the beach. Parked, and engines off—we could hear the roar of the surf.

Seth secured our gear and said to me, "You'll like this, I bet."

Grinning, he grabbed my hand and we both ran racing and stumbling down the path ahead of the others.

The waves were stormy and rough, crashing toward us in a frenzy—the salt spray stinging our eyes and wind whipping our jackets about like crazy flapping sails. We braced and slowly picked our way between the jumbled lines of smooth black rock, reaching out toward the surf to the open stretch of sand.

I'd seen many beaches in my day, but as Seth promised, Sandymouth was pure magic. Something about it evoked a new, unfamiliar sensation: I felt wildly thrilled and overwhelmed by this formidable stretch of sea and rock formation. "Blow your mind with this!" the place seemed to say, and it oozed with it—a feeling quite fiendishly black, dense and sleek, glistening from the never-ending motion of a Cornwall surf. This beach was extreme and intense to the core. An untold shifting and abrading mapped out nature's treacherous destruction, demanding continual transformation.

Immediately I understood why Seth's favorite beach was a shore I would always come back to, if only in my mind. Standing there, I felt as if I'd gone back—far, far back—in time. Everything ended at the beginning; the same waves and tides moving earth for billions of years. My ego meant nothing now, engulfed by the host of all life, the omniscient patriarch of ages gone by; the great mover and creator of life. My soul was the sea, and my body—just a ship, a means of passing through.

A brief witness.

"Hey Lauren, how about a dip into the Atlantic Ocean, where she touches the shores of old England?" Ian shouted through the wind, disturbing my reverie.

"Not a bad idea, but it's awfully cold," I shouted back.

I had to shake myself out of it. For a moment, nothing seemed solid or real.

"What's Seth doing?"

I looked around and eventually pinpointed Seth, braced high atop a cluster of rocks, standing fast and resistant—almost lost—in the swirling gale of surf and spray. He looked so vulnerable, yet stalwart and stubborn as a lighthouse.

"Shit, he's crazy!" Ian exclaimed, having spotted him as well.

We walked over to this cliff and Ian furiously waved his arms, yelling at Seth and trying to get his attention. Finally Seth turned and saw us gesturing below; he swiftly and deftly made his descent.

"What's the matter?" he shouted. "Had enough already?"

"No!" I sputtered through the rain. "Ian has suggested we take a ceremonial dip in the Atlantic."

"I wasn't serious," Ian interrupted.

"Hey, that's a good idea," said Seth.

"In this gale?"

"It's our only chance…"

"Why not?" Suddenly I no longer considered it a joke. Would I ever get an opportunity to visit this fantastic beach again? Probably not—so I had to do it now. My only chance…

Seth had already peeled off his rain-jacket, sweater, shirt, undershirt—then off came his pants. I followed suit (but keeping my bra on), laughing at the surprised look on Ian's face.

Ian's amazement quickly changed to glee as soon as he, too, stripped down to his underwear.

The others came running (automatically refusing to be left out), and a line of pale naked flesh in silly white pants dashed—screaming and pre-soaked by the drizzle—into the welcoming folds of icy Atlantic.

Whooping and cursing, we hit the water. Our impetuous dare lasted a good ten seconds, enough for two or three splashes, before we all dashed back out again—screaming and shivering—to the pile of rocks sheltering our clothes. Convulsed in giggles, I scrambled madly to pull my damp clothes over my wet body; then I stopped for a minute.

I stopped because I suddenly sensed something peculiar in the air, as if we were being watched.

I paused to survey the surrounding rocks, but of course no one else could be seen. No, it wasn't a person, but something else. I could feel it riding the salty blasts of the wind, pervading the shadows dividing the cliffs, whirling in the foam-edged tide pools, slipping in and out along the rocks. An invisible presence reached out to the sea like the black-boned finger joints of a giant octopus.

I looked at Seth, who—as if reading my thoughts—grinned and spread his arms out in a theatrical gesture, inviting the unseen to enjoy the show.

I threw up my shirt and we both doubled up with laughter. Could it be we'd amused our god called Sandymouth, audience to a small gathering of humans in the wind and rain? If so, he must have found it hilarious, a bunch of naked midgets hovering about his rocks—struggling to clothe themselves.

"Good, eh?"

Climbing up the hill back to the bikes, Seth reached for my hand. He placed it inside his coat pocket for warmth, pulling me close to his side. Of course Seth knew. He knew from the look on my face, that I'd never forget our swim at Sandymouth.

"Some things endure," he muttered fiercely in my ear. "Long after we've died and turned to dust. They carry on—for us."

"Sounds like something I read once," I answered. "Now I'm pretty convinced."

"Well?"

"Well what?"

"Don't be afraid when you feel it. Then maybe I won't."
As he said it, he was squeezing my hand...
Hard.

When I awoke the next morning it was still raining.

I stuck my head out the tent flap. A dark green rain mack stood—or more accurately humped—beside the second tent. Then the hump moved back a bit, ejecting a stream of piss that splattered in the drenched mat of grass.

"Shit," grumbled a voice inside the mack. "I've had enough of this."

"We're all going."

'We're all going' was definitely Seth's voice, rising out from the muffled drone of cursing and splashing.

The rain mack nodded, and stumbled back to the tent. An arm emerged, and thrust out a couple of plastic bags. The bags were tied tight, and stuffed with gear. I eventually realized it was Ian underneath that hooded hump; loading his stuff on his bike.

And it wasn't long before we all followed his example. No one even bothered to light the camping stove for a cup of tea—there wasn't time in the mad rush to get out of the mud and drizzle and back home to a warm house and some dry clothes.

"I'm not sorry we came, though, are you?" whispered Seth, before donning his helmet.

"No, I'm still glad we did it," I sputtered back, wiping away the drips from my chin and nose. "At least I got to see something of Cornwall and Sandymouth."

We headed north, in a line: spraying through an unending sea of puddles and half blinded by a dense mist.

A few hours later, and only twenty miles south of Lichfield, the clouds disappeared. The road was dry, the visibility cleared, and it felt like different world altogether—in the Midlands.

Basking in the sun at the final petrol stop, I said my goodbyes to the rest of the gang as Seth waved them on. He explained he needed to add some oil; make a few checks.

He did this, and yet he didn't seem satisfied.

Patiently waiting, I wondered if something had gone wrong with the bike.

"Everything all right?"

"Yep, you ready?"

"Whenever you are, Seth."

"Not far to go."

"I know."

"The weather's turned."

"Oh well."

"Typical."

"It is, isn't it?"

"There's still Monday. I took Monday off and we're back a day early."

He gazed at his bike, slapping his gloves against his thigh, before he looked back at me.

"I told Ian, if we didn't show up soon after, it meant we'd decided to camp somewhere up here for another night."

"Another night?"

"We can if you want."

Despite his off-hand tone, I couldn't help but notice the sharp, defensive edge hanging off the end of every word. And his expression: poised and ready to react as required, to the slightest hint of approval—or rejection.

"Do you want to, Seth?"

"Why else would I ask?"

I didn't know what to think. I hadn't anticipated anything quite like this, to say the least.

"Up near the river," Seth explained, "where we took that walk, there's a dairy farm. My parents are friends with the couple who run it, and they've let me camp there before."

"Sounds good to me," I confessed. "It's a shame to waste the rest of the day when the sun's finally come out."

"A crazy idea," Seth muttered. "But I thought I'd ask, just in case—like me—you suddenly weren't that keen to get back."

"So let's do it."

"Next stop, Willowby Farm, Hamstall Ridware."

I nodded and quickly reached for my helmet. At least with a helmet, Seth couldn't see exactly how keen.

The farm sat on the edge of a hill just outside the village of Hamstall Ridware. We pitched the small tent on the corner of a field with a pleasant view of the river Blythe and valley below. Then we walked along the narrow lane leading to the village and church.

"Ridware comes from the old English word r-y-d-ware," said Seth. "It means place of the riverfolk."

"How do you know that?"

"Something I read once."

"And how old is the church?"

"I'm not sure, but I think St. Michael's has been here since the 1400s."

"I'm glad I'll get to see it after all."

"Yeah, I meant to show you before we got…side-tracked…" Seth mumbled, and then smiled. "I take it I'm forgiven, by the way?"

"Yes, I mean no, I—"

"Not that I forgive you," he said. "For tempting me beyond all endurance…"

He leapt ahead and grabbed a twig off a nearby Alder, glancing back at me with a wry smile.

"Sticks and stones don't break my bones but words can always hurt me," he chanted, pointing the twig at me.

"Is that why we've never talked about it?"

"Which 'it' do you mean?"

"Seth, you know, when we kissed."

"Is there something more to say?"

"There could be."

"Yes." Seth stood, arms crossed, twig pressed against his chest. "I could say something more." And he waited for me to reach the tree he was leaning against.

When I did, Seth didn't speak. He simply put his mouth over mine and slipped a hand inside my jacket. "More," he breathed, pushing my back against the tree, the hand now reaching and cupping my breast.

"There could be more…"

He eventually let go.

Heart pounding madly and rooted to the spot, I could hardly believe his self-restraint.

"There, it's said," he muttered, lurching away from the tree. "Now let's not, for the second time, forget the poor old church."

St. Michael's was deserted. The church itself was in very good condition, considering its age. Sitting isolated at the far end of the village, I admired the humble structure of stone, adorned by a few narrow medieval windows. Of course the church was hardly as majestic as the great Cathedral, but nevertheless I was dumbfounded by a sense of reverence and awe.

"Want to go inside?" Seth asked.

"No," I answered. "I'd rather just look from the outside, and walk through the graveyard."

We passed an ancient Celtic cross, and I took a deep breath, moving behind the church to where a host of gravestones tumbled down the sloping field; some bent and leaning, some broken and black with age; others more recent. But they all had a place and they all faced the river. A silent sentry of souls, watching the sun rise and set, the seasons change, the sheep come and go, the birds fly, the great yellow cress bloom and fade. Down by the river Blythe.

And I envied this church, standing so close to Seth's favorite spot near the banks where the reeds hid the swans and there was nothing to feel but peace and bliss, lying in a true love's arms.

"I'll remember you," I whispered to a woman named Sarah Jane, lying in the ground below my feet. "Wife of William, in loving remembrance. Sarah Jane. And when I'm gone, would you mind—in return—keeping an eye on Seth? Would you do that for me?"

"Yes," a soundless voice whispered back.

"Hey, no messing around with the dead," Seth shouted. "Unless you want them to haunt you."

He stood waiting at the gate, probably wondering what on earth I was doing, hugging a Victorian grave.

But for the time being, Sarah Jane, wife of William, wasn't needed—not when I pretended all the way back to the farm that I'd never leave. How could I leave with Seth building a fire and cooking sausage and beans on the camping stove? We sat outside the tent until the stars appeared and an owl hooted, once, from a distance. Its cry, breaking through the black shrouded hush of a nearby wood—seemed to carry on forever.

We hadn't spoken much, as if to avoid the predicament. Perhaps the owl finally broke the spell, reminding us both how the night was passing quickly.

"Did you hear that?"

"Yes."

Turning his eyes away from the fire, Seth handed me his whiskey flask.

"What a shame that's all we've got left."

"That's it then? There isn't any—?" I couldn't finish.

"More?" Seth chuckled under his breath. He'd caught the connection.

More…I remembered the way he'd touched me as he said it. The prospect of 'more' still pulsating through my body so nothing else really mattered. I wanted more but I was scared of it. I was so confused.

Meanwhile Seth waited. He kept his distance. Why? I held my tongue, wondering if this was some kind of test. Or did he simply prefer to relish the mounting tension? Maybe he only wanted to see how long I could hold out and do nothing….except suffer.

But the owl was alert and hunting: eyes riveted on every movement made by its prey. I suddenly realized we, too, were playing the game of hunger. And I had to make the next move. Nothing would happen unless I took the risk and emerged from the dark where I'd been hiding.

So slowly, I inched forward. Got closer.

Close enough—as it turned out—by simply bending down to rest my cheek over the freckles on Seth's hand. Instantly his other hand clasped my neck and pulled me up.

"Lauren, you crazy fool," he hissed, kissing my lips and running his fingers through my hair.

Clasping my head and sighing, he pulled me in one swift motion toward the tent. Once inside, his heated kisses grew intense, almost frantic, but I realized my own pent-up frustration was even greater: willing us to go further by pushing down my jeans, flinging aside pants and sweater, my body mindlessly opening and urging Seth to…

Half moaning with wretched desire, I felt the swelling tide of his orgasm rush into my own…

Thank. You God….

The sudden release was a surprise, a sensation I'd never felt before. A strange thing, to melt under the lightning bolt. So deep, so natural, as if my body blossomed and every petal opened, completely and utterly, within the bursting light of Seth's being.

Going all the way with Seth closed the gap between my blood cells and his veins. No divide, riding this current. No flesh, no body—only a limitless exchange. And what had I ever experienced sexually before? Compared to that? So little, I was thinking, I might as well have been a virgin.

The feeling proved so exquisite we said nothing when it was over—just molded into each other's limbs like conjoined twins.

🍁   🍁   🍁

"Hoy there, Seth! G'morning to ya!"

Huddled naked under an unzipped sleeping bag, I opened my eyes.

Seth rolled away from the warmth of my side and unzipped the front of the tent. Through the opening, in the dim morning light, stood a pair of black wellies.

"Mr. Shaw?"

"I know it's early but I'm out this way and Mrs. Shaw, she's got breakfast up at the house if you care to have some."

"Thanks."

"Your mum and dad all right?"

"Fine."

"Glad to hear it. That's all I come for, then, so I best get on to the milkin'."

The boots turned and squelched out of sight.

Seth grabbed his crumpled T-shirt and sweater. "Lauren?"

"You want to go now?"

"Aren't you starving? I am. Come on, let's get dressed. You'll like Mrs. Shaw. And we'll stop at the barn on the way—I'd like to show you the milking machines."

I quickly dressed, deciding I'd better put on Elizabeth's borrowed wellies, and followed Seth. With a wink, he grabbed my hand and half-dragged me across the pasture. Then, whistling under his breath, he unhooked the nylon string looped over the nearby gate.

In the adjacent field, a dirt track led the way to the milking machines, now noisily churning away inside the barn. The chirping birds, mooing cows, dewy grass and low-lying mist seemed to envelop the sound, making the morning just perfect. The sight was as soothing as any dream I might have dreamed last night.

But surely last night had been more than a dream! Last night, when I touched with my lips, when my tongue wandered in a daze, discovering a world no longer hidden. All for me—this land of green eyes—bathed in lust, topped in subtle orange hues of tangled auburn hair; paths streaked in red freckles and rolling hills of pale white muscles. I crossed every inch, every bead of sweat; tumbled through the soft, thin forest of fur running down the slopes of his chest: Seth's landscape.

Yet I'd slept. Hours later, I found him distant again. And now the rumbling noise grew louder, and the dirt track widened into wiggling furrows of mud.

We leaped and mucked our way through the mire, dodging puddles and clumps of cow dung to reach the dry, graveled oasis in front of the barn. At this point a black-and-white sheep dog, wagging its tail excitedly at the sight of new friends, led us inside the building.

Rows upon rows of black cows were lined up on both sides of a center aisle, all connected to hoses that pumped and heaved as they milked. With the stench of cows, milk and sludge filling my nostrils, I followed Seth into a separate room at the back where a gigantic stainless steel drum churned its load of steaming white liquid.

Seth found a pitcher nearby and causally scooped up a sample from the swirling vat. He handed it to me.

"Is it safe to drink, like this? Straight from the cow?" I asked, peering into the milk expecting to see bits of dirt, blood, hair, or something strange.

Seth laughed. "What do you mean by *safe*?"

"Oh, you know, shouldn't it be treated with chemicals or pasteurized or homogenized or whatever they do—to remove impurities?" I felt pretty stupid as soon as I said it. As if people hadn't been drinking it straight from the cow for centuries! The milk looked perfect: unblemished and pure.

I took a sip. It tasted wonderfully sweet and thick, full of the true flavor of milk.

I smiled at Seth. A smile of pure happiness. Grinning back, Seth reached to take the pitcher from me, to take his drink. And very slowly, deliberately, he laced his fingers tightly over mine.

The vat churned away, more milk spilling endlessly into the tank, swirling around and around. The sheep dog kept jumping up against Seth's legs and I tried to loosen my fingers but no, Seth held them fast, telling me with his eyes the secret of the milk's taste.

The vat kept churning, the dog barked and still Seth's hand gripped mine. No, *don't let go*, his eyes seemed to say. He held firm until he was sure I understood. Then he loosened his grip and took it from me, lifting the pitcher to his lips and taking a good long swig.

We filled the pitcher again and wordlessly marched up the hill toward the house. By the time Mrs. Shaw had boiled the water for coffee, I began to wonder what that episode in the barn was really about.

"There, you see?" Seth said, apparently reading my mind as he buttered his last piece of toast.

"What?"

He tilted his head toward the pitcher. "It's safe."

I nodded.

Grinning, he said nothing more.

And when I checked the milk again, a thick layer of cream was already beginning to form...

Right on top.

CHAPTER 9

Hunger Hill

"We've got to go."

"I know."

"My parents will worry."

"We should ring them from a call box."

"Yes."

"Tell them we'll be back for dinner."

"Tea."

"All right, tea."

"But let's go back the long way."

"Yes."

"Where's the map?"

"Here."

I unfolded the intricate pages of the Ordinance Survey, and Seth pointed to the farm buildings. To the left of Hamstall Ridware, I noticed a small triangle marking a summit, called Hunger Hill.

"What's at Hunger Hill?" I asked him.

"A hill," he replied, still leaning over my shoulder, lips brushing my ear. "Let's have *more*," he muttered, hugging my waist.

But I held fast to the map. "First tell me what Hunger Hill stands for."

"Famished and hung like a horse."

"Seriously."

"You really want to know?"

"Yes!"

"Then we'll go there. I'll tell you the story and you can see it for yourself."

Seth let me go and reached for his helmet.

"Fold up the Pathfinder and put it away," he insisted. "As it happens I've been there many times."

The hill itself wasn't very high, but the view was good. A dirt road climbed straight to the summit, round and flat. We left the bike under a large oak tree and struggled through a field of weed-ridden grass toward a stone marker.

"Can we see Lichfield from here?"

"Look for the spires."

"I don't see any pointy...oh, wait...no, it's only a factory."

Seth wasn't looking. He'd disappeared into the grass, rustling the dry thistles and seed pods into a crackling chorus as he moved about on his hands and knees.

"Seth?"

"Come over here."

"What are you doing?"

"Getting ready to tell you the story of Hunger Hill."

I found him lying in a flattened circle just big enough to hide us both.

"Come hither," he entreated, mincing Shakespeare. "Come hither and lie thee down."

With my head resting on his lap, Seth stroked my hair and began his tale.

"This hill has always been a sacred place for the river people," he explained. "Around 60 AD, the ancient Celts built a fort here, made of high earth walls topped with wooden sticks. Inside the fort were circular huts made of mud and twigs, with bones and skulls hanging from the doorways. The Celts honored their conquests and worshipped the spirits of the thick forest and many rivers that surrounded them. But the Romans had arrived, and after the great battle against Boudicca, a legion of Roman soldiers surrounded the hill and commanded the Celts to surrender."

"And if they surrendered?"

"The Romans would take them as slaves, sack their homes, and rape their women—for a start."

"Go on," I said, but I was beginning to dread the ending.

"And so," stated Seth, "they were under siege and on the verge of starvation. For three months they held out, living off dried grain, roots and rainwater. On the fourth month they survived very nicely off their toenail squeezings. It's been said they even held their noses and drank the juice from crushed dung beetles. But eventually, on the fifth month, they reached the end of their stores and ingenuity. At this point the great Chief asked his hill-fort people what they wanted to do. 'Should we live—or die?' he asked them. 'We'd rather die, than settle for life ruled by Roman gods, under a Roman king!' they said."

"So they all died?"

"The Chief handed his wife his sword and commanded, 'If you love me, cut off my head.' So she did, and everyone else followed the Chief's example—until only one young girl remained."

"Really?"

"Of course the Roman soldiers, hearing all the ruckus, and smelling all the blood—knew they'd won. They marched up to the fort and were greeted by the young girl."

Seth paused, nipping off a wayward stem of grass tickling his nose. Solemnly, he placed it over my stomach.

"That's it," he finished.

"But the young girl?"

"Oh her. Well, she rushed up to the soldiers and said, 'Take me alive, please, won't you? Nobody loves me so I may as well carry on.'"

My jaw dropped. "No…"

Seth tried to keep a straight face, but as soon he saw my reaction, he broke out laughing.

"You made the whole thing up?"

"Yes!"

"You bastard! Just because I'm a gullible American doesn't mean—"

"Anyway, it might be true," Seth insisted. "And since I've never found out why it's called Hunger Hill—I had to think of something. I couldn't disappoint you."

"You never disappoint me, Seth," I replied. "Though now, more than ever, I wish you would."

He wasn't listening. Already his fingers were dislodging the stem he'd placed on my belly, and smooth as a snake—they slid under my shirt.

Moving closer, I wanted to find every inch of him, right then and there. A feast of fingers, lips, tongue, and breathless fumbling wasn't near enough: I had to feel heaven rushing in. Together we'd obliterate the hill.

"Tell me though, what's your point about the girl?" I asked. "I don't understand."

"It's a riddle to solve," whispered Seth.

"So she was the odd number left? And she couldn't face killing herself?"

"She said nobody loved her enough," Seth reminded me. "Someone else—anyone else—could have spared her that by cutting off her head."

"But then she wanted to go on living afterwards…"

"Hunger and love. Well, a different way of showing true love. Those are your clues."

All I could think about at the moment was my own hunger. I kissed Seth as if I'd never get enough of his lips…

"…Famished and hung like a horse," Seth finally murmured, unbuckling his belt. "I think I prefer that version."

❧   ❧   ❧

"Uncle Henry?"

No sign of recognition. But just like my Aunt Bea, I chatted away.

"Seth's taking me to the train station. I'm on my way back to America. It's time to say goodbye."

I would never excuse Henry's behavior as a softening of the brain. In my opinion Henry's brain was as sharp and hard as nails. His body was the culprit, the cause of all his trouble.

"Thanks for everything."

Henry didn't flinch. His eyes looked moist. But his eyes always looked moist—brimming but vacant—no matter what was happening.

"I loved staying here. I guess my grandpa left Lichfield to find his fame and fortune in America, but I'm sure he had his regrets. I think I know, now, what he left behind and couldn't begin to explain."

No comment.

I glanced over at Seth, with a strange feeling Henry had understood every word I'd said; or if nothing else, had caught a host of connections flying through the air like static electricity.

"Goodbye, Uncle Henry."

The blanket draped over his legs suddenly slipped to the floor.

"Have a safe trip, dear," piped Aunt Bea, as she bent down to retrieve the blanket. "And don't forget to ring Harriet when you get home."

I hugged them both. Just a ten-minute stop, then back into Chester's car. Seth drove me, in silence, straight to the station.

"I'm going with you to Birmingham," he announced, as I purchased my ticket. "One round-trip to Birmingham, please."

"What about work?"

"I called in this morning, told them I was ill."

"You did?"

"I didn't lie. I *am* sick."

So we both traveled to Birmingham station. Ironic, but it didn't help having Seth close by, right up to the end. Nothing would have helped—in the final hour, when the Twilight Zone kicks in. I was passing through in limbo, where nothing happens for real. And I was wondering how I'd handle the ghostly smiles or even the cursed goodbyes.

The only thing you can do is put on a mask, I was thinking. Like Darren. Don a mask with a smiling grimace—half reaper, half buffoon—so the words come easy. Goodbyes are best resolved as pre-scripted clichés.

Clichés are choke resistant, like cough drops—they slide down a burning throat with ease. 'Well, see you later' or 'This isn't goodbye' or 'Hasta Luego' or 'Let's keep in touch' or anything except the bare bones 'I can't say goodbye, I just can't.'

Full Stop.

Which is why I stood with Seth, mask on, at Platform 12, Birmingham station, almost wishing he hadn't managed to get me there alone. With no Chester and Elizabeth around, there were no excuses for keeping it secret and I was finding it difficult to successfully sustain that mask.

Five minutes to go.

"Goodbye Lauren. Have a safe trip." Hours of silence and that was all Seth said.

We both seemed to be standing on a battlefield. Lined up in one trench was a wavering flank of optimism; in the other, a reinforcement of geographic despair. In between, there might have been flashes of affection, hurt and anger swirling around Seth's face—but once again, he held back.

"Lor-en."

His light green eyes rested obstinately on my face. They seemed to be saying, "That's it—just a simple, easy goodbye."

So I hugged him, easy. A simple warm hug. The kind you'd expect between parting relatives.

"Don't let go," Seth muttered, taunt muscles shaking slightly.

His cheeks felt hot and hard; his physical desire blatantly bulged against my skirt.

I broke away and walked bristly to the nearest door of the train. Full stop. I didn't cry. Like having suddenly been told someone in the family had just died,

I moved through a vacant, unfeeling vacuum—a world of weird, unknowable grief.

A zombie managed a final wave; stepped on the train and rode from Birmingham to London; got on the plane; found the proper allocated seat; carefully stowed the hand luggage; tightly fastened the seat belt.

High up in the air, the dull, droning hours sat waiting to be filled.

A black space hovered endlessly outside the window, kids roamed restlessly up and down the aisles. England and Seth were already far, far in the background: a thing of the past, a mere recollection.

A stewardess approached. I opened my mouth and said, "Coke, please."

I've done this before, I've done this before, I kept reminding myself. A lifetime of goodbye experience. A lifetime of goodbyes. Moving away and promising to write, to keep on helloing, to keep it going; but soon the letters, the calls drift into the void. Sometimes it takes years—it inevitably happens. Any Navy brat knows. Vows to visit never manage to surmount the obstacles: busy lives, immediate concerns, good intentions—but no. Foolish commitments, keeping in touch.

It might have helped to simply drink the coke, but the liquid held no interest. Fingers clutched the plastic—refusing to let go—needing something to do, holding the coke until gradually the ice cubes disappeared, like memories. All melted now, hardly any fizz left.

I ignored the other passengers as if they didn't exist.

"Chicken or Beef?"

"Nothing, thank you."

I desired nothing more than oblivion, or a Celtic fairy tale, or a hum from a tune by Seth. I hungered for a feeling, playing on and on, or freckled arms flexed across the guitar, fingers dancing hard.

"Coffee or tea?"

"Water, please."

Water. I had my water, liquid, pond, beach. Ripples. Foam and white-feathered birds, rain-splattered bricks. Ladies of the Vale, bah-ing sheep, Georgian bedroom, milk. A river. A ghost. A tombstone wearing the epitaph of the old Lauren.

I kept thinking, was that me, in the airplane window, staring fixedly back in reflection? Out from the black space beyond?

Nobody would know for sure. And there might be a cousin Seth, whose music sent a shudder down my spine: so sweet, intense, ever changing and unrehearsed. But his music, his light, was all in my mind. Magic romantic worlds engulfed his image, his country; something beyond me, something I could never touch.

I could see it, feel it—but I knew I couldn't hold it. Here lies the mystery, I was thinking. The riddle up on Hunger Hill.

Staring into the black space outside the window, my mind flying back to St. Michael's Church, to where I'd be standing even now, watching the sun set over the moss-streaked grave of Sarah Jane…the silence broken only by the cawing of a crow, or the bleating of a sheep.

Until the flight ended: the plane lurched, hit the runway.

And boom. I was back home again.

❦   ❦   ❦

Nov. 10

Dear Seth,

I thought you might like to have a few of the pictures I took. My favorite is of you sitting by the River Blythe, with the swans in the background. Second favorite is you and Ian standing against the rocks at Sandymouth, looking profound in your underwear. Tell Ian I miss his witticisms (you know I miss yours, not to mention a few other amazing talents) and tell Aunt Bea I'm rationing the jar of pickles she gave me, thanks to my new addiction to cheese and pickle sandwiches…

My dad is a bit miffed over my homesickness for England but I'm sure he thinks it will wear off. So, it's all bare trees and choppy gray seas over here. Signs of winter. The winters can be pretty wicked in New England. Even colder than a well digger's ass, they say. I've promised Grandma to visit her in Boston before the ice-caps set in!

I guess I should be worried about my future and whether or not to go back to Santa Barbara, but you already know don't you—I can't go back, not now. Not when it isn't really, really what I want to do…True, I told my boyfriend Leo (in Santa Barbara) I was only visiting Newport. He thought my dad would convince me to

stay. Funny, but like you said, you don't have to SAY anything. Leo and I both knew it was time for me to move on.

I hadn't realized I'd decided for myself until yesterday. I was walking aimlessly around the town, when I saw a 'Help Wanted' sign in the window of a little French restaurant, and found myself talking the owner into hiring me as a dishwasher. When I got home and told my dad, he went BERSERK. How could I insult him like that, a smart young girl like me who just graduated with a degree, which HE PAID FOR, and then get a job as a DISH-WASHER? He was furious but I calmly looked him in the eye and said 'I really want a job here, any job, and I need the money.' 'What's got into you?' he shouted. I replied, 'Something I found again in England.' Okay, so I wanted to, but didn't say it. What I really said was 'Don't worry, I'm only taking this job until I find a decent one.' Of course my dad is nevertheless extremely pleased I've decided to stay.

I hope you don't mind if I write to you once in a while. You never said whether you wanted to write or not, so don't worry. No obligation to write back, it's just that I was an English major, remember. A sucker for written words. Stupid thing to say, but too late now. Say hi to your family for me. Hope you're all keeping warm and well.

Lauren.

ॐ

Nov. 30

Dear Lauren,

What a surprise when I got home from work to find your letter waiting for me in the dog's mouth last week. It cheered me up no end (the letter that is) to say the least. I really buzzed inside when I read it, so send me some more quick. You may be wondering from what I just said, that I may be uncheerful. I will list the reasons: Firstly, the weather is oh so bad. Secondly, my bike is oh so sad because the weather is bad. Thirdly, I am so mad that my bike is sad because the weather is bad. And last of all, my socks need washing.

What a depressing life it is since you left. It's enough to drive anyone to the end. Can you imagine being driven that far? You know, holding your thumb on a table's edge with a steel hammer wavering in line above it, clenched in the other hand, and saying to yourself—

"Shall I do it…shall I do it?…it will hurt…yeah but shall I do it?…the pain…but I'll do it…I can do it…I can't wait…"

No I can't really imagine it either.

People who think like that should be sent to live on the seabed, with Halibut fish. So. I lied. No, my socks do need washing but I also need a change, like a trip to the States. Sometime this century would be nice. Maybe around August? If a visit appeals to you, say the word and Seth will find a way to blast into America. Lock him in a steel cage and bury him at Earth's center and he'll burrow up to Newport. Stick him in orbit eternally round the Earth and he'll parachute in—using nothing more than his string vest. He'll sail across the Atlantic in a plastic bag if necessary—or even post himself in a letter.

I'm really glad to hear you're staying in Newport. The decision to go it on your own sounds really good to me, so good in fact, that if you don't do your best, I'll throw my unwashed socks at you. Get where you want to be and don't hang around.

Love,

Seth

P.S. Of course I want you to write. It's something I'd hoped for, but did not expect. Yes?

∾

Dec. 16

Dear Seth,

Of course I'd love for you to come over—any time. My dad would be more than happy to have you, too. Hmmm…I won't get too excited, just in case for some reason it doesn't happen…then again, that's a lie. I will get excited. Just not too. Meanwhile, what can I say? The past few weeks have been really dull and low key. Job-hunting gets pretty depressing because I don't have the sec-retarial skills or experience, and no matter how keen or intelligent you are it just isn't enough. I went for a receptionist job at a sailmaking place but they said I didn't type fast enough. I was really disappointed as it felt right, working for a boating business. Oh well, guess that job didn't have my name on it.

Love,

Your cousin Lauren

P.S. Inside this box is your Christmas present, a batch of honest-to-god homemade American Chocolate Chip cookies. I made them myself. Hope they don't arrive a bundle of crumbs.

∾

Jan 1. 1980

Dear Lauren, You Knob-head of a Second Cousin...

Happy New Year. As you probably know from the news, the weather over here has us in a Great Deep Freeze. If it doesn't snow for a few days, things will really be looking up. If it gets above zero degrees C, we can get out the deck chairs. Huddled in a chair under five layers of clothing and a wrapping blanket keeps me out of trouble, and yes, I have been doing a lot of thinking as well. Stuck in this chair. I've been trying to have an insight at what lies ahead and reconcile it with what must be done. You know, sometimes that seems like firing a rocket at Pluto. So maybe neither you nor I have any idea at the moment which wagon to jump on (the future is a mystery to most), but at least you can arrange things so that the present can unfold near enough the way you want it. Meanwhile, read the signposts, wait at the junction and the wagon will arrive—presto! You've got a map! Sorry, I didn't mean to go on like that. I'll try and get the stage version in production soon.

P.S. I want more American cookies. I'm hooked and won't survive without them...One now and again at bedtime or after washing the socks. The change is unbelievable. I put on my black gown and mask, and go out into the dark cold night. Sinister and

low, hunched and distorted, hunting cookies...(Ian begged but I wouldn't share)

Seth

Newport, Rhode Island, was no longer just a name for the place where I was born. I had expected a grotty naval shipyard hemming in a nondescript town—but what I discovered was a clean, quaint New England seaport. Despite the decline of a military presence (bar the War College) a boom of reconstruction was in progress. Rhode Island was steeped in history and the tourists loved the colonial monuments to verify it. So once again, Newport began to flourish.

The Naval shipyard, practically empty, was miles away. But in the town's main harbor, the Restoration Society kept builders at work year-round, turning every wharf and ruin into a shop, restaurant, or museum piece. Tourists flocked in from both land and sea, as the America's Cup lured yachts from all over the world. The fishing vessels, now a minority, were fighting for dock space; the crumbling summer mansions of Victorian New Yorkers were being converted into expensive condos to house the growing population.

Unlike Southern California, New England had a definite change of season. The extreme weather cycles appealed to me, mainly because they provided a true sense of transformation and diversity. And the East Coast was about as 'ancient' as America could get—though hundreds of years wasn't quite the same as thousands. New England still lacked the archaic magic of the Midlands.

So I spent most of my time scrubbing sauces out of copper-bottom pans, thinking about Lichfield and Seth's letters. I continued to search for a proper job, but building a career could wait. Of more crucial concern was how to devise an honest reply to a personal letter. A battle of strategy was at stake, and I hadn't yet deciphered the code. With Seth such an expert at innuendo, what did his words actually mean? Nothing? Or Everything? Uncertain, I couldn't decide what to say or not to say.

Washing dishes was simple. I could keep myself in limbo, waiting for the next cryptogram hidden inside an envelope—postmarked Britain. After all, Seth hadn't exactly explained this sudden urge "for a change" which would send him blasting his way to America. His tone implied a friendly sort of affection, punctuated by exclamations of comic exaggeration. I could hardly afford to misread his intentions. Why hadn't he just said "I must see you again?" Why hedge around the bush?

No, I kept thinking, he couldn't really be in love with me. Why would a lightning bolt choose a Common Alder, when it could have a Silver Monarch Birch? Wanting a definite answer, I composed a draft of a very explicit letter, only to tear it up. Five drafts later, I still faced the prospect of starting all over again.

However. I hadn't forgotten that first night with Seth in his kitchen, when we understood each other completely. Surely such lucid insights were inherent in any verbal exchange with Seth—coupled with a bottle of whiskey. Of course! Convinced I'd found the answer, I decided to try it again, one evening when my dad (in Washington DC attending some Navy thing) left me at home alone, holding the key to his liquor cabinet.

By three in the morning, I'd sampled some of his very best Glenfiddich and Glenmorangie in an attempt to prepare myself. Then, too drunk to dial but sufficiently fortified with courage, I reached for the phone.

Carefully scrutinizing each number before pressing the corresponding button, I managed to poke all the right digits.

"Nine-eight-five-two, hello?"

"Seth, isssthat you?"

"Lor-en, blimy! How nice of you to ring. How are you? All right?"

"Yeah well, I jusssssst thought, well, I just wanted to tell you the good news. Today I got a phone call—out of the blue—from that thailing company and they offered me a job."

"With pay?"

I laughed, a rather gurgly drawn-out giggle. "Yes, it turnsss out they need an assissstent for the girl they hired. Seems she can't handle the workload on her own. They figured it might be good...er...you know...to have someone like me who could edit and sssspell-rrect their letters and rerrr ports."

"Great news. Good to hear your voice, matey."

"Good to hear yours too." Vaguely annoyed by the fact I was speaking in slurs, I forced myself to slow down in the hope I'd sound more sober. "What are you doing right now?"

"Having a bong-hit. I'm blasted. Philip, John and Naomi are here...we've just got back from a wicked long trip to Derbyshire, on the bikes."

"Oh. I see, I won't keep you then."

"I'll sniff a sock for you, for good luck."

"Thanks…well…I better go now. Bye."

Damn.

I put down the receiver and stumbled up to bed.

Luckily my brain, heart, and nerve-endings were so numbed by the whiskey I can only remember blubbering the f-word a few times before I passed out cold.

But the next morning, foul-tempered and blinding sober, I was forced to face the torment. How could I possibly blot out Naomi, and all those other lovely nymphs swarming around Seth in libidinous Lichfield?

Two days later I started working at Shoreline Sails.

"You don't look very happy," stated my dad. "I thought you were thrilled about this new job."

"I'm just nervous," I answered.

My dad, at the best of times, was not the sort of person who empathized. Six feet tall, the epitome of masculine strength (both mental and physical), and the perfect military leader—he expected me to stand up straight and toe the line, no matter what happened. Personal feelings were irrelevant when the ultimate goal was the American ideal. In order for him to be proud of me, I had to fulfill these very simple requirements.

Which is why I hadn't told him about my feelings for Seth. Not to mention a few other things.

"I know how to cheer you up. Let's go out and celebrate over a nice lobster dinner," he said. "Let's make it a date for Friday night."

He knew, of course, I hadn't been on a date yet—not in Newport.

Using the new job as an excuse, I wrote Seth. I poured out my feelings like a drinking fountain, suddenly gushing at the turn of a knob but nevertheless quenching a deep thirst for humor. I joked over how nervous I'd been the first day; how the simple skills required of a receptionist were hell for someone like me; how socializing with strangers develops the ability to smile at will and fake the keenest interest.

Mimicking his sense of fun, I described how I answered the phone, 'Shoreline Sails,' about a sixty times, which at some point in the chain of repetition changed to 'Soreline Shails.'

But despite all my efforts, Seth apparently wasn't in the mood to reply. No letter came, and after a full month had passed, I began to worry. My worst fears seemed justified.

Meanwhile, my father, who must have noticed my muted state of despair, began to make matters worse. He probably figured if I didn't start dating soon, I'd get bored with Newport and want to go back to Leo in Santa Barbara. So he fixed me up with a date. He set his hopes on a young naval officer—a handsome upstart at the head of his class, who drove a red Corvette.

I figured why not, since I didn't have anything better to do and my dad (for once) would be immensely proud. Lieutenant Robert Roth was his name, or Buzz to his friends and colleagues. Tall, brown haired, clean cut, aggressively self-confident—Buzz was definitely four-star admiral material and the perfect choice for a captain's daughter.

He picked me up in the red Corvette and took me—of all places—to the little French restaurant. So I sat there, picking the almonds off my trout, with a huge grin on my face.

"What's so funny?" the Lieutenant kept asking.

"Oh nothing," I replied. "I'm just enjoying myself."

The waiter arrived with champagne, extremely pleasant and polite. He obviously knew Buzz well, from previous occasions, and I could see by the look on his face there'd be more than one bottle. Jesus, I was thinking, I knew this waiter and he was a completely different person backstage. A rude, impatient bastard, this particular waiter detested both the chefs and the lackeys in the lowly kitchen.

So why hadn't the waiter recognized me? Perhaps because I was wearing a bra, and fixed my hair in a twisty bun. Or more likely, the connection was simply too absurd: a dishwasher posing as a posh Navy upstart's date? At any rate, I relished the fact and waited until the bill was paid. Lieutenant Roth, as predicted, put down a very generous tip.

"Buzz, would you do me a favor?" I asked.

"Sure Lauren, what is it?"

"When the waiter comes back, ask him to take half of that tip to the kitchen. Tell him it's for chef."

Buzz looked puzzled, but agreed.

"I know what it's like in restaurants," I explained. "It's only fair the tips should be shared with cooks in the kitchen. But they never get their share. No tips, and no gratitude. Just watch. The waiter will be furious with you now!"

I was right. Buzz handed the waiter two tens, and asked him to give one to the chef. "Tell the cook the food was fabulous," Buzz said. The waiter frowned, then glared at us. All gooey and sweet as syrup before, he suddenly turned sour grapes. Snatching the bill from the table, he stomped off.

"He didn't even say thanks," muttered Buzz.

Smothering my face in my napkin, I was overcome by a fit of giggles and could hardly contain my delight. Buzz, however, wasn't quite as amused. He was more interested in getting me out of the restaurant and into his car. After "crepes a la cherry" for dessert, I'd given my consent to a nightcap at his place. He seemed keen to move on.

Rather too quickly I found myself back in his Corvette, speeding away—too fast for me to change my mind. Suddenly we were inside the apartment and I was sitting on an enormous white leather couch in the middle of his living room. And it was just as I'd imagined: an officer's bachelor pad quite sparse and spotless in decor, on the top floor of a renovated Victorian house. Very elegant, with a good view of the harbor.

I could hardly have pretended not to guess what he had in mind. First the antique stained-glass table lamps were turned off. Then the flames in fake-fire marble fireplace were turned on. Finally the latest in stereo console came to life, emitting soft soul music in the background.

"Now here's the perfect drink," he announced, pouring me a glass of vintage cognac. Our two crystal brandy snifters chinked in toast.

"Here's to you," he muttered, putting down his glass and deciding I was sufficiently prepared for a French kissing attack.

When I felt his hand go up between my legs, I abruptly pushed him away.

"Okay, nice girls don't do it on the first date," he groaned. "But don't you want to? I promise I won't tell anyone."

"I don't want to." The leather upholstery squeaked as I moved away, reminding me of Seth. I winced in silent agony at the thought.

"You don't want to?" he repeated.

"No, I don't." Unfortunately, at that moment I couldn't contain my bitter feelings, which erupted in a totally inappropriate fit of giggling. Again.

Buzz looked at me as if I'd just pulled the pin out of a grenade and tossed it in his lap.

"I'd better take you home, then," he muttered. When he stood up, I noticed his tackle erect and still on alert. But the battle was lost, and his ego floored.

"Sorry. Oh Buzz, believe me, I wasn't laughing at you."

"Let's just get you home, okay?"

Back in the Corvette, the young Lieutenant held the keys in the ignition, thinking. Before he started the engine he looked at me—really puzzled.

"What's wrong with me, then?" he muttered. (He didn't have a clue.) I wasn't sure it was a good idea trying to explain. Explain what? I couldn't help it. I liked Buzz, I even felt sorry for him. But I didn't want anything less than what I really, really wanted. And despite all his flash, his money, and his car, Lieutenant Robert Buzz Roth didn't have it.

"Nothing's wrong with you," I answered. "It's me. Maybe we just should have gone out for a pizza," I added, making some sort of effort.

"Yeah, a wasted hundred bucks," he exclaimed.

"No—that's not true," I said.

Buzz started the engine, and with a jolt the Corvette screeched in reverse out of the driveway.

"Not wasted at all," I repeated. And smiling wryly, I added, "I'm sure the chef felt it was worthwhile!"

Revenge is sweet. Or so they say. I do admit I told my dad I preferred smelly socks to after-shave, and the following weekend accepted a date with Jeff, a sail-cutter who worked 'on the floor' at Shore Sails. He took me straight to a bar on the shoddy side of town with a measly ten bucks in his pocket and marijuana on his breath. Listening to live Reggae and drinking shots of cheap whiskey, I kept thinking: I've got to find more people in Newport who are my type—because if I don't, by the time Seth gets here, he'll be hugging a volcano.

Then I starting thinking: If Seth *ever* gets here.

It had taken until the beginning of April for another letter to arrive; a wait long enough to convince me that distance does not make the heart grow fonder. Not when the heart is as fickle as a lightning bolt. At this point I could hardly bear to open the envelope.

∾
April 10

Dear Shailing Lauren…

It's 11 PM and nearly time to hit the sack. But as I look across the piles of old clothes on my bed I become worried about the moth colony asleep inside them. What will I wear tomorrow? Sometimes, like right now I wonder "What's Lauren doing?" Well I bet you've just got home from 'Soreline Shails,' undoing your canvass sailcloth overcoat which you have to wear (for the advertising), kicking off your keel-shaped shoes and then running a nice hot bath from a special tap which only delivers seawater. I imagine the place where you work has no stairs—only masts between

floors, and you've got to climb them with a dagger between your teeth....

My place of work is very nice. Every morning when we arrive the manager kicks us in the face and then discharges 60,000 volts from an electrically charged metal sphere into the nose of any person smiling. That is not all. If any employee fails to make £500 profit in the first hour, he is cut in half with an electron beam cutter and fired. But really, we all get along fine and the money is good. Last Friday I had a wage rise to 9 pence a week. Which means I can afford to send you a letter every month and hopefully have enough left over to buy a new pen. Lousy excuse? That's all I got, mate.

Seth

Somewhat confused and frustrated by the lousy excuse of a letter, I decided it was time to phone. I had to either phone, or go insane waiting another god knows how many weeks. But first I had to summon up the nerve to actually dial.

Without any whiskey, it took a bit longer. About three touch-and-go-no-don't-do-it weeks.

"Nine-eight-five-two."

"Hello, Seth?"

"No it's Ian."

"Oh—Ian. It's Lauren."

"Hi Lauren! How are you?"

"I'm fine, thanks. And you?"

"Shit." He chuckled. "Just kidding."

"Is Seth there?"

"No, no he isn't." Ian sounded unsure of what to say next.

"Will he back later? Shall I try again around dinner time?"

"No, he's moved out, Lauren. Didn't you know?"

"No, I didn't know."

Pause. "Well he left home...a week ago. Met some girl—a singer—from a band in Birmingham. He's living with her, I think. Quit his job, packed up and left home for the big time."

"Quit his job?" I was flabbergasted.

"That's my brother—you never know what he's going to do next. Now he's joined this band, as a stage hand."

"Stage hand?" My imagination immediately conjured up all sorts of pictures...

"Out on the road most of the time. They just got a gig over in Europe, I hear."

"Oh. Well, I'm sure he's having a great time."

I gulped for air, keeping my voice steady while my whole body felt like it had just been hit by a ten-ton truck.

"I'll tell him you phoned, next time he rings up," Ian said. "Though who knows when that might be."

"That's okay," I replied. "No big deal."

"I will tell him."

"Sure, well, bye for now then."

"Bye, Lauren."

No big deal.

I hung up, with 'some girl' and 'singer' hanging in the air like a...

Lead balloon.

Pushing down on that hit-and-run ten-ton truck.

CHAPTER 10

The Rival

A pile of stones sat on my dressing table. Every morning I picked them up, rolled them around in my fingers. I took comfort in their cold, hard surfaces—just a few sample pebbles—smoothly rounded and plucked from the River Blythe, that day with Seth, when I couldn't find any forget-me-nots.

Some might call them common, or nameless; but for me those rocks had become a vital necessity. They surely survived the intangible threads of memory. So I'd stand in front of my dressing table, rolling them around in my fingers. They were solid, real: they proved something.

Yet when I looked out through the window beyond—at the bare, eerie trees—I remembered Lauren's Law. And I felt just as naked and quaking as those poor trees in a freezing gale. The long, lonely winter pushed autumn passion—even the pebbles themselves—into a post-mortem void, hollow and unreal.

Eventually I realized the rocks were actually no better than transitory phantoms: mere ghosts of glacier peaks tumbling around in my hand. My solid things were no more rocks than mountains, because one day they'd simply crumble into sand—and disappear in the wind.

When the rocks lost their power I tried closing my eyes and visualizing how we made love up on Hunger Hill: skin to skin, hearts beating like a pair of Celtic drums, the soft prickles of Seth's beard caressing my cheek, hands cupping my breasts, fingertips milking my nipples, sliding his secret inside, exploding our divides.

The feeling stayed. The connection still persisted, as solid and real as any object. Or was I merely a dreamer—distorting and enhancing what I thought I'd felt? Could I rely on that? Or was it all made up? I only knew for sure that when life ceased to have any meaning, I felt exposed and stripped clean like a defeated soldier in a winter storm, shivering in the face of starvation. But death failed to seize love on Hunger Hill. Rolling those rocks around my hand, I tried in vain to recapture the saving grace.

Eventually, the vital 'alive' feeling diminished; the old Lauren was once again mislaid. Another excuse, I suppose, but in Newport there were few reminders: no post-and-beam pubs, no ancient stone churches, no nameless gravestones; no wispy auburn-haired Seths with light green eyes. The regimented green lawn at the War College was hardly a substitute for medieval hedge and field.

I grew lazy, settling for a regimented routine with my Dad in his house on the Base and bussing calls at Shoreline Sails forty hours a week. I ate, slept, repeated "Good morning, good afternoon, can I help you" and drove home, set the table, cooked a meal, argued with my father, cleaned up, watched TV, woke up to the alarm. I tried not to wonder too much whether Seth (with a singer) had bothered to save any of his own pebbles.

But stubbornly, I clung to the hope that one day I'd make another pilgrimage to Lichfield. Even if Seth wasn't home, I imagined his two-wheeled spirit wandering back from Europe just to give me advice and prompt me on.

By the end of April I'd purchased a rusty Ford Galaxy and took long drives in it, finding solace wherever I could in the beauty of Newport. When the harbor was calm I'd admire the moon and lights on the bridge; follow pink sunsets that glowed past the masts; laugh at gulls chasing dogs and marvel over the rubber boots worn by gruffy fishermen. While New England children splashed through puddles in the potholes on Bellevue Drive, I picked daffodils and bought myself a dictionary to learn the names of plants.

Regardless, nothing felt quite the same as it did in England and all manner of pleasure seemed hollow without Seth. Ashamed and disillusioned, I wrote to Leo across the miles, "Has anything really changed? Leo, am I just making a fool of myself?"

I almost wished I'd never been to Lichfield. 'Don't let go.' That's what he'd said, and what tangible gains had been made? None. Just heartache, and months of struggling alone in Newport. I should have gone back to California months ago. Yet another voice inside said 'wait.' Hold out a little bit longer. Seth would surely write again, with singer or without. And he was bound to say something to inspire me on. Please Seth, spark the fire, I prayed. Send me a glimmer of your lightning bolt.

But the weeks dragged by and my dad and I were beginning to get on each other's nerves. I was itching to get out from under his thumb. The morning frost still nipped the buds in May and no news from Seth. The arrival of spring—or a letter—seemed as plausible as an orchid sprouting in Northern Siberia.

❀   ❀   ❀

In the last week of May, a sudden announcement hit the headlines of the Aimes Family Evening Bulletin, under Weddings and Engagements. Slam bang out of the blue and dropped in my lap when I least expected it.

Ironically enough, I was reading the 'Apartments for Rent' section of the *Newport Daily News*. The pages were spread all over my bed when my dad burst into my room.

"Lauren, I've got some fantastic news."

Sitting next to me, he pushed aside the crumpled paper. "It's a major decision that will change my life. I hope you'll be happy for me."

"Happy about what, Dad?"

He hesitated, then smiled and said, "I'm getting married."

"You are? Really?"

"I asked Sally last night, and she said yes. You like Sally, don't you? Of course I realize this comes as a big surprise, but it's been a long time since your mother—"

"Died. You can say it, dad. She died. That means she's dead. It's okay to say, you know. I'm not a child any more."

"Precisely. Which is why I hope you don't mind if I move in with Sally. We'd rather not wait until the wedding…and she doesn't want to live here."

"Oh dad," I insisted, "of course I don't mind. I thought you'd been seeing a lot of her lately. Congratulations! As it happens, I've just starting looking for my own place. Now that I've got a fairly decent job and a car, I can do it."

"Good. I'll lend you more money if need be. But I still think you should take that Civil Service Exam. There's plenty of jobs at the War College for civil servants."

I nodded. It just so happened Sally Graham was a civil servant. She edited research papers at the War College, and probably composed a few letters as well. Or drafted memos for busy senior officers like my dad.

"I have your approval, then?"

"I'm happy if it makes you happy."

"I guess I'd better phone your brothers, and tell them the news. Though odds are, they won't answer the phone. Don't they ever stay at home?"

"I doubt it."

"Well, we can discuss all the details tomorrow. Sally's pretty anxious to get everything planned."

I didn't get a chance to say another word. My dad marched out just as quickly as he'd marched in. The next minute I could hear him talking on the phone downstairs, crooning to Sally.

Yes, yes, don't worry Lauren thinks it's great, he was probably saying. To reassure her. Great for him, but I was feeling pretty numb.

After a few minutes I carefully folded the newspaper. Then I turned off the light, pulled down the bedcovers and pretended to go to sleep.

Sally was a nice lady but certainly not the kind of woman who would sympathize with a daughter like me. Two against one, now.

"Mom?"

No answer. I knew my mother—if she really *were* watching over us—would agree and take my side. Two against two. Including Seth, possibly three. But what did it matter. I was all alone, left with nothing but ghostly whispers and dreams every night...fighting death and love...

In the dark.

🍁   🍁   🍁

Yet despite everything, May brought forth the long-awaited splash of color to shrubs and trees—bursting in yellows, whites, and pinks. Birds chirped outside the open windows; the sun felt warm and inviting. At least Mother Nature managed to cheer me up considerably.

As if on cue, the postman also saw fit to deliver a groundbreaking letter.

"Dear Lauren...So glad to hear the news about your dad..."

From Leo. In reply to my own long letter. It seemed best to inform him of my recent decision to return to Santa Barbara—immediately after my dad's wedding.

"*You're really coming back? I'm sincerely pleased to hear it. No hard feelings,*" Leo wrote. "*Always remember that, Lauren. Even though I'm in Los Angeles now, you can always come and stay with me if you can't find a life in S.B...We're still friends, right? I mean it, keep in touch.*"

I put the letter down. It looked like Leo had really forgiven me. He deserved someone who could properly love him in return. I was glad, for now he'd moved on and would meet the right girl to take my place.

Decisions can be made—so easily—by events, which are completely outside one's control. I had to hand it to fate. My dad's sudden plans to marry left me stranded in Newport with a boring receptionist job and a few friends whom I didn't like that much, while Seth's silence left me nothing but a crazy urge to travel and chuck it all in. And finally, Leo's letter promised a secure landing, right in home territory. Right where I belonged, in sunny, palm tree southern California.

Everything fit neatly into place. All I had to do was give my notice at work and wait for July. Then I'd advertise for a rider to share the expenses and help with the driving—a whopping three thousand miles to the West Coast. But I'd done it before, with my dad.

Folding up the letter, I propped it against the mirror standing on my dresser. Right where the pebbles and pictures used to sit. But not any more: I couldn't have any mementos from England lying around. It was all part of the cure.

No reminders of a perfect love. A triumph for Lauren's Law.

The question, after all, was how to survive in a world of limited possibilities. But the seasons change, all phases come and go. Some are destroyed, others must begin again. What better harbinger than Spring?

With the window open, I could hear the blades whizzing on my dad's lawn mower, and it wasn't long before the damp, sweet smell of freshly cut grass began to fill the room.

❦   ❦   ❦

"Are you sure you aren't bored?" asked Max, with a funny smile on his face.

"No, not at all," I replied.

"Though you're about to sunburn rather badly, by the looks of your legs," he murmured, placing his hand on my thigh and leaving a white mark against the pinkish-red skin.

We both looked at it for a minute. But then the first baseman stole second and Max turned his attention back to the game.

The stadium at Boston was packed. The Goddess of Summer Baseball had broken into a warm, voluptuous smile. She generously spread her devotees all over the bleachers, sending sparkling sunbeams across the aisles and graffiti all over the pitch. Her pleasure grew into gentle laughter, flowing through the quivering shouts of the crowds, the vibrant red stripes on the player's uniforms, and every movement behind the bench.

The referees, I noticed, couldn't keep still. The excitement would grow; a home run would come soon; we'd all be screaming in frenzy.

I was no exception, sitting among thousands of fellow devotees in the bright, scalding sun. Huddled in the stands between Anne and Anne's friend Max, I laughed, yelled and cheered as if I was truly a fan. But of course it wasn't so much the game, as the wonderful feeling of summer itself; of crisp cloudless blue sky and the perfection of the day; of the simple, neat *crack* of the bat as it collided with the speeding ball.

Crack! There it went: all heads looked up, all jaws dropped in awe. The batter disappeared in a cloud of dust. Ahhhhh…. safe as he slid on base. I was holding a plastic cup full of beer in one hand—which I almost dropped. With the other hand I pulled my wide-rimmed straw hat at a lower angle to shield the sun.

"Whew!"

"So you work with Anne?" asked Max, after the cheering subsided.

"Yes, but I'm leaving soon," I replied. "I just handed in my notice."

It just didn't occur to me—that hot, dry day in July—that Max might have been stealing fanciful side-swipes in my direction, although I was tempted to take my eyes off the pitch to look at *him*. I assumed the attraction was no doubt due to the excitement of the game and my sudden thirst for several beers. Yet even so, bewitched by the goddess of summer's smile, I felt bold and beautiful that afternoon: content to live for the moment, finding mystery and loveliness in the game, in the crowds of sweating faces anticipating a home run, in the clenched jaw in profile sitting next to me.

This innocent curiosity, however, took a sharp twist when we meandered downtown to Tony's Pizza after the game. In between the drunken, carefree laughs, Max managed to throw a fast ball. Quite unexpectedly (the minute Anne left the table) he leaned forward and thrust a sly invitation in my ear.

"Lauren, would you like to go to dinner sometime?"

I instantly swung back with a blind "yes" before Anne returned from the Ladies' Room.

When I told Anne about it afterwards, she reacted with envious glee.

"No! He asked you out? You lucky thing. Max is one of the few gorgeous, eligible bachelors left in town. He makes good money as an accountant, too. I'd always hoped he'd go for me, but I've had to settle for just friends."

As I lay in bed that evening, safe and sober at home—I was thinking in the cool darkness about how good it felt, starting something with Max. And he wasn't at all like Seth. Was it his smooth, handsome appearance? The maturity of a few years above my age? The firm mouth, strong cheekbones, narrow dark-brown secretive eyes? The dimples when he grinned? The head of tightly curled black hair, faintly tinged with gray? The aloofness or pensiveness? The strange reluctance to speak? Or the sum total of it all?

I turned over and tried to sleep. Max reminded me of a doll; a male doll made for a girl's favorite Barbie. I'd just have to explain to this doll-man it wouldn't be right to go out with him. I just couldn't take it further—I had this strange feeling I'd regret it. A premonition. Besides, why bother when I was leaving Newport for good in a few weeks?

I fluffed up my pillow to find a cool spot; positioned my head so I would sleep and stop thinking. But I kept on thinking…even my plan to leave Newport felt like a useless sham. Talk about excitement…I might as well have presented my boss with a wet rag, the day I handed in my notice. And what if I couldn't find someone suitable and willing to share the drive to California? What if Seth finally attempted to reach me again—with no forward address?

No, that would be good. Serve him right. Trying another position, I flung the pillow aside and turned over on my stomach.

Of course I wanted Seth to write and tell me what was going on more than anything else in the world, and yet I didn't want him to. I was scared to death of the truth. More than likely, this long-awaited letter would be the final, lethal blow to my precarious love. Whereas without the letter (aside from an aching heart riddled with scar tissue) nothing between us could actually turn to worms—my lifeline was secure.

I extended my arm toward the nightstand, feeling for the lamp. In another minute I knew I was doomed to sit up and read again—for the hundredth time—the cryptic contents of his three measly letters.

Just three.

And Jesus, some comfort.

CHAPTER 11

The Airport

A week later, Max and I were lovers. I had succumbed, feeling relieved and exuberant, as well as apprehensive and sad—as if perhaps I had either brilliantly saved myself or executed the ultimate error of judgment.

I suppose it took someone like Max (handsome, keen, clever Max) to short-cut his way into Seth's position. He had done the right thing: phoned several times to argue the point, sounding hurt and pained but humbly willing to wait (without a deadline) for me to decide.

When I gave in, he insisted I choose the restaurant. I picked the Lobster Trap, a quaint converted warehouse weathered by wind and salt, sitting on the lesser-known side of Narragansett Bay.

Staring at Max across the candlelight table, surrounded by the rich aroma of freshly cooked fish—I did most of the talking, groping for the hook. While Max, for the most part, kept his mouth shut. He didn't seem to mind mutual silence, or a shared reluctance to speak. We simply enjoyed the lobster, savored the wine, and studied each other, bemused, throughout the meal.

"So why are you leaving Newport?" he finally asked, out of the blue, after dessert.

"There's no good reason to stay," I replied.

"Won't you miss all this?" Max turned his head, gazing—with good reason—at the view.

In the distance, the lights atop the bridge arched across the bay, like a colossal arm studded in stars. Below, twinkling lights from passing boats inched through the ever-widening black expanse, heading out to sea.

"It's lovely here, I'll admit. But I don't feel as if I belong."

"You belong in California?"

"Don't laugh, but I really think I belong in England."

Max raised his eyebrows. He didn't laugh. But my answer left him rather mystified.

"I spent a month in England last fall," I went on. "My mother's father was English. They both died years ago…but I've got distant relatives there."

"Where? London?"

"No, in Lichfield. You wouldn't have heard of it."

"Where is it then?"

"In the middle of England, near Birmingham."

"Seduced by knights and their castles, eh?"

"Something like that."

"But you're headed for California."

"Yes…that's the plan…"

"Don't explain if you don't want to. I'm just glad Anne asked me along to that game. And I went."

He smiled for a second, but I think his attention wandered away from the original question—or was hedging in too close. Staring wistfully down at his plate, he said nothing more.

"I wish we'd met earlier," I ventured to add.

"Ditto. A bad sense of timing, my dear." He raised his glass. "Who shall we toast to thank? Or blame?"

I didn't join in. I'd already finished my wine. Why toast with an empty glass?

"Shall we go?"

"Yes."

"I'll ask for the bill. Then, what do you say? Back to my place? Or not?"

Right. Now I had to decide one way or the other really fast. If I didn't, I'd lose Max forever…

"Your place," I said.

It had to be. I was taking Seth's own advice: seizing the here-and-now. And why couldn't I be more like Seth, an adventurer who takes what comes, as and when it comes?

"I promise not to ask again why you're leaving Newport," Max replied, reaching for his jacket. "At least, not tonight."

Escorted inside his apartment, I knew I'd fit right in. On a sagging burgundy couch, I sat back and kicked off my shoes; leaned toward those out-stretched, all-American, Ken-to-Barbie arms; held firm in his comfortable embrace.

We eased into a long, concentrated kiss.

The initial guilt slipped away, as I lay in the warmth of Max's body. Grateful for the smooth, straightforward manner in which we'd had sex, I savored the honor of sharing his bed. Snuggled up against my breasts, Max was half-asleep.

"Well you've really done it now," he muttered, half-smiling and nuzzling my neck. "I think I'm pretty damn close to falling in love with you."

Maybe I was falling too. It felt good with Max. Good, right up until the next morning when I got home.

Good, until passing through the kitchen, I noticed something sitting on the table.

It couldn't be, but it was. Some joker had really juggled the balls, putting that thing on the table. Right before my very eyes. Just as I'd pinned my heart, my body, my hopes on someone else. The timing was even better than anything you'd expect to find in a Dickens novel. But this wasn't fiction: the writing on the envelope was Seth's.

Holding the letter in my hands, I turned it over and over again, inspecting the paper, the stamp, and the handwriting—for several minutes. It had to be a trick, or some sneaky, rabble-rousing...

God. No, no, no, I was thinking. Well. Whatever Seth had to say, at least I felt more ready than ever before to take it.

∾

July 16

Dear Lauren,

It's been an interesting couple of months, to say the least. Ian told me you called. I'm sorry but life on the road is wild. Not conducive to letters, good or bad. Do you forgive? Now somewhat sober, rather sore and definitely broke—I'm back in Lichfield—but listen—still scratching the itch for America. Will you be baking cookies?

I'm still coming, money or no.

Yesterday I fixed up the bike. Yep, dosh for the airfare, and after tuning the carburetors I took it for a spin. A few wheelies and watch how the cars disappear in plumes of blue smoke! I'll miss ripping the bends like that, feeling the wind rushing past, that

howling Cheetah engine whirring like a turbine, and that thump-
ing great kick in the pants when you give it some stick. Sort of
sorry to see it go, but I could be in the saddle of an even meaner
wildcat in the glorious U.S.A.!

Already booked it. Boston July 25th flight 104 British Air. Yes?
See you soon matey.

Love Seth

❧   ❧   ❧

July twenty-fifth turned out to be a scorching hot day. Max insisted on
going to the airport with me. I hadn't anticipated that, but I should have
known better.

"I'd rather go alone, Max."

"Why?"

"I just think it would be better that way."

"I can help with the driving."

"No, I can manage—"

"You don't want me around?"

"Of course I'd rather you came, but…I don't know…it might be better…"

"Why?"

"No, no, all right, I'm being silly."

I didn't know what to say or how to act. My realistic decision felt about as
comfortable as jumping off a chair with a noose around my neck, only to curse
the fact that I'd kicked the chair so hard it rolled completely out of reach.

Max suddenly turned talkative. He wasn't satisfied with silence during the
drive to Boston—instead he kept tightening the noose by asking questions.

"Will I like him?"

"Of course you will."

"How old is he?"

"My age…Twenty-one, or twenty-two."

"What suddenly made him decide to book a flight to America?"

"Well, I'm not sure, really. He's like that. Unpredictable sometimes."

"Remind me, though, to thank him for it. Because if he hadn't decided at
the drop of a hat to come—you'd already be on your way to California."

"Oh…that's true. How strange."

"So you see everything has a reason…"

"I guess so…"

"And what are you going to do after you take him across country to California?"

"Well, eventually Seth will go back home and I'll stay in Los Angeles with some friends. Then it's on to Santa Barbara where I'd prefer to live. If I can find a job."

"Are you sure you're making the right decision to give up on Newport?"

I looked over at Max, sitting so confidently behind the wheel. Nevertheless his jaw twitched and his lips puckered into one of his doll-faced pouts—beseeching me to give in. He turned his head so I could see the subtle hint of manly hurt in his eyes.

"Well?"

"Max, of course *now*—I'm not that sure," I ventured, carefully. "Are you asking, then, what about us?"

"No, I'm asking on behalf of your dad!" he retorted, "—I don't think I have to spell it out, Lauren. I'd be very, very sad if you left for good."

Silence. I pondered over his words 'if'…and 'for good.'

We had almost reached Boston when Max decided to say something again.

"You know, I could probably take a two-week vacation and drive out to California with you. That is, if you'd like me to come along."

"Really?"

"Sure. It would give us both a bit more time, maybe enough to talk you out of all this. Besides, I'd feel better knowing you had someone along other than a helpless British tourist—just in case you ran into any kind of trouble. Has this cousin of yours ever driven a car? How do you know he'll be able to drive on the right side of the road?"

"Don't be silly. He can drive! But of course I'd be thrilled if you could come. Do you really think you can manage it?" I exclaimed, choking over the words, which nevertheless gushed out—of their own accord—through the corners of the noose.

"Yep," Max stated, sitting once again quite comfortably as he drove on.

"Are you really serious?"

"I'm always serious. Haven't you noticed? If I bother to say something, I mean it."

So. He had made up his mind. I could hardly believe it. Suddenly the initial flattery and romance of a fling with someone like Max had exploded into a whirlwind of uncertainty and dread. I wasn't as happy or as thrilled as I should have been. Intensely infatuated yes—absolutely certain, no.

"I want to be with you, Lauren."

"We've hardly had time to really get to know each other, but…"

"I just can't let you go."

"Oh Max, *don't*. I'm not sure what to do. But things will work themselves out, given time."

"We don't have much time."

"You'll come with us, then, all the way to California?"

"Yes."

At that moment the hangman in charge of the noose yanked the lever and I felt myself hoisted above and beyond any urge to struggle. Then, blackness—as the bottom dropped out and I sank—shattered and utterly devastated by what I'd done.

Suddenly *I knew*. I knew in my heart a fact so undeniably true it might as well have been written all over the windscreen in black and white:

Seth wouldn't like this at all.

Meanwhile Max took the exit to Logan Airport as if nothing had happened. We parked. I gulped and got out of the car, forcing a smile on my face, trying to muster up a cloak of composure for the awkward confrontation. We approached the Arrivals entrance. My stomach began to churn in airy spasms; I felt as if I was walking through a dream world. But I carried on—desperately telling myself Seth should suffer, too. Let him squirm. Let him pay for his care-free life, his long silences and cryptic hints.

The sliding doors mechanically opened, people rushing about dragging luggage and whining children in a stream of zigzag traffic in front of us. Max and I merged.

Heading for the International Customs Exit, I noticed how Max maneuvered with methodical efficiency, detouring at the TV screen to catch the flight before taking a sharp left turn—weaving through the crowds. I followed close by his side, blindly, silently, like a mechanized corpse.

Max, wearing gray khaki pants and a white cotton polo shirt, smartly fitted, had dressed more carefully. Add tasseled leather loafers and a pair of Rayban Driver sunglasses, and he looked as if he knew exactly what he was doing. In contrast, I wore a washed-out blue T-shirt covered in stars and clouds, a wrinkled gauze skirt, and cheap K-Mart sandals.

Though at this point there was no need for sunglasses. Taking his off, Max turned to me and said: "Well, this is it."

Fighting for a good position among the crowd, we moved closer behind the barrier, waiting for the big blue doors to open and let out all the passengers from British Airways Flight 104.

I tried to bolster my composure, thinking to myself how Max looked so perfect, so mature and well groomed. Aside from his looks, he also held a decent job with a computer corporation (as a staff accountant), doing very well financially for himself at the age of twenty-six. And despite his obvious talent for picking up women, he'd managed to stay a bachelor. As to his shortcomings—well, whatever they were—he smugly kept them all to himself.

Standing behind that barrier, observing Max as a bystander, I started to feel better. What, after all, was the crime? I had to keep asking myself this, just to keep up my nerve. But then a new thought occurred to me, sending another wave of post-mortem up my spine. Max was Seth's opposite in every way. They would only have one thing in common: me.

Finally a stream of people poured out from the Customs Exit and my victim, Seth Henshaw, shot into view.

He innocently pushed his way nearer to the crowd of greeters. He may have been exhausted and humbled by the flight and strange surroundings, but his appearance hadn't changed. No, he looked just as I remembered him—Rock Band T-shirt, faded jeans full of holes, heavy black boots; wild, woolly, lean physique and wispy brown hair. He still sported his goatee beard, with those piercing green eyes behind a soft face of golden-red freckles, as if he might be, after all, some kind of pagan, half-wolf Celt.

I instantly rushed past the barrier towards him. Seth saw me and threw off his bulging backpack.

Rooted to the spot, we hugged.

"Oh Lorrrren…." he moaned in my ear, with his heart-rending accent—as always—turning my name into something strange and exotic.

His embrace locked me in a death-grip, so tight and hard and trembling I knew it had been, was, would always be true. *He loved me.* Feeling his heart pounding like a drum—faster and deeper than anything I'd known—pressed tight against my chest, I *knew*.

But there was Max and I was forced to pull away after what seemed an eternity.

Turning to face Max, still standing in the background—I had to practically wrench myself free. Seth let go; I smiled and diplomatically pointed to the man holding the Raybans.

"Seth, Seth," I stumbled. "Here, I want you to meet—my friend—boy-friend—Max—"

Seth's face froze. In an instant he spotted Max and read the meaning of my expression. Horrified, I watched Seth's demeanor quickly switch to casual mode as he reached out to shake Max's hand.

There was an uncomfortable pause. The look on Max's face suggested he wasn't going to accept my story about Seth being no more than a relative. That didn't bother me—not now. But what else could I say? To either Max, or Seth?

Seth's hazel eyes flashed at me, as if to implore "What do you want me to do?" and my own eyes had quickly answered him in defense: "Play the sham." At the same time Max was already putting his arm around me, enforcing his claim.

Nobody made another move. For a moment Seth stood there like a lost soul in Hades watching me drift through a speechless state of purgatory. Finally Max's cool, confident voice broke through the black hole.

"Well, Seth—welcome to America!"

❦   ❦   ❦

During the drive back to Newport—despite the pleasant flow of conversation—I could tell Seth was furious over Max. Outwardly calm and polite, he nevertheless hadn't made any effort to break the ice. Slumped in the corner of the back seat, he kept throwing me subtle, questioning looks—whenever I dared to turn around and look at him.

But ignoring this, I carried on, nervously chatting away like a stupid little monkey trying to keep a hungry lion at bay.

"The weather's been perfect, Seth. We'll have to go to the beach tomorrow."

"Whatever you say."

"I expect you're going to feel pretty strange for a few days, with a five-hour jet lag. I did."

"I feel lousy, that's for sure."

"Wait till you see my new car. A Ford Galaxy, paid only six hundred dollars for it too, hardly any rust, and the windows go up when you push a button."

"So this is Max's car. What is it, a Mercedes?"

"Yes," Max cut in.

"It's nice to see you've recognized the quality of German engineering over American."

Max ignored this last remark but I quickly changed the subject. "Oh, but tell me Seth, how's your parents?" I asked. "How's Ian? Aunt Bea and Uncle Henry?"

"Fine, all fine."

"My dad's getting married again next month. He and his fiancé are flying to Fuji to tie the knot. Just after we leave for California, in fact. He spends the weekends at her place these days. But I'm still living at the Quarters, cranking all the halyards, so to speak, until we both abandon ship."

While I was spouting all this, inwardly I was constructing the line of attack I'd use later in my defense: *Now wait just a minute, Seth. Who do you think I am? Joan of Arc? The Virgin Mary? Odysseus' Penelope? You can't expect me to wait around like a saint while you carry on with Naomi—or that singer, or God knows whom. Your ego is a bit bruised, that's all. Join the club. And after all's been said and done—why should I be such a fool as to give up Max for someone as unpredictable as you, with your biker's leathers, teasing looks, and renegade ways? Why should I sacrifice a tangible, dependable future for a summer's lightning bolt?*

"I'm shattered," Seth suddenly muttered. "Hope you both don't think it's rude if I fall asleep."

"Go right ahead," said Max, speaking for me as well and putting another stake in his claim.

The Mercedes swung across to the fast lane and the monkey—much to everyone's relief—stopped talking.

What would happen next? And, I kept thinking, what did Seth really want from me? Did he even consider the consequences—the aftermath—of a real reunion? Wouldn't it be just like him, to take it for the moment and then let it go? Wouldn't he say goodbye at the airport, just as before, a picture of sorrow but an honest nothing promised?

Ah, but not me. Not this time.

I showed the security guard my pass and we drove on to the Base. Seth was fast asleep when Max parked the car in the driveway. My dad was out with Sally, so Seth was led straight to the guestroom to sleep. I brewed Max some coffee; he drank it in silence; then we kissed good night. The worst was surely over.

"I'll phone tomorrow from work," Max promised. "I should know by the afternoon whether I'll get those two weeks off."

"Fine."

"You're sure you'd still like me to come?" he asked again, with a wry slant to his smile.

"Oh course," I repeated.

Yet I knew he could tell I wasn't sure. Not at all.

"You won't regret it," he promised.

And maybe I wouldn't. Though retiring to bed so soon, I expected either nightmares or a guilt-ridden sleep. I could hardly change what had happened already, but I could always pray for what was yet to come. So in the end, I prayed to God and my mother; I prayed to the Light in the Void; I prayed to whoever or whatever would listen. *Oh please*, I asked, *please let fate intervene.*

Perhaps Max wouldn't be granted his short-notice, two-week leave.

Could prayers work to change one's fate? At least I'd managed to fall asleep, for in the morning I woke to the sound of muffled voices coming from the kitchen. Dressing quickly, I rushed down to find Seth having breakfast with my father. They were sitting together at the breakfast bar, eating pancakes. Correction—my father was attempting to eat, while Seth (ignoring his own steaming plate) was talking up a storm. Something to do with officials, visas, and government Embassies.

"Even so, Captain Aimes, I wouldn't have asked for your help."

"Why not? Just a few phone calls, nothing to make a fuss about."

"But I shouldn't have been denied a visa in the first place!"

"These things happen…"

"What's all this about?" I interrupted.

"Seth's been telling me how the Embassy refused to give him a visa," my dad explained. "He says they took offence just because he showed up with long hair, in a leather motorcycle jacket."

"That's right," Seth insisted. "And they denied me a visa, point blank, on no other grounds. It took *two months* of humble pie and kiss-ass before they finally gave in. To their advantage, of course. One more day of delay and I would have torn their fat smug faces off."

I winced. But I wanted to hear more. "Seth, why didn't you write—about all this?"

"Pride, I suppose. There I was, promising you how determined and prepared I was to get to America, only to find the last little detail, the seemingly most insignificant trivia of red tape—" he paused, taking a deep breath, "—to be my downfall, the cruel ogre, the mad axeman, the ultimate executioner of hope."

My father laughed. "You've got a flair for drama."

"And annoying people," Seth muttered. "But I'm telling you the truth. The Embassy didn't want the likes of me coming over here. It took weeks of hanging around in their corridors and hammering on their doors. I even cut my hair and bought a suit."

"When I could have pulled some strings and you'd have pocketed that visa in a few minutes," said my dad.

"Jesus…" I mumbled. I couldn't bear to think about it. Could a little red tape change certain lives in such a big way?

"Which I never would have asked for, even if I knew," answered Seth.

"It wouldn't have been a *big deal*," replied my dad, shaking his head and beginning to look insulted.

"Even when the game is crooked," insisted Seth, "I prefer to play my own hand fair."

"Well it's all over and done with now!" I exclaimed, aware the issue was getting well out of hand. "So, how's your jet lag this morning?"

"Not bad, I feel much better," Seth replied, with an uneasy smile.

"It looks to me like you haven't touched your breakfast. Now why don't you relax and eat some of those pancakes?"

"Your wish is my command."

"And what should we do on your first day in Newport?"

Seth looked up, with a drop of Maple syrup on his beard, and mumbled, "This is good…. ummm, how about going to a music shop? I'm hoping to find myself a cheap used guitar. I didn't want to risk it, bringing mine."

Then we both smiled at each other as if nothing had ever come between that last night in England and the nine long months that followed.

"Oh yes, I'd love to hear you play again while you're here," I said.

"I thought so," Seth answered.

❧   ❧   ❧

"Well, cousin. I've finally arrived."

"I've missed you, ever since the day I left Lichfield," I said. "I think I even wrote you and told you so."

We were sitting together—alone—in my Galaxy, driving through Newport. On our way to the music shop.

Seth shook his head. "Letters are useless bits of paper. I just assumed you'd feel the same as me, about my coming here. You know—better late than never."

I didn't answer.

"I know it's all in the past," he went on, "but I suppose I should try and explain. No, I couldn't write, for several reasons. You wouldn't want to know…"

"Probably not," I said.

"The Birmingham episode, the bout with the rock band, I guess Ian told you I joined up, as part of the backup crew. A crazy time. Too crazy, and I'm no angel. But it turned out even crazier, coming back to Lichfield—trying to get that Visa."

"I'm sure it all must have been an interesting experience," I replied. "Well, I did wonder about you, and I'm really sorry it took all that time and trouble, getting the visa…."—thinking as I said it: god, what a *pathetic understatement!*

"And when did you start going out with Max?"

Abrupt change of subject.

"Not that long…I don't know…it's all very strange, but I didn't think you'd mind, considering what you've been doing—"

"If he's made you happy, then I'm glad for you. Are you happy?" Seth asked, placing his hands firmly on his thighs as if to brace himself.

"Well, yes. I'm sorry that it all turned out to be a surprise for you. But it won't make any difference to our plans."

"It won't?"

"Of course not."

"But Max is coming with us to California?"

"He might. We'll probably find out for sure today."

"Oh."

Seth kept his head turned away from me, staring fixedly out his window, as we paused in silence, each thinking our own private thoughts.

"Are we on the High Street now?" he finally asked, clearing his throat.

"Yes. But we call it Main Street, or, as in this case, Broadway."

Parking the car, I realized he wasn't going to say a thing about what was *really* going on—he was leaving it all up to me. Why did I ever hope it might be otherwise? True, I was the one who'd messed it all up *now*. But why wasn't he telling me that? Why couldn't he just tell me?

The Music Box was one of a few stores still standing midst the mini-malls and condo conversions of downtown Newport. It hadn't changed since the fifties—the same yellowed signs, cluttered shelves, and dusty, obsolete wares. An amazing variety of acoustic guitars hung from the walls; Seth and I wedged in between the piles of out-of-date sheet music and instruction books to take a few of them down for inspection. The old woman who owned the shop sat smiling and nodding behind the cash register, letting Seth do as he pleased.

When Seth's favorite tune burst forth from the first guitar, I felt wonderfully happy and sick. He looked up at me and grinned.

"Nice?"

"Yes!"

"Let's find the nicest of the nice."

After several tries, the guitar he chose sounded as near to his own as he could find. He assured me it would do as a substitute. (His own guitar—irreplaceable—was indeed worth keeping safe and sound in England.)

The old woman was so pleased she threw in an extra set of strings and a handful of pics at no charge.

"Well, I guess it's time for a tour," I suggested.

We returned to the car and I took Seth through the center of town, passing the picturesque colonial homes and shops, all carefully restored. The route included the narrow and cobbled streets with historic homes and shops tightly wedged together English-style, toward the tall pointed spire of Trinity Church rising above all the landmarks.

"There's our Lady of the Harbor," I said. "At least that's what I like to call it. But our spire isn't in the same league as your Lichfield Ladies. It's built of wood, painted a brilliant white, and in comparison—feels like a mere child."

"I didn't realize you felt so strongly about our Cathedral."

"It's all very pretty here, with some of the earliest colonial buildings in America," I explained. "But it doesn't feel English, does it? Now that I've actually *been* to England, all this comes across as a feeble copy, a mimic of history, a brand-New World. There aren't any man-made structures a thousand years old, and the hedges haven't been standing for centuries. So…I guess maybe that's why…you know….nothing in the air feels quite the same as Lichfield."

"Lichfield isn't unique, you know," Seth added. "That feeling comes with most of our towns and villages."

"That may be true," I answered. "Yet what *other* towns and villages have such—such—(I struggled to keep him out of it)—nice relatives—or—or—(I suddenly remembered) a gorgeous cathedral?"

I drove on, past the marinas and boatyards crammed along the harbor, heading beyond Fort Adams and Hammersmith Farm—until we'd reached the far end of the Island. Here the Atlantic Ocean gently buffeted against a pleasant contrasting contour of boulders, pebbles, wild rose bush, seaweed and drift-wood.

Without a word, I parked the car. The beach wasn't Sandymouth, but it offered its own unique beauty and sense of solace; I knew Seth would be impressed. We clambered over the rocks, disturbing a flock of sea gulls—the birds noisily relinquishing their post.

The sea glittered in the bright sun. For a long time we both gazed in medita-tion as the deep blue waves swelled peacefully against the rocks. Finally Seth turned and carefully took hold of my hand, gingerly cupping it between his hands—as if such a gesture was a tentative remembrance of something already beyond his reach.

I held my breath. I was finally touching it again—the electric current of a lightning bolt rushing up and down my skin.

The penetrating light in his eyes pierced right through me, as he searched for the right words. "I feel that I should say something to you, Lauren," he began.

"Then say it. I hope there will be nothing ever to keep you from telling me anything," I begged, "Please, whatever it is—"

Seth took a deep breath as if he was about to unleash a difficult (or tricky) confession.

"Well…it's just that…(clearing his throat) I'm not too happy about Max coming with us."

He glanced away from me, striving for a safer distance. "Daft, I know, but I didn't expect you to have a boyfriend when I arrived. Hmmm, well, I suppose I should have expected it. It's perfectly reasonable for you to have one. I don't blame you at all."

He took a deep breath.

"Like I said, Lauren, if you're happy, then I'm all for it. But at the same time I can't help but get this feeling about Max. To be honest, there's something about him I don't like."

He stole a quick look up into my eyes, which confirmed my raised eye-brows.

Of course I was surprised. "Go on," I insisted.

"Oh Lauren, I don't know—it's like he makes me very uneasy. It's a feeling that I'd rather not have—but it's there. I wish to god I could make it go away."

"Oh," I replied, miffed. This certainly wasn't at all what I'd hoped to hear.

"But you obviously are very taken with him," Seth stammered, "and I have no right to come along and discredit your relationships. It's your life and I want you to do exactly what you feel is right. But..." (inhale) "—as friends—" (exhale) "I think it's important to tell you truthfully how I feel."

"Yes, I agree you should tell me," I said, in a voice that seemed far removed from Earth, as if the place where we sat rested on some other planet, in some other universe.

"It's not easy...I don't want to make any fuss," Seth continued. Then, almost in a whisper, he added, "And it may be very selfish of me—but I don't trust Max and wish he wasn't going with us to California."

"So that's it?"

"What do you mean, that's it? I've just told you I dislike your new boy-friend!" Seth exclaimed, letting go of my hand.

"Well, I'm glad you told me," I managed to answer, shaken and disappointed. "Though I wish you could explain more about why you don't like him."

"You've not felt anything strange, rather covert, about Max?" Seth asked sheepishly.

"No...I admit I haven't known him very long, but I don't have any misgivings about his character," I said, my voice beginning to shake.

Seth straightened his back and inquired stiffly, "So—do you—do you—love him?"

"I don't know...it's too early to say..." I mumbled, annoyed at Seth's easy-feigned surrender to martyrdom.

"But you do really want him to come with us?"

I couldn't decide what I really wanted at that moment. I only knew that Seth's tantalizing physical presence engulfed me in a succession of hot flashes, making it extremely difficult to articulate anything at all.

But Seth expected an answer. He seemed distantly tormented and only slightly sad—without betraying the slightest flicker of totally selfish disapproval.

Looking at him I realized I wasn't going to hear what I wanted to hear. Rather than admit he might be in love with me, Seth seemed quite willing to accept Max if I asked him to. So what kind of love was that? Shy? Stupid? Sacrificial? Or *super*ficial?

"You really want Max to come with us?" Seth asked again.

To hell with it then, I thought. It was foolish giving up someone like Max for a question mark. Even so, I couldn't speak my true mind. Instead I offered a silent nod.

A nod of yes.

"Okay then," Seth sighed, trying to force a reassuring smile. "Don't worry. I'll never mention it again. Let's go on as before and forget about this silly little talk. As long as I'm sure of your feelings, I'll be fine—Seth's promise." And he once again took hold of my hand, briefly, in a tight, concluding squeeze.

Damn it all! Racked with overwhelming passion, I could hardly believe what was happening. Seth had twisted the issue, surely! All I could do was hold on. Keep my head. For Seth wasn't about to offer an easy way out of my predicament.

No guarantees. And if Seth really did love me with equal passion, I'd have to assume he was being a coward—just like me. But Seth was no coward.

"Are we finished?" I asked.

"Yep, now that's off my chest I'm ready to go."

Having completed the tour, I drove Seth back to the Quarters at the War College. By the time we'd crossed the causeway, my burning nerves had cooled under the grim knowledge of how I'd get my revenge. That was easy. If Seth could disguise his jealousy under a detached sense of distrust—I could stay equally aloof by keeping hold of Max.

And we would all stay happy.

CHAPTER 12

The Chase

Max, of course, got his leave. With only four days to prepare for the trip, we didn't have much time to waste. My battered Ford needed a tune-up and two new tires; camping gear had to be purchased; various other items had to be assembled and packed so the sum total would all fit neatly in the trunk or roof-rack. Plus we had to make room for Max and his luggage.

Seth kept his promise. He maintained a light-hearted attitude toward the news that Max was coming with us. I almost wondered whether he was really bothered by it. The excitement and enthusiasm over the cross-country trek seemed to liven him up and put a genuine sparkle in his eye.

But day two arrived and suddenly all organized efforts to prepare fell apart. Seth and I had just arrived at Max's apartment to show him the new tent and stove we'd found on sale at K-Mart. While assembling the stove to ensure that it worked properly, Max's phone rang. Oddly enough, it was my father. Puzzled, I picked up the receiver.

"Yeah dad, what's up?"

"*What* the *hell* does Seth think he's *doing*?" screamed my dad. "The *police* were just here! It seems the Post Office drug-dogs sniffed out a huge chunk of hash hidden in a small package addressed *here*, to Seth! And it came from Britain! I'll *kill* him if I ever get near that insane idiot cousin of yours again! My god! How could he be so stupid? *You* could have been arrested—luckily I've managed to convince the police you had nothing to do with it! But Seth is in big trouble. If they find him he'll be booked and deported."

"There must be some mistake!"

"Sorry honey, but there's no mistake. I suggest Seth make himself scarce *this minute*. The military police were here too, but they've passed the case back to the civilian police—who'll definitely go after Seth. Whatever you do, don't bring him back here!"

"I can't believe it," I whimpered, "Dad, I'm so sorry..."

"I'm too mad to talk about this now," my dad retorted. His voice was hoarse with rage. "But I sure hope you had *nothing* to do with this." He hung up.

"What's wrong?" Seth asked, noticing the shocked look on my face.

"Everything!" I exclaimed.

During the next fifteen minutes (which felt like a slow-motion time warp) my car was loaded up: a chaotic frenzy entailing a completely arbitrary and hap-hazard assortment of Max's clothes, blankets, jackets, shoes, road-maps, and whatever happened to be in his kitchen cupboards for food. We couldn't risk going back to the Quarters for anything (even though Seth bewailed his new guitar and me, my contraceptive pills). There was no choice but to high tail it out of Rhode Island and hope the police would not extend their search beyond the State.

"I never posted any hash!" Seth insisted, over and over again.

But what difference did it make now? I grabbed his shoulders and shook him. "All right, don't worry, I believe you! But we can't let the police get to you. You'd be in custody for days, maybe weeks! Who knows what would happen..."

While Max and I hastily scrambled to assemble a load of necessities, Seth stood aside watching—horrified. He was about as useful as a helpless, ignorant bystander who'd just witnessed a car accident.

He couldn't really do much, of course. So when Max, loading the car outside, shouted at him to fetch a certain map from his desk, he eagerly rushed to the task.

"Can you find it?" I asked, standing in the kitchen awaiting help in lifting a provisions box.

"Not yet."

"Shall I look?" I was losing patience.

Seth wasn't finding this map. He frantically scrambled through the top drawer; empty-handed, he continued his search to the second drawer. I was about to go over to help when Seth apparently spotted it. Stopping abruptly, he bent closer to inspect something in the messy pile of papers.

Suddenly Max came bounding up the stairs. Seth whirled around to face him—speedily shutting the drawer with his hip.

"Haven't you found it yet?" Max shouted impatiently.

"No, it's not there," Seth answered.

Max rushed over and threw open the top drawer. No map. "Oh damn, it's probably in the glove compartment of my car! I'll get it in a minute—is that everything?"

With a unanimous "Let's just GO!" we set off racing (scared shitless) towards Connecticut, using every back-road we could find.

"I didn't do it…who did it?…this isn't happening…" Seth's voice kept moaning. A string of angry curses ensued, all from the back seat, while I drove on in a frightened stupor. Seth, lying down on the floor, had strict instructions to keep his head down.

Max started to argue with me: "Maybe we shouldn't conceal him. We might be arrested as harboring a criminal."

"It won't come to that," I replied, looking at the rear view mirror every second for police. "But I think it's better if it looks like only two people are in the car."

Suddenly Seth's head popped up between the seats.

"It's Philip! It's got to be Philip! I'll tear him limb by limb if I ever get back! Bloody Hell! He's daft enough—and—I remember complaining to him about not being able to bring any blow with me—and didn't he offer to send it. Fuck! That imbecile—I told him not to, not until I checked out this end first."

"Some friends you have over there," Max muttered.

"Should I turn off here?" I exclaimed, "or will I just be heading in a circle?"

"Let me drive," Max insisted. "I've been in this part of Rhody before—"

"Get down!" I screeched to Seth, as the car veered off the road. "It's all academic; whoever did it can't rectify the situation now…Jesus, is that a cop behind us?"

"No. Now pull over," Max calmly commanded.

Switching places, it suddenly occurred to me that Max wasn't scared. In fact, he seemed amazingly unruffled by the whole situation—almost as if he wasn't very concerned over the danger of Seth's arrest. It made me wonder if maybe Max was even secretly hoping my cousin would be whisked right out of the picture.

No, I decided, that couldn't be it: Max was finding the best escape route—spreading out the map, carefully studying the secondary roads that side-swiped all possible towns with police stations. He was the one who suggested we travel as far north as possible, through the uninhabited swamplands, entering Connecticut just outside of Warrensville.

While Seth—in hiding—missed all the scenery: the woods, cornfields, vegetable stands and porched farmhouses; the rivers, marshes and bird-havens of Rhode Island. It seemed such a shame, but we raced on, saying nothing, until I read out a road sign: "Thirty miles to Warrensville."

By this time the cursing had ceased—the body on the floor had become as quiet and motionless as a corpse. I eventually began to relax a bit.

Too soon, however, Seth's head once again popped up and startled me like a Jack-in-the Box. This time he grabbed my shoulders and blurted "Yep! Of course, it *would* have to happen!"

"Jesus, Seth, what now?"

"Can't you feel it? We've got a flat tire!"

The car definitely agreed, lurching and bumping until Max turned off onto the hard shoulder.

As the dust-cloud settled, I found myself commenting dryly, "I told you this car needed two new back tires."

"But it's the front that's flat," said Seth.

"I suppose getting a spare was also on the list?" asked Max.

"No, no, of course I have a spare!"

We jumped out; I insisted it would be best if Max changed the tire and Seth hid in the woods in case a policeman stopped to see if we required help.

The tension and pressure merely heightened the animosity between the two rivals. If only I'd known how to change a tire! Max couldn't loosen the nuts. Seth kept emerging from behind the trees complaining it was taking too long; then they wrestled over the wheel spanner until it suspiciously flew out of Max's hands into Seth's knee. Howling, Seth had the bolts and tire off in a matter of seconds. He handed the spanner back to Max—with a superior smirk.

"I loosened them for you," Max insisted.

"If you say so."

"Why don't you let Max finish the job?" I implored, nervously squinting my eyes to study the features of an upcoming car in the distance.

"All right, but I'm not going to be eaten alive by mosquitoes for much longer," Seth muttered, rubbing his knee. "It's a swampy shit-hole behind those trees."

Luckily Max had just removed the jack before Seth trotted back to the car, scowling and scratching.

"What's that smell?" I asked, as we pulled away. "It's really foul—like rotten eggs!"

"It's the muck you made me wallow in," muttered Seth, and look—what's this?"

I turned around, holding my nose. Seth's jeans were rolled up and he was pointing at a tiny round black spot embedded in his ankle.

"Oh, that's a tick. You better get it off, but don't pull it out. Burn it with a match."

"I've never seen a tick before. Is it dangerous?"

"In your case, it's bound to be carrying Lime Disease," Max grumbled. "It won't be your normal, everyday, nondescript tick—not if it's attached to you!"

A few hours later we stopped at a gas station. I went to the rest room and when I returned Seth was sitting bolt upright—again—looking extremely agitated.

"Seth, what' wrong?"

"Look, Max went in the station to pay and now he's making a phone call."

"So?"

"I don't like it. You ask him who he rang when he gets back."

Max, slipping back into his seat, casually explained before I could even ask. "I made a brief call into work," he said. "I forgot to give my secretary some last minute instructions."

"So, let's move on," I said, giving Seth a don't-be-paranoid glare.

We were ten minutes away from Warrensville when I realized Seth hadn't stopped fidgeting. It sounded like fists banging the seat back in the fugitive corner.

"All right Max," Seth finally announced, employing a deep, slightly threatening tone, "Maybe it's time you considered changing your course."

"What?"

Max's eyes flared with anger. I noticed he instantly tightened his grip on the steering wheel.

"I said, you should change course. Because it might just be to your advantage, Max."

"What are you talking about?"

"I have a feeling we should stay clear of Warrensville."

"Seth—" I started to intercede, but then decided against it.

"Are you implying something?" Max asked, his voice cool and almost offhand, but his eyes still narrow and scowling with anger.

"No. I just think—on impulse—we should take another route—maybe we'd prevent the police from contacting a unit in Ohio at the same time."

"Ohio?"

"Yes Ohio," Seth insisted. "I read it somewhere. The police are on the lookout in Ohio. They've got a name, but no traceable address."

Dead silence. Max's jaw tightened.

"Look—if you'll feel better, then we'll waste another couple of hours zigzagging up and down Rhode Island," Max suddenly replied, wincing. But he immediately swung the car around in a U-turn.

I said nothing, only felt a hollow pit growing in the middle of my stomach. It gnawed and twisted as Max reached over and placed his hand firmly on my knee.

"It's all right. We'll detour a bit south," he said. "And I'll have to explain Ohio—later."

After the U-turn, the non-passenger in the back remained unnervingly quiet and motionless, all the way through the last-minute detour leg of Rhode Island, through to the Connecticut border, and into the early morning hours of the next day.

I'd never know for sure if the police were tipped and waiting to ambush us in Warrensville. We crossed into New York—around midnight—and we finally stopped to catch some sleep in a motel. Max insisted on two rooms; Seth quickly grabbed a six-pack of Heineken before disappearing into his.

"Good night."

"We made it, Seth."

"Yes, we'll be fine now."

"No hard feelings, Max."

"No. Let's just relax and enjoy the rest of the trip."

"Right."

"Good night."

In our room, I stood uneasily in front of the window, waiting for my explanation. Max had already taken off his shoes and was sprawled out across the bed as if he'd rather go right to sleep.

"So?"

"I didn't rat on Seth."

"You didn't?"

"Of course not. How could you even think I did?"

"Because you turned around so fast!"

"I didn't want to cause a scene. I thought it best to keep your visiting relative happy."

"And what was all that about the Ohio police?"

"Your cousin obviously went sneaking and prying into my desk drawer—he must have seen a Court Summons. It's true that I am avoiding the authorities in Ohio—for Child Support."

"Child Support!"

"Yes. I was going to tell you about it…you see, two years ago, when I lived in Ohio, I dated a girl and she got pregnant. She wouldn't consider an abortion and although I had misgivings, we got married. It didn't work out—but she insisted the baby was her problem and she didn't want my help—"

"*Her* problem?"

"I'm pretty sure she intentionally got pregnant in the first place, to hang on to me—and after we parted amicably she suddenly changed her mind and sued for child support. As you can understand, I'm not too inclined to let her get away with it," Max explained. By this time he'd sat up, both elbows sinking into the lumpy mattress. "So as soon as the Summons arrived I moved to Rhode Island—leaving no forwarding address."

"So you're *married?*"

"Only technically."

"I wish you'd told me." I felt betrayed.

"I'm sorry. But I felt it was none of your business—at least—not at this stage."

I tried to swallow all this and asked, "But why did you marry her?"

"I thought it was best at the time. I made a mistake." Max shrugged.

He did look pained, hurt, and ashamed. But was it for the right reasons? I stared back at him, somewhat unconvinced.

"I would have told you all this eventually," Max assured me. "It's not a part of my past life I'm proud of, but believe me—please—I'm not hiding anything."

"But Seth seemed so convinced you'd told the police where we were heading."

"I could get really mad at him for that insult—but I won't, because we both know he's crazy. You have to admit, Lauren, he's paranoid. And all right, he's your cousin and a good friend." Max smiled. "I'm going to prove to you that a friend of yours is a friend of mine too." He hesitated, and then added, "That is, if you still believe me."

I couldn't believe I might be wrong about Max. No, he just couldn't be lying!

"Come over here," Max said (stretching out his arms and looking much too sexy to resist).

I obeyed. Max's hands gently stroked my hair. His expression insisted I believe him: eyes sincerely pained, mouth delicately and solemnly leaning forward—poised for a kiss.

We kissed.

"You don't really think I called the police at that gas station—do you?" Max muttered, graciously placing a succession of little kisses along the base of my neck.

"No…of course not…" I mumbled.

But as I undressed and crawled under the covers next to Max, I couldn't help but add: "It still would have been better if you'd just gone ahead to Warrensville to prove it—for Seth's sake."

"I'll forget Seth's sneaky intrusion into my private affairs—for your sake," said Max. "And if he doesn't trust me, that's *his* problem."

His problem. Even so, I couldn't sleep. Instead, I struggled against the restless, nagging urge to get up and go see Seth. But I couldn't do that—Max wouldn't like it at all. He'd made it clear enough: either I trusted him or I didn't. And if I were Max, wouldn't I prefer to wait awhile before telling my new lover about a previous affair? God, I was so confused. What had Max called Seth? *A fugitive.* I winced every time I thought about it. *Fugitive.* The image kept eating away at my conscience, as I tossed and turned in bed—long after Max's snores offered a chance to sneak away.

I didn't dare go see Seth. And besides, no amount of consolation (from me or anyone) would alleviate the stark fact that Seth was doomed. Like an overloaded missile on it's launch pad, he'd misfired; now he could do nothing but wait to be hit by an unseen enemy.

Scared of my own feelings and what I might find in the next room, I chose not to budge. Lying next to Max, rigid and racked with guilt, I fought back the tears—unable to bear my own remorse.

For no matter what happened, this would surely be Seth's last trip…

To America.

❋   ❋   ❋

The next morning I phoned my father to tell him we were safe in New York—heading straight on to California. He seemed relieved. The civilian police had questioned him again, but apparently they believed his story.

"What story?" I asked.

"Don't be alarmed," my dad replied, "I told them I only knew for sure that you, Max and Seth had left on a trip across country, with plans to end up at your uncle's place in Colorado." Then he admitted he had gladly given the police the address—knowing we didn't intend to visit Colorado at all.

I tried to explain that Seth's crazy friend Philip had sent the hash, but of course my dad didn't believe it. At any rate, he agreed that Seth was relatively safe—outside of Rhode Island. He told me to be careful; he also reminded me that he never wanted to see Seth's troublesome face again—innocent or not.

It may not have been a pleasant phone call, but at least it calmed everyone's fears. Now we could continue our cross-country trek at a reasonable pace; we had every reason to relax and make the most of it. At least—on the surface—the worst was over.

Even Seth seemed a lot happier, as if he'd managed to put the whole episode behind him. But despite the many laughs and jokes we made about it afterwards, I was still worried. And baffled. Because Seth wasn't the same Seth. His carefree manner often hid a slightly bitter twist and his actions seemed much too strange and unpredictable. He also had this crazy new look in his eyes, like a wild animal on the verge of attack.

I asked him several times if he was all right, but he'd always say "Fine, fine, dandy. Why do you keep asking me?" So I left it at that.

The present circumstances demanded a 'save face' strategy on all three sides. To avoid further confrontation, I pretended to completely trust Max; Max pretended to half-heartedly forgive Seth; Seth pretended to care about nothing at all. It looked as if the three thousand mile adventure would prove nothing more than a vague collection of polite tittle-tattle, half-hearted laughs, and nebulous roadside scenery.

And so it passed, mile after mile, all through the midwestern prairies and Kansas plains, the Rocky Mountains, and the deserts of Arizona. Nobody really cared too much to stop and enjoy the surrounding landscape or detour to an off-road change-of-scene. Seth acted indifferent; Max turned too impatient;

and I, in dismay, tucked my heart safely under my sleeve. For the time being, I accepted the quieter punishment of not taking sides.

The final blow to the trip came when I gave Seth my camera. He immediately became obsessed with it—and rarely surfaced from behind the focuslens. Pictures clicked and flashed away as we drove. Restricted by Max's two-week deadline, Seth didn't even bother asking if we could stop. Too late for regrets: the journey had to fit Max's tight eight-day schedule.

By the time we reached Flagstaff, only half a day could be spared for the entire Grand Canyon. At that point I realized just how terribly naive I'd been, telling Seth 'it would make no difference to our plans.' (Scrap naivety; it was a downright lie.)

If there was any place in the entire United States befitting dramatic action, it was the Grand Canyon. The Great American Wilderness. Finally I couldn't stand it any longer. I *had* to do something.

"Max, we have to spend more than a half day here," I insisted.

"But that means one less day in California," Max replied, frowning.

We were standing together on the viewpoint platform. As usual, Seth had stationed himself a good twenty yards away, snapping photos from all sorts of different positions and angles.

"I don't care! Do you? I mean, look at this! The Grand Canyon—doesn't it take your breath away?" I gazed at the fantastic expanse of rock formations cutting a gargantuan cleft in the desert plains. I was desperate—imagining the colors at sunset.

"It's amazing, I agree. Of course it would be a shame not to stay longer...."

"Please, Max. We have to stay the night."

"All right then—if the Lodge has a room left."

The minute Max disappeared inside the Lodge to enquire about a room, I rushed over to Seth. When he put his camera down, I couldn't resist. I threw my arms around him.

"Seth, isn't this fabulous?" I whispered, suddenly realizing how badly I had wanted to touch him.

Seth held me tight, until a deep shudder seemed to run up and down his body. Frightened by my own response to what we might have shared again (even so briefly), I quickly pulled away.

"I wish we could stay here longer," muttered Seth, staring at me as if it might be possible. His flashing eyes shot straight into mine, saying *I wish you'd shoot me, or put me out my misery...*

"Don't worry—I won't allow you to be cheated out of *this*," I said, almost in a whisper. "I've already told Max we've got to stay till tomorrow. Right now he's trying to get us a room for the night at the Lodge."

Max reappeared: the two of us waited anxiously to hear the news.

"No rooms left."

I groaned. But looking at Seth, I knew exactly what to do. I had promised....

"So what? Good! We'll just have to camp!" I exclaimed. "Come on," I entreated. "Let's make the best of it and take a long hike, okay?"

Max shook his head. "I'm no so keen on camping—or strenuous walking."

I stood firm. "Seth?"

"We've got the kit, haven't we? Let's camp."

"Two against one," I stated. "The vote is to camp. And you don't have to go on a hike, Max, you can stay here and wait."

Before Max could say another word, I grabbed Seth's arm and pulled him toward the nearest trail marker. We disappeared out of sight, racing down the winding trail—laughing like hyenas.

Laughing all the way down the ravine, we were holding hands; fingers entwined as the tears rolled down our cheeks. Like two wild animals, we dashed deep into the bowels of the Grand Canyon for safety. A place to unwind, vast and magical: truly an ancient land. We managed to cover several breath-taking miles, gawking blissfully at the views. Three stolen hours.

"This comes close," I said.

"To what?"

"A feeling I had, standing next to a church. With a view not quite as grand, but…"

"Pretty damn good."

"Yes, wonderful. And it seems to make a difference, your being with me to see it."

I gazed at the magnificent canyon, the deep layers of rock curving and twisting in shapes and colors too complex and mysterious to comprehend.

"So simple and eternal," Seth whispered.

"Not like the rest of the world."

"Where nothing endures," he was quick to add, throwing me that look.

"But I thought you meant, well…some things do."

"Maybe I was wrong," he replied.

When we appeared back at the Lodge, as I predicted, Max had been spending his time in the bar—getting drunk. He didn't ask why we'd taken so long;

he obviously sensed it was time to loosen the reins. He sobered up soon enough, however, when we arrived at the camp. And unpacked the tent in the woods.

"Have you ever put this thing up?" he asked me.

"My dad usually—"

"Twelve poles, thirty-five holes, three different brackets and no directions." Max's cold displeasure at having to erect a tent began to get on my nerves.

"Forget the tent then," I declared, refusing to let him dampen my high spirits. "Let's sleep out in the open air. Look at all the millions of stars up there—I could stare at them all night."

"Yep, that's why I'm going to," Seth said, rolling out his sleeping bag next to the campfire. "Bloody hell, I've never seen so many blinking galaxies, except once on a bike trip to Scotland."

"Lauren and I are sleeping in a tent," Max repeated, thrusting the four-man tent poles up at an even faster pace. He obviously had his own plan, for after luring me inside the newly erected shelter, he began to undress. Then he undressed me. With the woeful sound of Seth's guitar playing a Scottish ballad in the background, mingled with the crackling fire—Max and I made love. Quietly.

Max was satisfied. I couldn't feel anything except guilt.

Later, I could hear Seth zip up his sleeping bag. The fire must have gone out; only the hoot of an owl and a chorus of crickets disturbed the peaceful quiet of the woods.

I'd been thinking of Seth (and hating him) the whole time I'd been making love with Max. Perhaps Max made love more like a skilled craftsman than any slave of passion. But who knows, sex with Seth might end up like that—if we tried it more than twice. That's what I was wondering. Would gazing at a multitude of stars twinkling in the heavens above seem less wonderful if one saw them every night?

I was becoming hopelessly depressed stuck in that tent. But didn't love have the same pitfalls? When my parents bought a house in San Diego with a swimming pool, it seemed like a dream come true. My brothers and I swore we'd use it every single day. After a few months the novelty wore off and the pool was abandoned. In the real world, what joy ever really endures?

True, Max wasn't much of an outdoorsman, but would my own passion turn stale if I indulged in hiking more often? Lying in the darkness next to Max, I fought back the tears. I just couldn't let that restless figure—lying under the stars outside—turn me into a scarecrow.

Our last stop: Las Vegas. We arrived late in the afternoon and booked into a casino hotel. Eyes gawking, lights blinking, chips chinking, pulses rising, we were ready. After the strain of the Grand Canyon we needed some kind—any kind—of easy thrill.

Max headed straight for the Blackjack table. He sat down and stayed there. He lost consistently.

"I'll wait it out," he stammered. "Don't feel obliged to stay here and watch."

Bored, I sauntered off with Seth. We decided to try a team-effort at the slot machines.

"I've got an idea," Seth said. "I'll pull the handles, holding your hand at the same time for luck."

I didn't mind that idea. With my heart pounding, Seth squeezed my hand and kept his eyes on me, ignoring the whizzing blur of fruit until the machine either clanged to a stop or clinked out a rushing stream of coins.

As the bell clinks...

With unbelievable results, the prize money dropped at out feet. With more clinking than clanging, and giggling like children stuffing our pockets with sweets, we could hardly carry away our mutual winnings.

"The Gods are with us!" Seth proclaimed to the gawking bystanders.

Max was not impressed. After we'd shown him our winnings, he waved us off, refusing to abandon the Blackjack table until he'd recouped his losses. I could say nothing to dissuade him: Seth and I would have to celebrate on our own.

"You're free," announced Seth, with a rather bewitching smile. "Max has set you free. So, matey, hang 'em high 'n follow me!"

With Seth taking the lead, we walked hand-in-hand through the neon-lit streets, gleefully sampling more casinos, more slot machines, and just enough booze to drown any sense of guilt.

Las Vegas itself was a fluke, an impossible win: haven for all sinners, gamblers, pimps and whores. Seth loved roaming the streets blessed by the golden hand of Midas and the magic enchantment of all-night hours. The possibilities seemed endless...until suddenly it was four in the morning.

We stumbled back to the hotel and managed to find the elevator—even the right floor—but we couldn't remember the room number. Luckily I found the extra key in my pocket. Seth opened the door.

Max was wide awake.

"Oh," I mumbled.

Sitting on one of the beds with a glass of scotch in his hand, Max kept watching whatever he'd been watching on satellite TV.

To save money, we'd agreed to share a single room—which didn't seem like a very good idea, now.

Nobody bothered to speak. Seth was so drunk he flopped on the second bed and instantly fell asleep with his clothes on. I rushed straight for the toilet. Suddenly I realized Max was following me; he shut the bathroom door behind us.

"I want you," he insisted, slamming the toilet seat down.

"But Seth, he'll hear us—"

"He's passed out. Besides, he must know we do it. Who cares if he hears us?"

So Max claimed me again. Not cool this time, but hot. *Intense.* High as a kite, I suddenly found myself devouring those lips; that fire, that lust, for touch. I had it so easily with Max. His own desire, pushing impatiently between my legs, was perfectly clear. He wanted me. I might have imagined someone or something else. But I came, in a wave of pulsating ripples rushing up and down my spine. Heart pounding. Standing up...

Against the bathroom wall.

❦   ❦   ❦

Pushing on, in waves of heat and dust, we passed through Death Valley and headed toward the San Fernando hills. Soon we'd hit the smog-lined valley and outer fringes of Los Angeles.

After Vegas I could really feel it: my love for Seth burned relentlessly; scorching and seething like the desert. Miles and miles of it. Yet still no sign, no promise of relief from the dry, parched question mark.

In sure-fire contrast, Max openly declared his love. And I couldn't have both. I had to choose, and Max must have known, despite my efforts to hide it. He seemed even more determined than ever to keep me from slipping away.

Though he needn't have worried. After Las Vegas, Seth's rekindled spark snuffed itself out. His mood had changed; his attention focused elsewhere. Out came the wild-eyed animal again, with that blasted camera.

A few more rolls of film and we'd reached the end of the road.

"California, here we come, right back where we started from," sang Max. "Hey Seth, would you like me to tune in to some country western on the radio?"

"Why?"

"You've probably never heard anything like it in England. And as soon as we get closer to Los Angeles, I'm switching to a tape of the Beach Boys."

We'd arranged to stay with my younger brothers, who shared an apartment in Santa Monica. My brothers were still in college, so as far as Max was concerned, they might as well have been beach bums. Being long-distance brothers, they were thrilled to see me, and much to my relief welcomed Max and Seth with genuine enthusiasm. But it was Seth who really won them over. They liked him so much they promised to whisk him off to every surf spot in town.

With a lets-go-out-and-show-our-British-cousin attitude, my brothers lined up a busy schedule of surfing, drinking, skiing, skateboarding, drugging, volleyballing and partying.

Meanwhile, Max arranged his own more sophisticated pursuits (i.e. L.A. Symphony, Rodeo Drive, Universal Studios) and I hardly saw anything of Seth for the next five days.

The end of the journey changed everything. I was hardly aware of the significance of those five hectic days—caught in this whirlwind of sightseeing, uncertainties and conflicting desires. I felt utterly lost in California. With Seth out gallivanting with my brothers, our time together was running out. It had to end, so how could I judge, or choose? I didn't know what to do: instead I waited for something to happen.

And it happened. In fact, Max had apparently worked it out, prior to the day of his departure. I was sure he had, looking at his face that day. We were eating lunch, sitting outside in the sun. He didn't seem the least upset, with his dirty clothes in the dryer and his bags already half packed.

"Lauren?"

"What?"

"Here's a little farewell gift," he said. "From me."

Swallowing the last bite of ham sandwich, he handed me a plane ticket—with my name on it—to fly back to Rhode Island with him.

"You don't *have* to take it," he said. But his eyes begged me to, full of love and hope.

"I know."

"What's keeping you here? Come back and live with me. I'll take care of you..."

Max always knew just what to do. Wasn't he forcing me to choose, instantly?

I hesitated. Of course I didn't want to cut short my time with Seth—or did I? What could possibly happen if I stayed? We might have a few weeks of frenzied happiness before facing another airport scene. I envisioned the worst: watching the crazy lightning bolt disappear again, back to England.

I'll take care of you: Max. I need my freedom: Seth.

"What's keeping you here?" Max repeated his question, knowing he'd hit the crucial point.

"Probably nothing," I said.

Having decided the answer to *that* question, I accepted his offer.

It wasn't easy, but the next morning I managed to corner Seth alone in the kitchen. I told him, as briefly as possible, what had happened last night.

Seth listened, remarkably stone-faced.

"You're leaving tomorrow, right?"

"Yes."

"Then would it be too much to ask if you'd spend the day with me?"

"Oh yes, I mean no, I'd really like that."

"But not Max. Just you." For a second, Seth's eyes had the same look as when he'd found out about the hash.

"Of course. Max is in the shower. I'll tell him when he gets out."

"Good."

"I wish we'd spent more time together the past few days, but you've been busy with my brothers and all…"

"What else is there for me to do?" (Stone-faced again)

Damn it, Seth, I was thinking. You have no right blaming *me alone* for that.

I nevertheless went on: "I hope you understand that really, for me, I have to give Max a chance. It seems like now that I'm here, Southern Cal isn't really where I want to live."

"But you don't have to leave so soon."

"I know…but I've run out of money, so either I start job-hunting here, or go back to Newport—now—with Max."

"It's not going to be the same, without you," Seth said, much too quickly, but keeping his voice steady and matter-of-fact.

"Let's do something special together today…" I broke off, unable to finish.

But Seth was already prepared. "I've thought about that," he said. "I'll be back in two hours to get you, all right?"

"Yes! Why two hours?"

"You'll see."

Two hours later, as promised, Seth returned. He immediately commanded: "Right, follow me outside."

As soon as I opened the front door, I gasped in surprise. Standing gloriously in expectation on the front walk, a specter of gleaming chrome and black metal stood before me, poised and ready for action. The frame was bright red; the tank emblazoned with the word Harley. Harley Davidson.

"Where'd you get it?" I exclaimed.

"It's rented," said Seth, with a cunning grin. "Yep, from what was left of the Vegas money."

He pointed to a pair of helmets positioned together in the grass next to the bike. Then, leisurely moving to the machine, he flicked the ignition on. The wildcat trilled and quivered in anticipation for the kill.

"So, would you like to go for a ride?"

I hammered his arm, shouting, "Damn it, you know I would!"

And then we jumped on the growling cheetah and headed for the hills.

Seth handled the bike brilliantly; I fought against a constant surge of tears, keeping my visor down during our brief stops so Seth wouldn't see.

Swerving and winding the severe corners of the Malibu canyon hills, we climbed and dived at breath-taking speed, Seth opening up to what seemed full throttle on the straight sections. He'd never driven so fast with me before, but I wasn't afraid—the ride seemed to carry us beyond the bounds of safety.

Were we flying back in time? Speeding like crazy past the spires, past Abnalls Lane, and on to Willowby Farm? Knowing this was our one last chance to be together? While the prospect of fleeing behind Seth—completely wild, senseless and out of control—seemed at that moment such a good way to go: to put an end to it all. *To feel the eternal indifference of my very own soul...*

Yet it was not to be. As we approached slower cars ahead, Seth either pulled over or diverted to another road. He wasn't risking any dangerous overtakes; his high-speed runs halted abruptly at hairpin turns. At times I found myself lurching forward against his immobile, supportive frame.

If this wasn't suicide, it was a ride to end all rides: Seth instinctively mastering that fine line between a daring equilibrium in precipitous flight and a crazy flirtation with danger. Neither he nor I, his pillion, were meant to notice the scenery. We seemed to lunge forward, further and further, into another dimension—floating magically above the ground.

Finally, all Seth's nerve and energy gave out. He stopped the bike—at a wayside picnic area deep in the canyons, surrounded by oak and sycamore trees.

I got off, removing my helmet and quickly wiping away the tears which had been streaming down my cheeks. Seth secured the bike. He threw aside his helmet as if it were possessed; stumbled over to the nearest picnic table; and then, without a word, flung himself on top of it.

I humbly followed. Stood there. On the table Seth's torso and limbs remained motionless, but his heavy breathing continued. He looked like a cadaver laid out on a funeral slab, hyper-ventilating. Straddling the bench next to him, I sat down knowing I'd have to speak first. Whatever I said would be incredibly inadequate.

"Man, Seth—that was something."

"Good, wasn't it?"

We were completely alone. A slight breeze ruffled the leaves of the trees; blackbirds cawed in the distance and Seth's body (heated and trembling—lying blatantly inches away) shifted suddenly.

Leaning on his elbow and gazing pensively at me, he said, "Something happened, I had to let loose. I just assumed you understood. Scared you, though, eh?"

"Not really. I'm never scared riding with you."

"You know—of course it happens on the bike—but just now it felt so perfect and right, like having you there at the dairy farm. Or taking you round Las Vegas, when the gods were with us. Like we couldn't lose: I've never ridden so fast, with so much confidence…"

"I think I know what you mean. And I felt it too—"

I wistfully lowered my head against Seth's heaving chest, but he didn't seem to want to touch me in return.

But after a few awkward minutes he said, "Lauren, if we continue like this my heartbeat won't ever slow down, it will explode…"

Reluctantly raising my head—I caught Seth trying to contain a disobedient rim of moisture swelling in the corners of his eyes.

Enough. I tossed my doubts to the wind; I threw my arms around him. With my lips locked tightly over his, I could feel his hands seize my hair, encircle my neck. Pressed against him, the danger of his heartbeat exploding felt so possible I half-sobbed with fear.

Still clutching my head, Seth held firm, smothering my sob with the force of his tongue; slipping his arms down my back, in a desperate and deadly kiss.

The same kiss which had been waiting to happen ever since that first day at the airport.

❦   ❦   ❦

"I just want you to be happy," Seth said, the next morning. Before I left.

"I know," I answered.

CHAPTER 13

The Silence

I flew back to Newport with Max. But of course I couldn't get that ride on the Harley out of my mind. Seth had seen to that. Though what was the point in hanging on? Max had seen to that. He offered a permanent home, a definite 'I want you with me' answer. Scarecrows don't last very long in the wind—not without sturdy clothes and some decent shelter.

Max had won. And now that Seth was well out my reach, my relationship with his rival—in one sense—seemed to be getting somewhere. Like two peas in a pod, Max and I did all the things couples living together do, enjoying all the benefits of a joint income. I'd managed to get employment again with Shoreline Sales—but this time as Sales bookkeeper.

The weeks passed quickly, heading toward autumn. Yet no word from Seth. I had given my brothers Max's phone and address, but I didn't know for sure if Seth was still there. Maybe he'd left Santa Monica…heading for Colorado, or Utah…who knows? I was petrified of finding out. It seemed safer not to know.

October went by, the leaves beginning to fall like a strip tease in slow motion. I couldn't fake it any longer. The trees were growing bare; the scarecrow was cracking up.

But who can say why it was on *that* particular day, I knew the time had come to face the truth? Awareness suddenly chooses a moment: hanging in balanced suspension, until something nameless bends the supporting stick too far—and bam—the scarecrow falls.

For three months we never fought, we never disagreed, we never complained. Then came autumn—splinters everywhere. The last rags of conscience blew free, bouncing off Max's Wall. Max's appeal, his mystery, his sexual prowess and intelligence—they all failed to express the true spirit of love.

Difficult to admit at first, but I'd been wrong about Max. There's a big difference, it must be said, between depth of feeling and reserved distance. Hadn't Seth tried to warn me about Max's lack of feeling? Well, I'd refused to listen. And how much did I know, even now, about Max? He never really let me in; he kept his deep, soulful self carefully shrouded under wraps. That self would always stay a mystery.

"Max's Wall," is what I came to call it, and no one, not even I, was allowed to go past it. Max had nothing to share. I finally discovered that for myself. I couldn't understand Seth's vague reservations that day, but now it was obvious. Some men never, ever share their heartblood—instead they prefer to latch on to a woman, using her emotions—her flesh and blood—to clothe their own flimsy disguise.

That kind of love wasn't what I'd had in mind at all. And once I knew for sure, it was time to leave without looking back. I left, thinking Max would probably feel just as relieved. He had his own Law. No knocking, prying, or climbing behind the Wall. I'd given up trying; I doubted either of us wanted to be there when we hit the peak, and passed over to a downhill slide.

I think it was the first week in November when I got up one morning and started to pack. Throwing all my things into boxes and bags, I simply walked out. In a few hours Max would come home from work to discover I'd gone.

I went to live with my old boss and good friend Anne. Luckily Anne, who still worked at Shoreline Sails, had just heard about a job vacancy with a fast-growing yachting company, International Marine. I applied and was hired: proving my ability to learn fast and work hard, I set my sights on being promoted to charter-broker.

My new job was the lifeboat on a sinking ship. Knowing I would be financially secure and optimistic about my prospects with International Marine, I was able to get over Max and begin again. I could concentrate on the exciting possibilities that lay ahead.

And I was totally free at last to think about Seth, which I often did. But had he forgiven me for all that had happened? Ashamed of my past actions, I simply waited, hoping Seth himself might—after a while—initiate some form of correspondence. But he never wrote or phoned. He might have left California altogether, but that was pure speculation. At any rate, his visa would have expired on October twenty-fifth. Seth had once joked it really didn't matter when it expired—he was already in trouble over the hash. So maybe he was still staying with my brothers…

Go out and get what you really want for yourself, a voice whispered softly in my ear.

What I really wanted was a life with Seth. No one else. It was that simple, that stupid and crazy.

On November twenty-fourth I risked it. I took a deep breath and dialed my brother's number.

"Hi David? It's Lauren."

"Hello! How are things?"

"Fine. Well, Max and I aren't together any more…"

"No? Wow, that's a surprise!"

"Anyway, I called to find out if Seth is still there—is he?"

"No, Lauren, as a matter of fact he left two weeks ago."

"Two weeks ago?"

"Yeah—what a bummer—I was heartbroken."

"Why sound so sarcastic? I thought you liked him!"

"I did, but what can I say? He wore me out. The whole scene turned a bit weird, after you left. And then, to top it off, I was stupid enough to let him use my car. I never let anyone use my car—but Seth—I figured okay and the next thing I know he's calling me from the police station. 'Speeding?' I asked him. 'No,' he said. 'They called it an illegal U-turn.' So I told him, 'That's nonsense—they can't put you in the slammer for a U-turn!' Then he said 'I think they can—anything's possible in the USA.' I would have gone straight there, except Seth admitted he wasn't at the Police Station. He told me the police would contact me when I could fetch my car and not to worry—he'd phone me again when it was all sorted out."

"Go on," I insisted, my voice sounding hollow.

"I guess the shit hit the fan. What kind of drugs did the dude smuggle in, anyway? He calls me back all right, this time from L.A.X. Airport. He wouldn't explain why, just that he was being deported straight back to England! It must have been dope, I figure."

"Oh no! But weren't they going to prosecute him here first?"

"No way. He said he'd be sent home in disgrace, that's all."

"Thank God."

"I was thanking god too. We all gave one big sigh of relief when he left…I was convinced by then that he'd be going back in a coffin."

"Come on, David—"

"No, really. Lauren, you won't believe what went on after you left."

"Like what? Go on, tell me—what difference does it make?" I said. "It's all history now."

"Well—you know what Seth's like—he wanted to try out everything. But after you left, he went sort of crazy about it. Just about topped himself a few times!"

"Really?"

"One time we all went to our usual skateboarding place—Demolition Hill we call it—and Seth insisted on giving it a try. This was a hairy steep hill going straight down for three miles. I wouldn't let him use my board, but Seth grabbed somebody else's board and off he went, not knowing how to slow or stop—I think he tried to jump off before the board took him over the edge of the cliff—"

"No..."

"If he'd gone over, that would have been the end of him, but luckily he landed on the hard shoulder and only lost a good bit of his chin..."

"Was it bad?"

"There was blood everywhere! We had to rush him to the hospital for stitches. He's got an ugly scar where his beard used to be..."

"Jesus..."

"And when we found him lying there, holding his chin together with his hands, he laughed and said it was just his luck choosing a board with wobbly wheels!"

"Sounds just like Seth."

"But wait till you hear the rest!"

"There's more?"

"We went to a party one night and Seth got really drunk. So drunk he decided to climb a nearby water tower. I don't know how he made it all the way to the top, but he did. He sat up there like a guy out of his mind on LSD, shouting and singing near the edge. I yelled up at him to stop, or he'd fall off—but he didn't care, he said. Completely off-the-wall crazy. He acted like that sometimes. Once when we took him to the Quarry for a swim, he disappeared down some underwater caves. He didn't find an opening at first, and came out with his lungs full of water...sputtering and coughing and scaring us to death, for what he called a little mistake, mis-calculation..."

"That's not like Seth, to be so careless," I gasped.

"In the end, I refused to let him use my extra surf-board any more…after it bashed into his neck after a flip-out. That guy is a walking disaster. I don't know what got into him, but I'm glad it's all over and he's back home."

"He stayed with you until the cops caught up with him?"

"He hung out with us the whole while he was here," David said. "He did thank us for putting him up for so long—guess it was pretty mind-blowing for him too."

Then David changed the subject, moving on to other family matters. But I couldn't concentrate on anything else. I kept wondering why Seth had acted the way he did. If it wasn't a desire to self-destruct, was it some kind of sick revenge?

I shuddered. On my part, it seemed too late to *ever* make amends.

❀　　　　　❀　　　　　❀

The silence grew into months. I wanted desperately to write to Seth but composing that first letter became a nightmare. Several attempts were aborted as too disgusting and pitiful. No matter what tone I tried—apologetic, sarcastic, prophetic, pathetic, or emphatic—every possible approach sounded either absurd or inadequate. My crippling sense of guilt and remorse seemed insurmountable.

The months grew into three years.

Three years.

Though one little thread still remained, thanks to Elizabeth. Every Christmas Elizabeth would send me a card with some news of the family. A sentence or two about Seth would be devoured and cherished until the following year: Seth lived, Seth studied to become a photographer, Seth traveled over Europe, Seth had a girlfriend.

But Seth himself never wrote. And I accepted my banishment as a retaliation…

I justly deserved.

The Build-up

Business at International Marine was booming. Riding high on their tide of success, I'd established a reputation as a first-rate charter broker. My position put me well within the affluent yachting sector of Newport, acting as a mediator, booking boats for all kinds of clients. Having inherited my dad's sailor instincts, I guess I was naturally suited for the job.

Luxurious power-yachts and sleek classic sailing vessels became my specialty. As the contacts and commissions grew higher, I became an exclusive agent for corporate and private moguls; matching personal taste and a generous budget to whatever might be their cruising heart's desire, from the Caribbean all the way up the eastern Coast to Maine, and across the Atlantic to the Mediterranean.

For someone who began a career in Newport as a dishwasher, I'd miraculously moved up to one of the most enviable positions in town. My job became my main passion. Captains and crew in the charter business all over the world would report to me when calling port in Newport. It was promising and exciting work—and best of all, it incorporated my affinity for the sea.

Even my dad was proud. He could hardly complain. He had Sally to keep him busy and his daughter was doing her bit, too—towing the line.

So as it happened, I never did leave Newport. Most of the men I dated were connected to boats, though I wasn't dating that much. Nor was I looking very hard for a future husband. I had this feeling I'd never marry a roving sailor. No, I secretly yearned for a lover of rocks and roads, a man of two wheels. Someone who'd take me through farms and rivers and fields.

A landlubber.

❦   ❦   ❦

In the spring of 1985 I wrote Chester and Elizabeth to tell them Harriet had died. The year before I'd stopped visiting her at the old folks home. There didn't seem much point. She was much worse off than Henry by then. She never recognized me. Though I suppose I'd changed a bit myself, five years on. But I had my work. And there wasn't much time to mourn or reminisce. About anything.

But when it came to music, or more precisely the sound of a live guitar, I was still making an effort to show up at 'Bluebird Club' on a Saturday night. I often went alone. There was never trouble or hassle at the Bluebird and the music was always good.

So I was sitting there, as usual, one summer night: tapping my foot and drinking a bottled beer—listening to a local rock band let loose on a tiny stage just opposite the bar—when I felt something.

It felt like a hand. A light fingering on my bare back. And not moving or seeming to notice, I savored that touch: physical sensation, pure and simple.

It turned out the hand belonged to a stranger, sitting at the next table. Apparently this stranger assumed it was all right to put his arm behind my chair and then carelessly let it slide off its perch—into the realm of my skin.

To my surprise, I didn't mind the arrogance of such a gesture, which, after all, might be expected—considering I was alone. A lone woman sitting in a Club, ordering her own drinks from the bar.

The feeling of a hand, a male hand, on my female skin—I suddenly realized—was a shocking, painful remembrance of months without it. *Without touch.*

The hand, as if sensing my thoughts, sympathetically brushed my shoulder.

"I'll buy you drink," said the man who owned it, leaning closer.

For some reason that night I didn't care who he was, or whether or not I might want another drink. I could only feel that other realm, where his hand lightly fingered my bare back.

"What's your name?"

"Lauren."

"Mine's Paul. Paul Thaos."

He had bright blue eyes. His hair was jet black; his nose long and thin. The top buttons on his smooth black shirt were undone, exposing the dark hairs on his chest. His physique, lean and rugged, permitted tight, sexy jeans.

I noticed the tight jeans and how they made him swagger like a cowboy when he got up and strode to the bar. While his touch lingered on, I couldn't stop this sudden yearning—*for more.*

I could have him, I was thinking. This man who—just now—had so boldly placed his hand on my body. He returned with my drink, stretching his leg over further, inch-by-inch, until it rested against mine.

I thought: why stop now? For at that moment what I really, really wanted was to feel close, to fall under the soothing spell of seductive flesh—give in to the weakness. It no longer mattered whom with.

But Paul Thaos was patient. Even though he must have known, he didn't push. Instead he leaned away and listened to the band: the blaring boom-boom rhythm of wailing guitars and drums, the guttural lyrics thrust into microphones dripping with sweat and spit.

The band: faces contorted and ecstatic, lips pursed, hair flying, chests heaving—asking everyone to join in. Let's rock and roll.

"Have you ever been to the Mythos for dinner?" he asked, when the band took a break.

"The Greek place? No."

"Well, I'm the owner. I like to know what people think—if they like the food, the service, the menu. So try it out some time, and tell me what you think. Okay?"

"All right."

He smiled. "You're so polite. And generous. I don't usually touch strange women—without permission—but with you it just seemed to happen quite naturally."

"Yes."

"But in a way, I do know you, Lauren. I've chartered one of your boats. The *Isabelle*, last week. Remember?"

Then he excused himself, and disappeared toward the men's room. The band re-assembled for the second half, and I still didn't remember. Though I was glad Paul Thaos had. So he didn't usually touch strange women, I was thinking. Now, had I ever touched a strange man?

Yes, once, at Monty's Disco, in fact. Only last week. Anne and Sandra were there too, at Monty's 'girls only' male stripper show. Well, what the heck? We'd all gone for a bit of fun. A show of hunks, tight asses, flexing muscles, and bulging G-strings: Johnny the DJ, Magic the Greek, Lenny the Lifeguard, and the Italian Stallion.

I screamed with all the rest, I had to admit. And oh boy, how we all screamed at the Stallion: tall and sleek, smooth as silk, with flawless muscles, dark flashing eyes and black sculptured hair. All us girls gave him our best whistles, hooting and waving dollar bills in the air; earrings bobbing, breasts bouncing, inner thighs aching.

Paul, with his jet-black hair, made me think of the Stallion again: how I'd waited until the grand finale to do it. I had thought 'but only if he struts by and stops right next to me,' and he kept getting closer, the women all screeching in a high pitched frenzy now, hysterical at their own bold depravity. Yes women: lusting after mere flesh, treating men like animals, even pinching their butts as they passed by.

I vowed I'd do it. But only if he stopped right next to me. Surely I couldn't expect the stripper to know that, but it seemed like the Stallion did. Me, standing shyly silent and half crushed by the surging crowd; and he, boldly weaving, whirling, plowing a path through the bodies—coming straight at me! The crumpled dollar bill, clenched tight in my hand, was well out of sight.

But he knew, or guessed, and *now, now*, he seemed to say to me with his eyes, stopping and standing directly in front, his soft olive skin taunt and glistening with oil…pelvis forward…. poised…

Moving my hand across his navel, I slipped my fingers inside his G-string. The Stallion smiled.

"How I love you babe," he whispered. And winked.

Which made me wonder if he was really some kind of demon, or ghost. Bringing a curse from Seth.

"Thank you, thank you. We appreciate your support and we'll be back again next month!"

The band had finished. So soon? I realized I hadn't been paying much attention. Lost in thought, and dreaming of Stallions, I closed my eyes for the encore.

With the music pounding and the deep bass rhythm sounding like a distant chant *'just a dream, just a dream,'* inside my head, I turned to look at Paul.

His arm still rested on the back of my chair.

"Thanks for the drink."

"Where's your boyfriend?" he asked, as the lights came on and people moved about clearing tables.

"Where's your girlfriend?" I replied.

He chuckled. "Maybe she's out with your boyfriend, having a good time."

"Could be." I smiled. "Time to leave. Thanks for the drink."

"Yes. But I'll see you soon, at the restaurant. Promise?"

"I promise."

He shook my hand and I found it hard to let go.

🍁   🍁   🍁

That Christmas, I added a P.S. on my card to Elizabeth and Chester. Maybe it sounded rather sudden, I wrote, but I just got married.

My new name, I said, was Thaos...

Mrs. Paul.

CHAPTER 15

The Awakening

"Lauren, have you opened your mail?"

"Will in a minute. Here's a few contracts to type up. I've written some notes on the additional arrangements. Shall we go over them, Sandra, or can you read my scribble?"

My assistant smiled. "I think I can decipher it." She turned on the VHF before sitting down to tap away on the keyboard. The soft drone of the latest marine weather forecast filled the room.

I opened the first letter, from the International Boat Show Committee. Once I'd read it I couldn't help blurting out the news.

"In London!"

"What?" Sandra stopped typing.

"Oh, sorry. I'm just a bit shocked by the announcement. The Boat Show isn't going to be in New York this year. It's going to be in London."

"London? But it's always in New York."

"Not any longer, it seems. The committee has decided to hold it over in Europe, every other year. It's only fair. And more convenient for the Med fleet. Turkey too."

I held the letter in my hands, pensive and silent. Sandra shrugged and went back to her typing.

Of course the possibility had never occurred to me before. Now I would just have to deal with it. I'd have to convince Paul why it was necessary; why I really must go. Business was business…But why should Paul mind if I went to London? I just had a funny feeling. He would. I was his wife now—I knew his every mood.

My stallion, with his bright blue eyes and jet-black hair, was quick to temper and prone to fight. A hot-blooded sire, Paul Thaos, of Greek descent: but how refreshingly different from the ice-stoniness of Max! No, I didn't mind Paul's emotion-charged trepidations—I was fascinated. Here was a man who let it all hang out. A boiling cauldron of open feelings!

Yet Paul could be calm and quiet, too. His sense of humor was subtle, dry and sarcastic. He was patient with his customers and friends. And he treated women with great respect.

Growing up in the tough, aggressive lower-class world of Boston, Paul was the youngest of six children. He'd managed to fight his way through the uneducated, ethnically biased barriers (starting out as a bus-boy) to make himself just as good—or even better—as the top Italian chefs. The end result produced the *Mythos* legend. Mr. Thaos, an emblematic figure sitting comfortably in the middle of aristocratic Newport; catered to every aspiring trend-following snob in town. If Paul's 'world' was different to mine, initially it wasn't a problem since Paul loved everything about me—including my easy-going, bourgeois upbringing.

Our relationship seemed to delicately bridge the gap, a healthy counterbalance of opposing worlds. (Or so I thought.) So why did I have this feeling of dread? After all, what was the problem? It was perfectly clear Paul adored me. His overwhelming, vehement devotion was part of his charm.

"If I were you, I'd be excited," Sandra said. "You've been to New York loads of times. London will be so much more interesting."

"I know, but Paul won't be happy about my going," I answered. "He gets worried when I travel alone. New York is just around the corner. London is three thousand miles away."

In the beginning I'd felt a bit dubious about his passionate temper, but having lived with him for four months—without any major complaints—I naturally accepted his marriage proposal. But after the legal ceremony, Paul started to change. It was as if he'd been given permission to start treating me as personal property, and a commodity such as a wife must always obey. Not only that, but all previous emphatic encouragement toward my job and outside interests disappeared. In its place, I encountered a growing atmosphere of possessive suspicion.

"Shall I ring the airlines for fares and reservations?" asked Sandra.

"No, not yet. Let me talk to Paul first," I replied.

It was as if our legal commitment exempted him from any further pretexts, on all fronts. Paul's jealousy could sometimes turn to brutal disrespect, aimed mainly at my job and associates, as well as anything else that threatened Paul's world and thus Paul's control. It was easier to simply avoid his insulting accusations and outbursts, which I did by carefully poising myself between his unrelenting demands and my own dwindling personal needs.

A far cry from what I'd encountered in the beginning.

Which is why now, sitting at my desk, I grew pensive and quiet for the rest of the day. I was astonished by the news, intrigued by London, and rather uneasy about the whole situation.

I picked up the Committee's newsletter and read it over several times. Attached to the Boat Show brochure was a list of hotels, but I didn't dare compare any prices until I was certain Paul would approve.

Everything was wonderful as long as I behaved as he wanted me to. At Paul's insistence I'd stopped working late and spending evenings with the charter crowd. If I risked it and went for a drink after work, I'd creep home petrified. For if Paul phoned from the restaurant and discovered I wasn't home, he'd rush back and wait. Then, hiding behind the front door—he'd grab me as I'd come in and fling me right across the room. Followed by embittered shouts of 'You cunt, you sneaking stinking whore!' the furniture and other handy objects would be smashed on the floor.

The situation improved once I'd learned to anticipate—and avoid altogether—Paul's depressive rages and paranoia. Luckily my career had turned me into the perfect mediator. I became the dedicated servant of two separate entities: the dutiful wife enslaved to her husband's viewpoint, and the professional compromised by her own clever devices.

After the wedding, we'd moved to a comfortable, newly renovated Victorian home on the Narragansett Bay. Paul wanted to start a family; I promised to leave International Yachting as soon as I got pregnant. So there hadn't been a temper tantrum for several months running.

But now there might be trouble—all because the International Charter Show switched from New York to London. Jesus, I thought to myself, of all places, it had to be London. Seven years on and I still couldn't bear the thought of going—not without trying to make contact with Seth again first.

Fate, England and Seth...suddenly that was all I needed. And work. Work had always been my main excuse.

It took the entire afternoon to compose the letter. Wrestling over every word, I finally compacted a quagmire of fact and emotion into two paragraphs. It felt as if I'd just summed up a chain of events which had happened only yesterday. As such, I faced my inner self—addressed to Seth—and mailed it off as proof: a plaintive voice resounding through the vacuous, cobwebbed corridors of a prison long forsaken—but not quite forgotten.

With no address I simply posted it to Lichfield. Care of Elizabeth.

∾

Sept 3, 1987

Dear Seth

I can't think of how many times I have thought about writing you, but each time I thought about it, I got bogged down with trying to choose a way to say something that would make it all good again, so I kept putting it off—waiting for a better time. So—waiting for what? Some kind of Benevolent Nod to intervene and obliterate the cursed memory of that summer? I guess. And meanwhile, I wondered why you never wrote me. I hoped maybe for the same reasons—though at the back of my mind I knew that when you were here, you were finally here, I disappointed you in many different ways. But it's almost autumn now, a time having so many cherished memories for me. I came to England in September...so whenever I find myself in the adult-prone rut, or the doldrums of normalcy, I remember that autumn in Lichfield when life was just as it should be: exciting and magical, full of discovery and intensity! There lies the spirit, the beauty of the Midlands, and a friendship which I hope even now is still...alive...

Is it possible you might feel likewise, seven years on? I assume Elizabeth told you I got married. She sends a card every Christmas, never asking why we didn't stay in touch, you and I. It may seem absurd, but I'd still like you to know you were right—Max was no good for me. At the time I thought you felt that way solely because his being around put so many clogs in what we might have done. How could I so blindly disregard the very essence of your mirror—which always proves true for me? I don't know. I found it more convenient then to see things the untrue way. As it happened, Max kept getting letters from some lawyer in Connecticut. He refused to show them to me, or explain.

Soon after we split up I found out he'd quit his job and moved away. He'll always be hard to track down. He'll live with his lies. But what is true—and always will be—is the fact that it means a lot to me, just to know you.

I hope you'll forgive my not having written sooner, and all the past errors of judgment that have hampered our friendship.

As always—Your cousin Lauren.

I added a P.S. to explain I'd be in London soon for a Boat Show, and would phone his parents with the flight details and dates. Then I mentioned I might be able to add a few days to the trip so I could visit them in Lichfield after the Show…

Exactly seven days later, I received Seth's reply.

Dear Cousin,

Here is my letter which you have been waiting so long (too long) to receive. I've been a very bad boy I know, and like you, I always got stuck when I tried to write. There's a million different things I wanted to say and when they're all trying to leap from the end of your pen it becomes impossible to sort any of it out. I don't know why I never wrote something (anything) but then again, maybe I do. It appears that while you waited for your permissive Nod, I stood inert under an invisible Stern Arm which bitterly and consistently placed pressure on my wrist. This happened whenever I managed, spasmodically, to motion pen and paper in your direction.

It's a mystery to me sometimes—when I think of the number of times I have thought about you, and times we have been together, and all of those things that happened. It seems so stupid that I left it, only for Time to bring upon us a big gaping void, which we now must try to fill. You hinted things in your letter which up until now I have shut away inside my mind—emotions so strong that repression was the only way I could hold them at bay. But I hope you'll stop thinking you had disappointed me! Because you didn't! I was annoyed at the fact that I'd buggered up the proceedings in the first place by failing to write, then arriving so unexpectedly, and finally behaving as I did. I had no

right to put my foot in your affairs like that, for whatever reason. So. Now we ARE writing to each other again. I guess we're both saying sorry. Our friendship means a lot to me too. A bit of an understatement, that. Because nothing will ever change the fact that, Lauren—I feel a closeness to you which will never die. I'll always long to see you again some day, to see those sparkling eyes and your smile. In the time that has elapsed I guess some of that boyish arrogance has gone and perhaps a little wisdom is taking its place. Maybe my ego isn't quite the size of the Grand Canyon now!

A long bout of persistence finally got me into freelancing as a TV news cameraman (you probably aren't surprised I found my calling as a photomaniac who travels around the world seeking to capture all the excitement). I paid my dues existing as a bum, basically, for the last four years, but I've finally broken in—actually making a decent living out of it. I could write a whole book. You too? But we'll have to accomplish this gradually. (I keep retrieving your letter for another look. Really, it's too good to be true)

I'll check the dates with my bookings and let you know. Note my home-base address is a flat in London!

With all my deepest Love and Affection,

SETH

I was so overjoyed with the letter it hardly mattered, a week later, when a second letter arrived—Seth sadly announcing he'd be in Africa on assignment during the week of the Charter Boat Show. Still reeling from the first letter, I took the bad news as a minor, slightly irritating setback. After all, I could return to London any time; I didn't need a Boat Show to get there. Besides, it might be easier to see Seth again in person after I had just a little more time to adjust to the idea.

And then Paul: wouldn't he get suspicious over my excitement? How could I honestly admit to Paul that I intended to see another man, especially when the man was Seth—without looking guilty? Yet I wanted nothing more than to re-establish a platonic relationship with my distant cousin, who happened to be male. Paul would never believe me. He'd never understand *that* kind of spiritual friendship...which is why I'd asked Seth to send his letters via International Marine. I knew Paul too well. And it was bad enough resorting to this first deception.

But Seth's letter fuelled my resolve to bend Paul's will in order to have exactly what I really wanted.

"When the Boat Show is over, I'd like to catch a train to Lichfield," I explained to Paul. "My mother's relatives live there, and they'd be heartbroken if I didn't go and see them."

Paul eyed me for a minute, considering. "How far away is Lichfield?"

"A few hours by train. I've been there before, a few years ago. With my grandmother."

Thank god, I was thinking, Paul wasn't kicking up a fuss after all.

"Well, you'd best go see them, then," he muttered. "Family is family, and this will probably be your last Show. Right?"

I looked at him. I nodded. To get his consent I'd agree to anything.

CHAPTER 16

The Reunion

I was still smiling to myself as I stepped off the plane at Heathrow Airport. Confident and gingerly strolling down the aisles, my hair cut short, wearing a business-type suit, high heels, stockings—I'd matured into a clean-cut career-minded Lauren. Quite a change, I was thinking, from the original young vagabond-girl in jeans and sneakers who'd once shuffled so shyly and insipidly along this same route.

What else had changed in the space of seven years?

I had to admit, with some sadness, that Harriet had passed on, and Henry had died last year...but I knew Elizabeth, Chester, Aunt Bea, Lichfield's shops, the Ladies of the Vale, the farms, brick houses, footpaths, thatched-roof villages—would all be just as I'd left them—unchanging and fascinating.

First I'd have to attend the Boat Show, but soon enough I'd be free again, clack-clacking over the rails on the rocking, bumping train; inhaling the medieval breath of hedges, bricks and fields; absorbing the ghosts and subdued British chatter...

With my heeled shoes clicking across the gray polished floor—I passed the lines of airport faces, signs held high by inquiring contacts, waves and shouts of welcome intermixed by hoots of "Taxi, Taxi!" and garbled intercom announcements.

Remembering I'd have to change currency, I suddenly stopped in my tracks. The hand-baggage and briefcase were quickly becoming heavy and cumbersome, bumping against my legs. With some relief I put down my bags and looked for a Bureau de Exchange.

Then a strange thing happened.

I thought I saw a familiar face float past the moving swarm of people. I scanned the crowd to find it again. It looked a bit like—it might have been—Seth?

I decided not. But nevertheless, this very face grinned insanely back at me, as if suffering from a strange bewitching disease. I flushed, feeling feverish—I was sure I must be hallucinating. Yet this impossible green-eyed, slightly freckled, intimidating expression resembled Seth's. Though it couldn't be him: the body behind it was all wrong. This was the physique of a well rounded, solidly built man, his face immaculately shaved, his hair cut extremely short and *bald* on top.

Despite these misgivings, I moved toward him. And as we grew closer, I felt my face turn a burning, burning red.

Seth leaned over to catch me as I fell (half-fainting) into his arms.

"I meant to warn you—there's not much left of my hair," he said, stroking my bundle of curls.

"Oh, oh I don't care about *that*," I sputtered, now nothing more than the sobbing effigy of a charter-broker.

"Well it seems to me it's the only reasonable thing to be crying about," Seth insisted.

My sobs gave way to a muted chuckle. And as soon as I laughed, the blood seemed to ebb back into my body. I opened my eyes. Still clinging to Seth, I looked over his shoulder and noticed the crowds had disappeared. Even so, decorum dictated it was time to end our embrace.

Jesus. How could I let go? Right now, or ever? No, not ever. For Seth's touch triggered a deep feeling of remembrance; a completeness that seemed to wash over me like the first desert rain seeping into the cracks of a drought-stricken riverbed. Life trickled back; a vibrant, soothing current of hope had returned to nourish a barren soul.

The sensation made me think of the banks by the River Blythe, when I stood watching the clouds break after a storm, the grass and fields glistening with moisture and the mist slipping into light: a gracious light, without self, sparked by Love.

Nothing had changed! I slowly withdrew from Seth's embrace, infused with the bittersweet knowledge that what existed between us had never diminished, never changed, never betrayed. Nothing in my life—ever—had felt as wonderful as this.

Did my face tell him so? I couldn't be sure.

Seth turned his eyes away and stepped back, fumbling in his coat pocket until he managed to pull out a flask, which he held out like a flag of truce. The airport closed in again around us. I stared, flabbergasted, at both the flask and the indomitable freckles on Seth's extended arm.

"Have some of this—you need it," he said.

"What is it?" I don't know why I asked, because I'd already taken the flask and gulped down a generous swig.

"Well?" said Seth.

"Ah, it's whiskey…I don't think I've had any of this since…"

"Feel better now?"

"Yes. What an exhausting flight. I can't believe you're here! But how and what—?"

"Simple," Seth answered. "Once I decided it was ridiculous *not* to be here. I gave the African assignment to a colleague and rang my mum to find out the flight details."

Incredulously, I studied every angle of this new Seth. He looked remarkably self-controlled and clean-cut. The skinny Celtic-wolf had shed all his hair and dressed himself in brand-new, spotless jeans; his shirt was collar-less but pressed white cotton, the sleeves neatly rolled up. With no flyaway mop of auburn hair, I could trace every contour of his head; the balding crown smooth and distinguished-looking, enhanced by the transparent-thin haircut on the sides edging neatly around his ears and neck.

My image of Seth—frozen in time—would now have to discard not only the hair, but also the leather jacket, the goatee beard, the heavy black riding boots…

"You look different too," he said suddenly, as if he'd read my thoughts. "Like a proper married working housewife—permed locks, fashionable suit, match-ing stockings and two-inch heels…"

"It was bound to happen."

"Yes. But I'm sad you've cut off all that long beautiful hair," he muttered. "Can you believe I'm losing *mine* at twenty-six? At least you had the choice. Why did you cut yours?"

"I don't know. I guess it's easier to deal with short."

Now that Seth mentioned it, I wondered why I'd cut my hair, really. At that moment it struck me as an embarrassing conformity. Of course Seth must be equally surprised by my change of appearance—and how did it happen? When did I start thinking it was par-for-the-course to gain ten pounds and allow my figure to slump, or shed every one of my past bohemian tendencies? What made me decide to quit smoking pot and drinking whiskey? Or switch to wearing dresses and cutting my hair to fit the current fad? Jesus! Seth was right—I had degenerated into a typical 'working housewife!'

"Do you still play guitar?" I asked, hoping to subvert the present by reviving the past.

"Yes. But not half as much as I used to," Seth answered. "It's a bit like riding my motorcycle. I've hung on to both for purely sentimental reasons, it seems. Both the guitar and the bike sit around unused, taking up room and collecting dust."

Seth paused—his voice beginning to waver. He shook his head, then leaned down to retrieve my bags. "Well, let's get you out of here," he mumbled, quickly changing the subject. "Can I give you a lift to your hotel?"

"Oh yes, thanks."

"I'm sure you have things to do and could use some sleep. What about tomorrow, then? Will you have any free time?"

"I'll be finished at the Show by four o'clock. And after the weekend I'm off to see your parents for three days."

"I can't believe you're here."

"I can't believe it either," I replied, handing over the flask and wishing Seth hadn't been so adept at taking it back.

Our fingers hadn't touched and yet I had no right to expect anything physical beyond that first hug. I was a married woman now.

As we drove to the hotel, I was feeling just as guilty in Seth's car. That one desire wavering over a flask was only the start. In fact, I was enormously relieved he wasn't married, and this sort of selfishness seemed utterly wrong. Why couldn't Seth have someone, like I did? But for obvious reasons I realized I was really glad he didn't.

Seth drove through London wordlessly, the drone of city traffic throwing us both into silence. Our progress was slow moving and often at a standstill, which was fine for now, I was thinking. Taking it slow.

Closing my eyes, I tried to calm my racing pulse and accept the dream-like atmosphere whirling around in the car as a feeling one should expect. Given the circumstances.

Fifteen minutes later, Seth suddenly pulled over to the nearest curb and shut off the ignition.

I opened my eyes. His arms were flung across the steering wheel, shielding his drooping head. I couldn't see his face.

"I'm sorry," he muttered, "but I have to stop. I'm feeling a bit odd—just give me a minute."

"Are you all right?"

Seth leaned back from the steering wheel, now covering his face with his hands. I sat motionless, wondering what was wrong. Could it be a delayed reaction to the same unnerving, burning fever that had hit me?

"It's the shock of seeing you again," Seth finally muttered, as if he'd read my thoughts. He rubbed his face, took a few deep breaths.

"Sorry. I'm all right now. The worst is over."

But was it over? I wondered. He said nothing more as we pulled away from the curb, just cursed the traffic the rest of the way to the hotel.

🍁   🍁   🍁

Seth's flat was small and sparsely decorated, but several large pots of indoor plants—mostly palms—positioned in just the right places happily filled the gaps. A folding table had obviously been pulled out of a closet to sit as it did now, in the middle of the lounge, complete with tablecloth, dinner setting and candles.

High on the tenth floor of a towerblock, his windows pointed toward the Canary Wharf skyscraper, towering well above the lower expanse of twinkling city lights.

A simple, pleasant meal of pasta and salad accompanied our long strain of conversation. We comfortably covered the events in both our lives during the past seven years. Still lingering on, we opened yet another bottle of wine.

Seth's face glowed in the candlelight. "You know, we should have a toast," he insisted.

"Okay."

"I'd like to toast in thanks. To a wish come true."

"A wish come true?"

"Yes, tonight. Right now," he confessed, raising his glass to me, "has been one of my little dreams—and I'm naughty for telling you this—that someday we'd be alone together again."

Alone together.

He paused a minute. My hand tightened its grip on the wineglass, but I said nothing. I hardly dared to breathe, in case it might discourage him from saying anything more…about this dream.

"It's true," he went on, "I always wished that what we'd started so long ago would become real and happen once more. I thought I was wishing for a window in my life which wouldn't ever open again."

Seth was staring at me, eyes moist with emotion, waiting for a reaction. I felt so confused and overwhelmed I couldn't reply.

"I hope you don't mind me saying that," he finally muttered. He said it lowering his eyes; caressing the stem of his wineglass. Deep in thought.

And I still couldn't find any words.

"Maybe I shouldn't have said it, Lauren, but I also have a feeling *deep* down, that you knew it anyway."

I sighed, then nodded.

"Now fate has given us this time alone, I could talk my head off to you all night long."

"That's fine with me," I whispered.

Seth smiled and offered me another glass of wine.

"But so far we've been talking about my life and you haven't said much about yours," I managed to blurt, groping for something easier to discuss. At least so my voice would grow stronger, and louder than a whisper.

"All right. What would you like to know? Yep, my socks still need washing…"

Seth moved the wine bottle, which was standing between us, though not really breaking our line of vision. He had an unnerving glint in his eye, as if the toast had unleashed an open space. Go on, his look seemed to imply. *Go for it.*

"What would you like to know?" he repeated.

"Well, I've wondered if you have a girlfriend…"

"Scrap the socks," he exclaimed. "Now on to the hormones—" he paused, and tapped the table with his fingers for a minute, before answering. "Well, Lauren, I did go out with one girl, Jenny, for over two years. We had some great times together and I still love her, but we split up a few months ago."

"You split up?"

"I can't really explain why, except that I had this nagging feeling that the relationship was going nowhere."

"But you stayed together for two years?" I was puzzled. "Something must have kept it going."

"True enough, but when—no matter how often you try telling yourself otherwise—you know deep down that things just aren't quite right, well, there's not a lot of choice left but to end it."

"But you just said you still love her."

"Lauren, you know as well as I do, there are many different kinds of love."

I had to agree.

"Guess I'm old fashioned in that sense," Seth muttered, "because when I finally marry and settle down with someone, there must be absolutely no twinge of doubt in my mind. I've got to feel as certain as death…drawn to it like the earth orbiting around the sun…then yes. Otherwise no."

"So you had this twinge of doubt?"

"I had the feeling that Jenny really wanted a peaceful, home-loving type guy. Not someone like me, who needs constant change, craves adventure—who rattles around like a pea in a policeman's whistle. She never liked my line of work. She didn't complain, but I knew she wanted to. I guess I loved her, but I wasn't really 'in love' with her. Know what I mean? I've only ever been 'in love' with one person before and it's a fantastic feeling you can't describe." Seth paused, carefully pushing a spoon aside and keeping his eyes on the table. "Maybe I'll never be lucky enough to feel it again," he went on. "But you can't—having known the other—just settle for something less."

"But Seth, don't you think you might be waiting for something that's *too perfect?*"

"Does that make me an incurable romantic?" Seth smiled. He'd averted his eyes from me when speaking of the 'one person.' But now he gazed at me fixedly, ready to play the mirror game.

"I'm not so sure about your 'twinge' theory," I stammered. "I mean, there must be some doubts hanging around, even with the highest kind of love."

"I won't deny that," Seth said, leaning closer toward the flickering candles, "but I'm talking about doubts—the kind that whisper inside your mind. Voices in here—" (pointing to his heart), "that are trying to tell you what you already know. You ignore them, only to discover they're never wrong. Never ever wrong."

I felt myself turning red. Seth's words rang in my ears, sending off an alarm of fear and dread. I had married Paul knowing all too well the distant sound of those inner twinges.

"And how about you, Lauren? Are you really happy?"

"Yes, pretty much so," I answered. Though I knew it sounded awfully flat and half-hearted.

Seth wasn't fooled. I knew that because he flinched and replied, "Pretty much? That sounds to me like…bollocks."

"I'm not sure what's relevant to that question," I mumbled. "Do you mean happy with my career, or personal life, or both?"

"Anything. It just seems like you're hiding something that's bothering you."

I thought to myself: Ah yes, but we all have something we're hiding, all the time.

"No, nothing's bothering me—except your high-minded utopian ideal," I retorted. "How can I answer a question like 'Are you happy?' It's silly and impossible to answer."

"Well I remember asking you if you were happy all the time…before…and you answered it quite simply. Without having to think about it."

"I was younger then—things were much simpler!"

"Oh, all right."

It wasn't all right. We both knew it. Seeing myself through Seth's eyes, I'd suddenly discovered a woman who was secretly very unhappy: a sad, defeated, disguised replica of the old Lauren we both once knew. And working hard to maintain the illusion I was quite satisfied with what was left.

"You don't want to talk about it?"

I shook my head. No.

"But you have some of those little voices festering inside the cupboards of your subconscious?"

"It's not a major problem," I mumbled, staring into the candle's flickering fire for strength. An enormous pressure of discomfort was beginning to weigh against my chest.

Suddenly the candle sputtered; I felt extremely hot and agitated. The air was close, suffocating; the wine beginning to make my head swim; Seth's face, shining in the candle's light, had become almost surreal. His eyes seemed to beckon like the fire—compelling me to succumb to their trance, and sway toward the mystic's snare. Those gleaming hazel eyes looked straight through me, exposing the disease and offering the relief of an instant cure.

"You can tell me," Seth whispered.

I could feel the tears running down my face, silently, of their own accord. I wanted to say something but the words seemed millions of miles away, cowering beneath a long dark tunnel that belonged to another world.

I hadn't even thought about what was wrong, let alone mention it to Seth or anyone else. Suddenly this cauldron of wretchedness surfaced—I could feel the repulsive mire erupting from my guts—rushing up my throat. I couldn't stop it.

"Oh Seth…"

"Tell me, please…"

I had to retch it out, the words kicking and shoving against my mouth: little monsters of truth emerging in guttural yowls and snivels of disgust.

"I—I've been beaten up—a few times—it's not that bad—but I'm scared. No, it is bad—Paul, he hurts me—hits me—I haven't wanted to face it—I'm not myself any more—I have to be what he wants—I hate it. I hate him sometimes, and I'm so afraid of him…"

"Oh Lauren…."

"No, it's my fault—I thought I—could handle it. He's fine if I don't make him mad."

"But how can you say that? What's he done to you?"

I tried to swallow the sobs so I could speak more clearly, but it wasn't easy. "It's stopped now but I know that's because—I've been good—oh god, I've been walking around on a tightrope, frightened there'll be a next time, because I can't stand—how he treats me—he—he throws me on the floor—he ss—smacks me. Spits in my face."

I stopped.

"He *spits* in your face?" Seth looked so horrified I couldn't go on. But now that it had finally come out, I felt so much better.

"It's my fault, I know. I should have realized he could be like that, before I married him," I said. Gradually the words were spilling out with much less effort.

"Why, how could you?"

"He'd lose his temper, rage at me, but kept promising he'd stop. I believed him; you see, he loves me, he really does…. I ignored the little warning voices and it's too late to get out of it now," I explained. "I wanted to find love, I wanted to have someone, and nobody's perfect. But I misjudged, I thought it would be all right. But really, I can't do anything now. It's not right. I've become someone else."

Seth shook his head in disbelief.

"So when you asked me if I was happy," I mumbled, "I suddenly thought, yes, I'm really happy that I've managed keep Paul from wacking me for over six months now. And that's it: the gauge of everything I do."

The light in Seth's face, glowing with such contentment just a few minutes ago, had instantly shadowed, as if he'd just received the force of one of Paul's blows himself. Looking horrified and deeply hurt, he stared at me in shock. Not even Seth could have suspected this kind of confession.

"It's crazy, isn't it? I've managed to hide it so well that even admitting it to you seems like it's coming from another person, another life. Not mine." I shuddered. Then I took a big gulp of wine. "Now I'm so ashamed. I feel so guilty. And I can't blame Paul, because I didn't have to be part of it. I've allowed it to happen."

"Lauren, nobody deserves to be abused. If only there was some way I could help you."

"You have already." Managing a feeble smile, I picked up my napkin and wiped the tears from my face. "Now that I've admitted it to myself, I'll have to find a way to work it out."

Seth threw back his chair. The next minute he was kneeling by my side. Both arms were wrapped around me, tight and secure. I was forgiven.

"Let's not talk any more."

"No."

We slowly rose and sat together on the couch. For a long time we just sat there, my head resting against Seth's chest. He simply held me in his arms until the darkness faded into the early hours of dawn and it was time to take me back to my hotel.

CHAPTER 17

The Church

A sea of glimmering lines, in a crisscrossed tapestry, spread across the open field as far as the eye could see. The morning sun, having broken through a gray wall of cloud like a gleam of light through the broken panes of a window, suddenly revealed the translucent sparkle of millions of tiny spider webs.

Seth and I, walking through what had first appeared to be a rather boring expanse of field-grass, stopped in our tracks.

"Oh, isn't it lovely?" I exclaimed.

"It's hard to believe—the creators of this colossal woven network are about the size of a pin-head," Seth mused.

"It's so beautiful I don't want to walk on it now."

"Good, isn't it? Yet a minute ago, it was invisible. With the early morning dew, and the sun's perfectly angled gaze, at this chosen moment we find a simple field of grass—pretty damn marvelous."

Only in Lichfield, I was thinking. Thank god for people like Seth and country walks in Lichfield.

As for the Boat Show, I couldn't have cared less. I made my three-day appearance but hardly remember any of it. Nothing meant more to my survival—right then—than simply getting back to the feeling I was having right now.

With six cans of lager tucked away in my hand luggage, I'd met Seth at Victoria Station and we both took the train. Listening to his stories about Africa, Israel and South America kept me enthralled for hours. But even more amazing—to me—was a simple journey to the Midlands, carrying me once again through the magical dales, fells, heaths, hedgerows and grassy fields of England. Every touch, thought, smell, sensation seemed magnified; every detail vividly striking a chord in my heart. The black-eared wool-laden sheep, the ancient cookie-cutter church-spires, the lumpy moss-covered brick, the clay-white clods of earth lining the furrows of plowed fields, the fragile arch of every eyelash gilding Seth's attentive gaze.

Elizabeth and Chester greeted me like a long-lost daughter. They'd even arranged a big reunion dinner at a local Indian restaurant. We picked up Bea and celebrated over curry and sparkling wine. Ian drove over from Birmingham, where he now lived with his new wife Sarah, four months pregnant.

Despite the inevitable hangovers, Seth wanted to begin our country walk early the next morning, to make the day last as long as possible. So promptly at seven, he'd knocked on the door to wake me, sleeping in the Henshaws' tiny spare bedroom…

Waiting outside was his dusty old motorcycle—tucked in a far corner of the garage. At my request we headed straight for Willowby Farm. Using his Ordinance Survey Map, Seth suggested a hike from Hamstall Ridware to Hunger Hill.

We'd just started down a footpath from the top of a ridge, to a peaceful stretch of fields below. Traversing the sea of spider webs, we came upon a patchwork of vivid green cushions, dotted with white cotton balls.

Seth pointed to the far corner of the field, where a large group of sheep huddled together.

"That's our stile, over there."

I followed from behind—deliberately—in order to enjoy the sight of Seth's figure ahead, walking with such confident stride. I could hear the water sloshing inside the bottle strapped to his backpack, as he marched, his legs thrusting forward, hiking boots lodging solidly over the clumps of grass and wet mud. His mood, his gait, even the swinging motion of the strings hanging from his gaiters seemed strangely wonderful.

A simple walk. Yet we might have been wandering through the scenes of an ancient fable and Seth, too, seemed to appreciate every legendary character. Each fence, tree, hedge, bird, hay, sheep, rabbit, cow, manure, dog, mud, barn, thistle, and brook was bound together, making up a woven tapestry that had taken thousands of years to make. Each humble thread was a hint of all creation.

"I know it sounds silly, but all this seems so different," I tried to explain, "from rural areas in America—and why?"

"You must have hiked through similar countryside at home," said Seth. "How could it be so different?"

"For one thing, access for walkers is limited to areas set aside by State or National parks," I answered. "It's purposely set up, if you know what I mean. But even the legitimate farmland you're likely to see driving through New England, for example: it's pretty, but not quite the same. Don't you think? Remember what you saw when we drove to New York?"

"I don't think I was allowed to look at anything," Seth reminded me.

"But what you *did* see," I went on, keen to reach my point, "you didn't get the same kind of feeling from it, did you? If you ask me, everything here really blends, artistically pleases the eye, in a natural sense. Like the gray stone farm buildings, with moss and ivy growing all over them—and the lovely hedges and stone walls. Nothing seems to be marred by man's bad taste. No junk lying around, no barbed metal fences, no plastic or synthetic materials. All the fields are so well kept. I haven't seen a single piece of litter or, for that matter, a garbage heap."

"I agree, most farmers over here are proud of their heritage. They don't like rubbish demeaning their ancestral land. But I could take you to other areas in this country where you'd be disappointed." Seth grinned. "We're not all compulsively tidy."

"Okay then, you'll have to show me. Take me to your trash."

"Fine."

We both ignored the fact that such an opportunity would not happen.

Leaning against the stile, Seth studied his map for the footpath leading to Blythe House Farm. We skirted the road, then detoured to the river. I collected my souvenir rocks and a few winter thistles; we stopped for a picnic lunch. Suddenly it was late afternoon. The sun dipped lower and lower, on the brink of impending twilight.

Only then did he softly ask me, "Have you been thinking about what you're going to do, when you get home?"

"Yes," I said. That was all, and it seemed to be enough.

As we crossed a field of tall grass, I spotted a church ahead, the flesh-colored sandstone walls half obscured by the giant truck of a tree. But the tower of St. Michaels rose up just as I remembered it, with the holly, the graves, and Celtic cross by its side.

"Look Seth—the church—did I ever tell you it's my favorite?

"What about the Cathedral?"

"No, it's too grand and much too popular. I prefer the little village church of St. Michaels."

Seth grabbed my hand. "Come on. That church is positively begging for a couple of visitors!"

We ran. The sun had just disappeared behind the hills, the pastures bathed in the subtle golden-hued tones of dusk. We laughed and stumbled over the grass, leaping like young deer across the open meadow toward safety.

As the deserted church loomed closer, Seth's hand tightened its grip. I wished we'd never get there so we'd be holding hands forever; running, laughing together across all the fields from Cornwall to Scotland.

Stopping abruptly at the parish fence, Seth reluctantly released my hand and unlatched the gate. The rows of ancient gravestones, slumped austerely on the other side, instantly silenced our mirth. Solemnly, Seth proceeded ahead, wandering though the cemetery, pausing occasionally to read the cryptic, fossilized inscriptions.

I immediately veered left, to that one particular tombstone—sitting at the far end of the churchyard, with the best view of the surrounding fields and hills we had just traversed.

"I'm back," I announced to the stone. "Did you know I'd come back, all along? Oh Sarah Jane, I wish, like you, I could leave a piece of myself here forever," I whispered.

A thousand years from now, the same feeling. And Sarah Jane a nameless, dateless slab. But I felt truly at home near this church and its river. Nowhere else had I found what every pilgrim seeks: knowledge of the true self through love. This was the real me; the Lauren who always dreamed of existing, the Lauren who truly existed and always would exist—despite everything.

Seth's footsteps crunched over the gravel path, as he walked over to where I stood.

Smiling and pointing at an anonymous gravestone lying next to Sarah Jane's, I blurted "Here Lies Lauren!"

Seth grinned, and winked. "So we finally learn the identity of the unknown marker!"

"I'm serious," I muttered, staring at the grave. "Well, a part of her, anyway," I said. "The best part."

"And what about Hunger Hill?"

"That's where both you and I...will always be, along with the Celtic ghosts," I insisted. "That's where we'll never die."

The dumplings were consumed with grunts and groans of amazement. Seth was starving: returning to London we'd forgotten to eat any lunch. By the time we'd reached his flat it was already past nine o'clock. I'd offered to cook. "Something American," I promised. "It's the least I can do for all your hospitality."

"You're a naughty girl," Seth mumbled, reaching for more stew. "This is fantastic. Now I'll want dumplings for me tea—and can't have 'em."

"I'll leave you the recipe," I offered. But the thought of leaving put a lump bigger than a dumpling in my throat.

"Forget it. I can just about manage boiling a packet of pasta. And besides, you've cleaned up my kitchen. I'm sure I won't be able to find anything in there any more."

"Sorry."

"You haven't eaten much," Seth remarked, looking at my plate.

"I know. I gave myself too much. I'm just not that hungry."

"Do you feel okay?"

"Oh yes, fine."

"My parents loved having you, even if it was such a bloody short time. And you had fun yesterday? Was the walk all right?"

"It was great! I can't explain how…how good it's been…"

"A shame we didn't make it to Hunger Hill," Seth muttered. "But it gets dark so early in winter. We simply ran out of time."

"Yes." I bit my tongue. What else was there to say? Was Seth secretly relieved—like me—that we didn't stand face to face with the memory?

"If we'd gone, we'd have been wallowing in the pitch black, bumping into a sword-buckling Chief," he added.

"Or even worse, Roman soldiers."

"I'm getting drunk," Seth cut in. "So I won't be conscious tomorrow—when you leave. I'll open some wine to chase the whiskey."

"That's okay, I can get a taxi back to my hotel."

Seth said nothing. There was a long silence, during which I could sense the futility of keeping the mood light and cheerful. Which meant more whiskey. Seth was losing his diehard grip—I could tell by the way he held the wine bottle.

"I still can't believe I'm here," I mumbled.

"Damn this cork," Seth answered. "It won't budge."

"I'm already wondering if all this really happened," I went on. "Maybe it's just a weird dream."

"*You* think it's a weird dream?" Seth exclaimed, flinging the corkscrew aside. Suddenly his pleasant tone turned sour. "What about me?" he half shouted. "Yes, and what about ME? How do you think I feel?"

His sudden bitter outburst caught me by surprise. "I know it's been awkward for both of us," I stammered, "trying to pretend our friendship hasn't changed after that silence—that gap—of seven years."

"Fuck the friendship," Seth shouted.

"What?"

"I said *fuck* the friendship!"

So. The sword had fallen. With no warning, it came crashing down. Seth's self-restraint had completely disappeared. I watched his face change color. His anger was rising. On the brink…

"This isn't easy, you know," he muttered, managing to lower his voice. "I'm quite amazed at myself, in fact, at how well I've handled it. You have no idea…"

"No idea about what?"

But as he spoke, Seth seemed far removed from me, as if he was talking to an unseen enemy. He looked like a tortured prisoner so distraught he was driven to crash the barriers—quite hopelessly.

"You've got no idea how I feel!" he exclaimed. "Or what I feel! I can't believe any of this. It took years for me to get over you. I couldn't stop thinking of you, even when I knew I was crazy, a stupid fool…you were always there, the center of my thoughts, the bright star in my dreams, the woman of my fantasies…"

He paused, eyes still avoiding me. "It took a long time, but eventually I managed to get free of you, to accept a life without you in it. Time passes, wounds heal. I could never forget that kind of love, but I had to forget YOU."

Suddenly looking up, he glared across the table. At me. As if checking—just to make sure—that I was still really there.

Then, pointing his finger accusingly, he said, "And now, all of that, bloody all of it, has been turned upside down. Here you are, a blasted curse from another lifetime, sitting right here next to me, in my flat!"

"Seth…I didn't realize…" I couldn't finish. I wasn't sure I'd really heard what I just thought I'd heard.

When it did sink in, I said, "My god Seth, why didn't you ever tell me?"

"Why didn't I ever tell you? Come on—wasn't it obvious enough? I was gobsmacked, from the first moment I saw you. All right, I knew you liked me, but I wasn't going to flatter myself by thinking you might feel quite the same way."

"But I did!" I blurted.

"No. You couldn't have—I knew for sure the moment I got off that plane and saw you with Max..."

"Oh, I didn't know! I thought you might have loved me, but in your letters all you mentioned was how you wanted to see America."

"The only reason I wanted to go to America so badly was because *you* happened to be there."

"But what about that singer?"

"What about her? Do you mean to tell me that you were completely celibate that winter?"

"But wasn't she beautiful, like Naomi? Don't you see how I thought you couldn't possibly be in love with me? And then you didn't write. You just expected me to know!"

Seth stared at me in dismay. "You *knew*, Lauren," he exclaimed, banging down his glass of whiskey which spilled all over the table. "Don't try and pretend to me that you didn't know."

Tears swelled in my eyes, spilling out over my cheeks. "I wanted to believe it, Seth. But whenever I believe, really believe, it never turns out to be true."

"So none of this is true, then." Seth's hand reached across the table and held my cheek. I could feel the lightning bolt race across my face; rush hot all the way down my body. I closed my eyes.

His hand fell away. "The minute I saw Max, I realized how foolish I'd been, thinking I'd have you all to myself."

"Seth, listen to me—" I said. "I wasn't head over heels in love with Max. Even when you asked, I never said that! No. Nobody else has even come close to what I feel for you...but it all seemed so impossible. And sometimes you acted so casual about it. I didn't dare presume that—"

"What you already suspected?"

"Why didn't you spend more time with me when I was staying in England, at your house? I waited in agony for you to get home from work, and when you did, you weren't that interested!"

"Wait a minute. You say you were waiting for me? But you were always reading, and it felt like I was intruding."

"Oh no...I had to pretend to be doing something besides waiting for you."

"Well, maybe that's true, but in America, why did you stay glued to Max like that?"

"If you had just told me in your letters that you were coming over because you wanted to see *me*, if you had only admitted *that*, I would have waited for you! But no, you wouldn't commit to that—just clever innuendos. All jokes and hints! And then, when we had that talk on the beach in New-port—remember? I wanted you to tell me then, so badly! But you didn't."

"I told you how I screwed things up with that bloody visa. I wasn't too keen on blowing my case with you, too. Was I supposed to tell you that I loved you more than Max? That I deserved you more than he did? I wonder what good it would have done, for either of us."

Seth waited for me to answer, his face looking flushed and defensive.

I fought to keep my voice steady. "I know, I know," I answered. "And what would have come of it? I couldn't face the thought of wanting and missing you, yet again. You'd go back to England and...."

"But I didn't know what I was going to do, not then," Seth insisted. "Maybe I might have stayed in America, if things worked out. Nothing seemed impos-sible—forget the hash—I only worried about how I could stay near you."

"And I wanted to be safe," I muttered. "Going back to Newport with Max seemed the best solution."

"Maybe you were right," Seth muttered, calming down a bit. "We were young and immature. Who knows what would have happened? So ill-equipped at that stage...We'd probably have burned up, and then burst apart—before we'd realized what hit us."

We gazed sadly across the table at each other.

"Though I almost burned up and burst apart anyway...without you..." Seth added.

"Oh Seth, don't. Let's not torture ourselves any more over the past," I implored. "At least we know the truth now, even though it's seven years too late."

Seth bowed his head.

The truth! Suddenly the dark despair dividing his fury and my frustration simply floated away. The whole room seemed to sigh with relief.

And softly, before he looked up again, I rose and found myself kneeling next to his chair; sinking my head in his lap. In the silence, pressing my face where I could feel his bulge, his warm pulse, grow taut with desire, a little voice kept saying *wait, you haven't quite finished, there's something you still have to say*. I still had to say it—out loud.

"I love you, Seth." My voice sounded strange, like a glacier melting into a mountain spring, running freely toward the sea. "I love you," I repeated. "I have always been in love with you."

Seth's fingers, in reply, passed gently through my hair, smoothing out the curls. Each stroke a fervent return to Hunger Hill. I hadn't moved, my face still hidden in the curve of his lap.

A few seconds passed, when we both might have imagined our platonic resolve would stay intact. Then, overpowered by flesh, my own call for passion discovered impatient hands pulling my head upwards. And Seth was mine.

Forcing my lips to his mouth, his kiss obliterated any sense of wrongdoing. With an urgency that ached with impatience, we consumed each other. No rules, no shame—just the heat of the lightning bolt's fire. The chair toppled over, Seth clutching and ripping off my clothes; his hands, groping to reach the source of his torment.

I moaned as skin to skin we finally clung together, my body limp and melting, disintegrating—hurtling wildly towards a bottomless pit of touch.

Seth's mouth roughly devoured my neck, impatient to claim more; moving down, his lips pressed lightly now, across the soft round contours of my breasts, over the rigid, aroused peaks of my nipples, pausing to savor them slowly, one by one.

Clutching Seth's head, I closed my eyes, half-sobbing from the re-awakened sensation; dissolving into the same sweet-pitched vibrations that came out of knowing him…gripping his head and forcing it back, I wanted to see his face.

While Seth, sensing my eager permission, said not a word, but raised his head for a brief second, like a hopeless soul tottering over a bridge before taking that final leap. His rigid body bent over me—last focused gaze formidable, desperately resigned.

We were one. Now I understood Seth's implied fear, for sex could go beyond sexuality, when two souls felt as close as ours. The dark, deep endless pulse of love, the secret of the river's source—that was what really bound us together.

Did Seth enter and feel it too? My womb a cradle of infinite space: I could barely feel the throbbing boundaries of his flesh, now furiously seeking refuge; now enveloped within the mystery of my embrace.

"Oh no, I'm going to…" Seth's husky voice broke out reluctantly, as if he couldn't bear to let it all go.

Astonished by the acute sensation of a simultaneous climax, I cried out in surprise.

And our bodies, why should they part? It seemed crazy to end the union; we'd rest inside each other all night, until every wasted year without it had been fulfilled. But eventually he pulled away, and lifted me up.

"It's done," he said, and sighed, before leading me straight to his bed.

❧   ❧   ❧

"Trust in yourself," Seth reminded me. His goodbye had been brief, trailing off into the unknown. "Don't worry. Neither of us can expect to know *right now* what to do." He'd looked so sad and guilt-ridden.

"How can we know?" he said. "It's like trying to figure out the universe—with a pocket calculator!"

Remembering his anguished, disconcerted face, even today—I end up smiling to myself. As if that moment was yesterday. And wasn't it just like Seth?

"Goodbye Lauren," he'd said, as I stepped into the cab. Full stop. And of course. You guessed it.

No false promises.

CHAPTER 18

The Reckoning

"Well, how was the Show?" asked Paul.

"Really good," I answered.

"Did you find something new to add to your portfolio?"

"Yes—it was worth the trip." I tried not to stumble over the words.

"So aren't you going to tell me about it?"

"I guess the highlight of the show was an old English 12-Meter yacht being refurbished. She was purchased by someone in New York, and as soon as the renovation work is finished, she'll be available for charter." I cleared my throat and summoned up what I hoped to be a more convincing smile. "They intend to have her ready this summer. And best of all, she's going to berth right here at Fort Adams."

"Sounds interesting. But how is a 12-Meter going to attract charter clients? I can't imagine there's much to offer—for accommodation—on a racing yacht."

"We intend to attract clients who'd rather experience good fast sailing rather than sitting comfortably down below, playing poker and getting smashed."

"I see. What else?"

I thought a minute. "Oh, I met some of the London agents. It was nice seeing the faces of those I'd only spoken to on the phone before."

"And your English relatives?"

"They haven't aged a bit. Or at least they don't look to me like they've gotten any older. I suppose it's the climate over there—not enough sun to produce the tell-tale wrinkles."

"Did you pass on my regards?"

"Of course. Anyway, at the Show," I quickly added, "I managed to co-ordi-nate with some charter companies around Lymington, who agreed to co-bro-ker with me. I'm excited about that, as it will mean a lot of new clients…"

"Wait a minute," Paul cut in. "You won't be involved with all that for much longer anyway. Don't forget, you'll soon be busy with Paul Junior."

"But I thought I still might be able to earn commissions part-time."

"Why? We don't need the money."

"It wouldn't interfere with a baby, not if I worked from home."

"Are you listening to me? I said no."

I flinched, but kept my nerve. I would now be crossing that forbidden line, purposely defying Paul's will.

"Paul, can't we discuss this reasonably? I'm trying to tell you that my work is important to me, and I'm not sure I want to give it up completely—even if we have a baby."

At the same time I was wondering why I'd been so meticulous about taking the pill. Didn't I want to be mother? Or was I dreading the prospect of raising a child with a father like Paul?

"So I thought we might compromise—I'd have the baby but continue to work part-time," I said.

"You're the one who's not being reasonable." Paul shouted. "You're being selfish and thoughtless! Don't you care about being a proper mother to our baby?"

"Yes I care!"

"The mother of my child stays home, she doesn't go gallivanting around lick-my-ass powerboats with a bunch of slimy, arrogant sailors," sneered Paul.

"I like my work," I insisted, "and you can't prevent me from—"

"You conniving little liar!" Paul lunged toward me, pointing a threatening fist in front of my face. "You agreed you'd quit at the end of the year, and now you think you can suddenly change your mind, to suit yourself?"

"No…" I faltered, unsure of what to say next.

What a sad, terrible state to be in, I was thinking. To see with open eyes, and hear the true meaning ring loud and clear with every word. Once I was finally willing to….

"Well I can see it was a big mistake letting you go to that blasted Boat Show in London," groaned Paul. "Now you think you're Miss Ta-Dee-Dah, and your job's more important than me!"

"It has nothing to do with you—"

"No, because you'd rather to be with them, not me. I'm no fool, I know when I'm being hoodwinked," he yelled, pacing the room.

"I'm not listening any more to this," I said, fearing Paul's verbal anger had worked itself up to a rather dangerous pitch.

"Why not? Because you know I'm right?"

"Forget it," I pleaded.

Paul glared at me, waiting—just in case—I might dare ignite his wrath even further. If he exploded, it would be my fault—not his.

"Let's not fight tonight, please? I've just got back from London, I'm jet-lagged and really tired," I admitted, making it all right again.

"You better go to bed then," Paul said, satisfied with my meek response. He waved his arm as if to motion "Get out of my sight." Then, harshly turning away, he disappeared into the kitchen.

I could hear the refrigerator door squeak open, followed by the pop of a beer can. Slowly retreating up the stairs, I felt utterly frustrated and alone. But there would be other opportunities to try again. My only hope of salvation would be to assert myself and fight back. In future, I planned to revive the old Lauren in smaller, subtler doses. Otherwise Paul would surely suspect something very peculiar had happened to me while I was away.

Lying alone in bed, I hoped Paul would drink several beers before deciding to come up and join me. I tried to sleep, but it was useless. Little voices kept whispering inside my head. I was glad about them, though—they were a *good* sign.

I knew I'd made a big mistake, ignoring those voices in the past. I'd got it all wrong, trying to follow my dad's don't-be-so-intense advice. Being true to my own nature was best. Anything else was simply floundering in a world of darkness and lies.

And what *was* the darkness? I'd needed Seth to remind me: loving a man who would not return such love; fear and intimidation and guilt; a slow, slow, giving up for the sake of years not finding the magic; simply *settling for less.*

Yes—I'd been a coward. I had betrayed my dreams, accepting a life of darkness. On rare occasions I might have encountered a streak of light—a tiny flicker resembling the real Lauren—which I pretended was enough. Now the horror of Paul's anger was nothing compared to the ghoulish image I had discovered staring back at me in Seth's candid mirror.

The next morning, however, I discovered an annoying rash on my legs. It started out as a small pink blemish on my right thigh, which by the time I showered, had grown into an ominous red blotch. The blotch moved to my other leg. It grew bigger and bigger by the hour.

Having never had a rash like that before, I was mystified. Then I started to worry. The rash was definitely a bad sign. Considering my present mental state, the affliction was probably psychosomatic. Going to see a doctor seemed pointless.

"Please, just go away," I murmured, rubbing it in dismay. "Give me some time and I'll sort myself out!"

But the rash apparently disagreed. It stayed, impatient to be recognized: a mounting pressure needing attention. Panic-stricken, I realized the futility of attempting to conceal the redness now seeping through my skin.

Sure enough, the second night Paul noticed it, sitting next to me on the bed as he pulled up my nightgown—a gesture he often used to signal his desire for sex.

"Look at that!" he exclaimed. "What's happened to you?"

"I don't know, I've got this strange rash all of a sudden," I answered, gently pushing his hands away. "I hope you don't mind, but it's so itchy and tender I don't want—"

"All right," Paul said. "But maybe you better have a doctor look at it."

"No. I'm sure it will go away in a few days," I replied. I didn't sound very convinced and Paul instantly noticed.

"It looks to me like it's taking over, not subsiding," argued Paul. "I've wondered why you've looked so worried—ever since you got back. Did you eat something you might be allergic to?"

"I guess I must have."

Paul looked fixedly at me, slowly recognizing the reluctant and terrified wave of fear passing across my face.

"What's happened to you? Something's happened, hasn't it? It's obvious, Lauren, you aren't good at disguising it. So you better just tell me."

"It's nothing. I'm just worried about this rash. Anything might have caused it."

"What the hell did they feed you over there? Rotten smoked salmon?"

My brain recoiled, twisting and twirling in a spasm of fear, incapable of constructing deception. I could feel my face flushing—soon it would match my leg's dreaded hue of scarlet red.

"I didn't have any fish," I answered.

"Then what's making you look so uncomfortable? I know you're hiding something, aren't you?" Paul exclaimed. He knew I couldn't lie to him. This was a proven weakness contributing to his power.

The rash ended everything. It was all over—I'd have to admit to my crime. For a fleeting instant, I envisioned Paul killing me, and yet nothing seemed more terrible than the unbearable pressure of hiding from the truth.

"Yes, something happened..."

"Well, what? Come on!"

I cowered—stammered words which had no sound. My mouth moved, but I would never be able to explain to Paul, who was now extremely agitated. To say the least.

"What is it?"

I continued to shake. I trembled and shook like a frozen animal caught without shelter in a blinding snowstorm.

Paul's eyes flashed with contempt. "I can guess, can't I?" Then it hit him. "Did you spread your legs for some British cock? Is that it—did you let some guy *fuck you* in London?"

I didn't answer. I acknowledged the truth with eyes spilling over in tears.

"You bitch! You *whoring* cunt!" Paul's arm swung out and knocked me off the side of the bed.

Lying on the floor, I instantly curled up into a defensive ball, shielding my head with my arms, while Paul resumed his verbal paroxysm of rage, flinging objects across the room, smashing the lamp and breaking the glass on pictures wrenched from the walls.

"I trusted you! I let you go, like a fool, thinking you wouldn't do that—but no—you couldn't wait, could you? Like a bitch on heat, you let some stranger thrust his dick up your cunt! Did you get off on it? Did you come, did your sticky vagina enjoy making a cuckold of me?"

Paul moved toward my crumpled body. "You whore. You selfish fucking cunt!"

He was kicking me, but I didn't cry out. Instead I retreated beyond the physical pain, and in the darkness shut the great wooden gates of the Fort at Hunger Hill. I held firm through the pounding and pounding, closed my ears to the screams and shouts, dug a hole and hid from the smoke and bedlam. Then I heard a crash, and opened my eyes. A shattered lamp lay in pieces near my head and I wondered whether the moisture on my face might be blood.

Suddenly the kicking ended and Paul hovered over me, panting heavily. I was being jolted upright by his steel grip.

"Well, you whore, you can fuck your husband can't you? I'm just as entitled as everybody else. Come on, let me stick it up yours."

Spitting my own blood, I tried giving Paul a dose of his own medicine. He ducked, then threw me on the bed, roughly grabbing my arms and pinning me down. Whimpering and choking, I watched Paul's fiendish aberration moving grimly over my rigid body. His grotesque smile swarmed above my face.

I shrieked; grunting with perverted pleasure, he jerked my legs apart...

And raped me.

Hearing the front door slam, I slowly raised my head. The room was spinning; looking down I tried to focus through the haze. My own flesh seemed strange and indistinct, lost beneath a heavy fog.

I blinked and rubbed my eyes. Gradually I could make out two legs. What must be legs—my legs—lying flat on the bed. Sobbing, I rolled over and covered my eyes so I couldn't see my pathetic state, or any part of the room.

Still, if those were my legs, I was thinking, that was good. Because at least now there was no sign of any rash.

❧   ❧   ❧

Two months later, Paul contested my filing for divorce. Convinced that my decision to separate was a temporary aberration, he told me I'd be sorry for taking such a hasty, impetuous step. He wanted me back and he promised to change. He'd never lay another hand on me. Or the furniture. Didn't I realize just how much he loved me? I, Lauren, was the only thing that mattered to him—didn't that mean anything?

I no longer thought so. I simply followed the warnings of those little voices, which told me in my heart that Paul would never change. *Don't let his clever arguments play upon your guilt*, they said. *Don't let him fool you.* So I persisted in resisting Paul's entreaties, waiting out the year to obtain my legal freedom.

Meanwhile, Paul resorted to harassment and wild, outrageous threats. He followed me home from work, sitting in his car outside the apartment where I lived. Sandra, (a sympathetic colleague who'd taken me in as a room-mate) began to resent the inconvenience of having her phone number changed, of peeking out her windows day and night, of listening to me creeping around and incessantly complaining about it all.

"Can't the police do something?" she asked.

"Not yet," I told her. "They say it's not enough to justify a Restraining Order. But sooner or later they'll have to. I know they will."

For Paul wasn't about to let me go. I knew he'd try every possible means. And I was fully prepared to go through every stage of the cycle: first violent and irrational; then calm and sentimental; as a last resort, a good hard tug at my heart and conscience.

There came a day when I realized I'd have to face him. As usual, at five o'clock I spotted his truck parked outside International Marine—waiting. When I came out I decided not to race blindly to my car, but let him have his say. I stood there. Shrugged. He jumped out his truck, a blue, four-wheel drive pick-up, and waved.

"Can't a man even talk to his own wife?" he shouted. "Just sit with me for a minute," he begged. "I really need to talk to you."

I went to his truck. I opened the door and got in.

"Lauren, we've had such good times together," Paul began. "I'm sorry that I've got a bad temper. Can you honestly say that it's all right for you to suddenly ditch our marriage—without giving me a chance to prove to you that I can control it? If I had known you were that unhappy—hell—things would have changed! But you never said a word…"

"I'm sorry Paul," I insisted, "but I can't give it another chance. Whatever we had before—it's dead. Something snapped inside me. I'll never get it back."

"Yes you can! Look, just try it for a while, and if you still feel the same, I'll agree with you. I'm begging you please…you're my wife…"

"I can't. Please don't cry, Paul. Try to understand."

His tears were desperate and sincere. I wavered. Jesus. He looked so defenseless and overwhelmed with despair. Covering his face with his hands, he groaned and sobbed, "I love you so much…what will I do without you?"

"Oh Paul, just let it go, please—"

"Nobody's perfect. What do you want? You'll never find it…nobody will love you as much as I do…you'll see…men are all the same…you're chasing after a fantasy, a dream—all for nothing."

The word 'dream' echoed inside my head, taunting and unbearable. Was I refusing to let Paul have another chance because I was secretly afraid he *would* stop the abuse—and *then* what reason would I have for wanting to leave? The reason could never be Seth. No. I had to be doing this for me, just me. I believed in that. There was nothing else I could willfully claim.

The dream. I couldn't bear to sit in that car any longer, watching helplessly as the wreckage of my thoughtlessness—my once beloved husband—moaned and writhed in pain.

I opened the door. I had to be free. I knew my life depended on it, all for nothing or not. So I rushed away like a madwoman, zig-zagging in a frantic attempt to evade the laughing demons blocking my way through the parking lot.

Of course it wasn't over. Paul had an amazing reserve of tenacity. His tactics turned again into a desperate aggressiveness—professing he'd rather die, or kill me, or destroy us both if I didn't come back. His insane remarks were hard to ignore, and I wondered if such threats were indeed only words—merely intended to scare. I couldn't know for sure.

Such was the power of fear. Perhaps that too was why it had been so difficult admitting to myself the extent of Paul's abuse. My repressed fears had protected me from the formidable consequences which now—much to my horror—I had to face. I guess the proof in the pudding was happening now. Paul would make my life hell, rather than let me go. But I surprised us both by stubbornly sticking with hell, rather than Paul. Though I was still scared of what he might do.

What next but to wait for the final confrontation? The day he would play his last hand? There was bound to be some hidden ace in the hole.

The game finally ended when he sent me a postcard (which couldn't be torn up without seeing the message) stating if I didn't see him the next morning, he would kill himself. Could I live with that? All he asked—he said—was for one last opportunity to talk...nothing more.

I gave in. The next morning I knocked on the door of a house that had become nothing more than a bad dream. A voice from inside called "Lauren!" and asked me to enter. I walked slowly down the hall, my hand clasping a weapon of mace—but somehow I sensed I wouldn't need it. I found Paul standing next to the hearth in the living room. He was stark naked.

"I know you love me," he entreated. "We've been together for four years! Can you honestly say to me now, that all of it was a lie?" His nakedness made him look weak and vulnerable; trembling, he leaned against the hearth for support.

I stared back at him, numb and speechless. What on earth was he doing? Completely naked? Did he think that by stripping off everything, quite literally, he might humble himself enough to win me back?

"Can you be so heartless? When all I ask is one more chance?" he whispered. "Just one more chance to prove—"

"No," I insisted, flatly, closing my eyes and ears against the agony of his plight.

"That's it, then? You don't give a damn about me? I don't believe it. Tell me now—straight to my face—that you *never* loved me." His own eyes, so blue against his black hair, pleaded like those of a broken stallion.

"No. I can't."

"Then you should give me another chance."

"No."

"I can't believe you've become so cruel…" Paul whispered, "but if you are, then you won't care—you can watch the end."

His body, shaking, moved toward the back door. I watched his nude figure trotting down the hill, right down to the Bay, which in Arctic-cold March was covered in ice. Then he stepped straight into the frozen water, until the cracking ice settled around his shivering pink shoulders.

Standing by the window, so Paul could see me witness his plunge, I wondered how long he would endure such a dip. I knew that fishermen had slipped overboard into the sea, and in winter they'd go unconscious in the space of three minutes. The victims had no chance to either struggle or swim. They actually drowned before they froze to death.

For three minutes I fought against the urge to run out and save him. How could he do this, my instincts wailed, how might I know if he's really going to go through with it? But those little voices, which I could still hear murmuring inside my heart, held me fast. *He wants you to give in,* they argued, *he won't really kill himself. You know that, don't you?*

Paul wavered, slowly drifting deeper into the hole he'd made in the ice. His face was turning blue and yet he continued to stare at the window where I stood, his dumbfounded gaze begging for forgiveness.

I couldn't stand it any longer; I turned away, rushing wildly out the front door and into my car. The next minute I was speeding down the street, then skidding around a sharp corner—to a position where I could view the spot where I'd last seen Paul.

The car screeched to a halt.

"Thank God," I exclaimed as I caught a final glimpse of Paul's cold-blooded nakedness heaving up the lawn toward safety. His figure, hunched and quivering but alive—sent a shiver of triumph up my spine.

CHAPTER 19

The Smuggle

The real me did it. I struggled for four months, fighting my own war which meant keeping Seth out of it. So I hadn't written him—not a word—since the Boat Show. But the silence was not silence. I could hear his voice, imagine his face, feel his pride in my efforts to come clean every time I moved one step further—toward the day when I could, in my newfound freedom, write him again.

We both must have agreed without saying: I would contact him first, when the time was right.

Now I was ready. I could give my love in way that was true and pure: a love not tarnished by betrayal. I felt oddly resigned to whatever might or might not lie ahead with Seth. I even considered the possibility we might never see each other again. But I wasn't scared of that. I'd simply ask myself 'Now do you believe in the highest kind of love?' And the answer was 'yes,' again and again.

April 15, 1988

Dear Seth,

Paul and I separated. I moved in with my friend Sandra (in town) but found it necessary to obtain a Court Restraining Order, which hasn't helped much. You're probably not surprised, after what I've told you. I'm sure he won't really hurt me physically at this point, but I need proof to get the police to arrest him. How

can I prove it was Paul who keeps slashing my tires, trampling Sandra's flowerbeds, or breaking the windows with rocks? That it was Paul who sent my charter clients insulting letters signed by "The Whore?" I've heard about women who have begged the Police for protection, to no avail, until they're actually murdered—then the police take notice. Paul won't kill me, he just keeps on harassing.

I've come to the point where for sanity's sake I've got to leave Newport. Fortunately International Marine has a partner outfit in San Diego, California, so if I move there I'll have a job waiting for me. I think the change is a good thing, and San Diego is a lovely city. Back to the west coast again! As soon as I've settled I will write and let you know my address. Hope all this doesn't sound too morbid. Really I am all right and very excited about finally getting myself back on track.

With all My Love,

Lauren

April 30, 1988

Oh Lauren, Lauren!

I've been shooting right here in London for the past few months. But I haven't really noticed. I only seem to notice how the sound of your voice is still fresh in my ears, as if your visit happened just yesterday...the sound never fades. My longing grows. I wait. I have you deep within. I believe that the mystery—no matter how strange or difficult to understand—will gradually unfold and begin to show us both a way.

Bloody hell.

I have pondered many, many times (you too?), wishing for a crystal ball; daring to ask of it to bear fruit, as they say, to bring forth a golden crucible laden with answers to illuminate the pathway. But none of this can be hurried. To try and do so is to cheat the journey. Occasionally we are allowed a glimpse of the way, but only that. The glimpse is a guide but never the road. A map reference but never the whole map. You may tread wearily some-

times, with sharp rocks underfoot and spiteful twists and turns along every stretch. But every sharp stone brings a lesson, every twist an insight, every turn a gain in wisdom—no matter how imperceptible. Yes? So nothing is wasted, as long as we have the heart to really know this.

It's taken me all night to write this letter, but I wanted to prove to you, dear cousin Lauren, that I can be dead serious.

We tread our different pathways, you and I. But we may yet find our River, or magical place where two brooks, born so far apart, yet meet and merge. Meanwhile—Lauren—I assume nothing, I demand nothing. I can only hope, wish, and pray with you that we may find the way. And in so doing, we cheat not on this journey.

As always, Seth

By the end of May I'd moved to San Diego; settled into my new job in the middle of June. Renting a studio apartment in a complex near the marina, I felt ready to come out of hiding. I felt safe enough to re-establish contact with Seth—even talk to him on the phone. Though I still poured myself a glass of whiskey before I dialed.

"Hello, Seth?"

"My god Lauren, why haven't you called me sooner?"

"I didn't want to burden you with all my troubles."

"Christ, you've carried the burden all by yourself long enough!"

"No, I'm fine, Seth. It feels great being on my own again. What else can I say?"

"I miss you."

"I miss you too." I relaxed a bit.

"There. So what's keeping us from seeing each other again? I will—I can. I'll get to you."

"You can?"

"I'll find a way. Screw the ban on my U.S. Visa! I've been thinking about it. I can fly into Mexico, befriend a few illegal aliens and follow them across the border."

I chuckled. "No way, Seth. It'll never work."

"I mean it," he replied. "I'm going to hang up now. I've got ten minutes before the travel agent shuts. Sit tight, I'll call you once I'm sitting in a hotel in Tijuanna."

And apparently he did mean it, because after I'd given him my phone number, he instantly hung up. I sat there listening to the click, the dial tone—in dismay.

The next morning the phone rang, early. My alarm hadn't even gone off yet.

"Hello Lauren?"

"Seth!"

"It's nice to hear the sound of your voice again—like a cure from the plague in the Dark Ages. The fever's gone…speak again, don't stop!"

"Where are you? Not in Mexico?"

"Yes, in Mexico. Tijuanna. I've been here for at least an hour already. It's taken me that long to get the right coins to put in this phone box and figure out how to dial your number. So how far is San Diego?"

"Not far. Oh Seth, I'd love to see you but this is *crazy*. What if you get caught?"

"I won't."

"But you don't have any idea how hard it is to sneak over here. The border is crawling with Immigration. They patrol in hoards—all the way to Texas!"

"So I'll get my hands on an Immigration uniform, and pretend I'm patrolling."

"No, come on, you're being dramatic. I've been so nervous thinking about this—worried you'll try something too risky."

"Feels good. Like I'm young again. What's wrong with that?"

"The thought of you locked away in a Mexican Jail!" I shuddered. Then I suddenly got an idea. "Wait. Wait a minute."

"What is it?"

"I think I know of a way to get you in. How about this—I'll drive to Tijuanna, pick you up, and we can cross back over together."

"You sure about that?"

"I think it's pretty safe. I've been to Tijuanna before, and US border people never ask for a passport—not if you're definitely Caucasian. Not if you're a white tourist and it's obvious you've just been shopping."

I paused, thinking it over. I'd done it a few times and the idea seemed sound. "Yes, I can even ask my landlady if she'd come along, for support, because she's quite elderly. She can be my mother. We'd definitely look the part—your typical family bargain hunting in Tijuanna."

"That sounds promising. But what about hiding me in the boot?"

"No—they always check the trunk for over-the-limit cases of liqueur, or drugs…"

"And if they unexpectedly ask to see passports?"

"They won't. Not unless we look suspicious."

"Well, your idea sounds like the best one to me, as long as you can't get into any trouble if they do catch me."

I didn't want to consider the possibility. Though I immediately answered, "Well, if for some reason we have to show our passports, they'd send you to their Admin Office to get your visa checked and stamped for entry. American citizens are exempt from all that, so you just have to look nerdy and keep your mouth shut!"

"All right. When can you get here?"

"Tomorrow morning, as long as my landlady agrees. I'm hoping she doesn't need much notice."

"Shall I call you in a few hours to make sure it's on?—blast—wait a minute while I put some coins in."

"Seth? Are you still there?"

"Yes, but I've now run out of change, so we might be cut off. So, why don't I call you around eight o'clock?"

"Okay. Yes—and can you try to find out the directions to your hotel for me?"

"Easy. Anything else?"

"Well, if you want, you can purchase some of our props. You know, stuff like leather belts, paper flowers, cowboy hats, clay pots, Mexican blankets."

"A bottle or two of Tequila?"

"That's it."

"I might drink some of it while I'm killing time."

"Just don't get too drunk…Seth…you've just given me another idea. Yes, that's it! If you pretend you're really drunk tomorrow—passed out—then they won't be able to ask you any questions!"

"You're brilliant. I'll call you at eight."

"I guess we better hang up."

"Yeah, I guess so."

"I can't wait till tomorrow!"

"Me neither, matey. Bye for now."

❋   ❋   ❋

Mrs. Marlowe, the landlady, had been talked into it. Or rather begged. But nevertheless she'd agreed and I got the day off from work. So far, then, the plan was running smoothly. I fetched my 'mother' promptly at ten o'clock the next morning for the daring smuggle operation. Although I would have preferred to meet Seth alone, an older chaperon would help us look even more inconspicuous.

During the half-hour journey to Tijuanna, I tried in vain to calm my nerves and keep to the speed limit. My landlady, given the explanation that Seth merely wanted to avoid the inconvenience of obtaining an entry stamp, seemed unbelievably naive and cooperative.

Though after a few minutes of mulling it over in my car, she was beginning to have her doubts.

"So this English fellow, you say, is your boyfriend?"

"That's right."

"And you're anxious to see him again, aren't you?"

"Yes I am," I replied, biting my lips.

"I can tell because your arms are shaking," said Mrs. Marlowe, "and all the color has gone out of your face. So how long has it been since you've seen him?"

"Seven months."

"And before that?"

"Seven years."

"Oh my! And you say he's your boyfriend?"

"More than that," I said. "But it's a long story."

"It sounds a little strange to me, but to each his own," Mrs. Marlowe muttered. "But I suppose if he's a news man then he probably doesn't have much time for romance."

"No," I agreed. "And living in different countries doesn't help either."

"And neither of you wants to go where the other is?"

"We haven't made any decisions about that yet."

"I see," said Mrs. Marlowe.

At that moment the freeway narrowed into two lanes—the first sign of the approaching border. Peering at the signs warning that U.S. territory was about to end, Mrs. Marlowe tightened her grip on her handbag. I frowned.

"Oh great," I mumbled. A long ribbon of cars was already waiting to cross into Tijuanna. We'd have to endure another half-hour at least, sitting in that line.

"Would you like to listen to the radio?" I asked.

"Yes, could you put on the news station?"

"Sure."

My mind skirted the noise of the radio, racing in circles around Mrs. Marlowe's simple questions. Why had my answers sounded so feeble? I'd finally see Seth again as a free woman, but even my divorce would not erase the onerous aspect of a transatlantic affair. We'd both still suffer the pains of separation.

Suddenly I remembered Seth's very first question, "Why not go out and get what you really want for yourself? and the whole issue of *not* settling for less was staring me in the face. Yet again. So indeed, why settle for these brief interludes?

Why doesn't one of you go where the other is? in Mrs. Marlowe's words. I repeated them to myself and suddenly it all seemed so easy. What could ever really keep us apart now? Nothing. What really mattered to me, other than my love for Seth? Nothing. What prevented me from moving to England if I wanted to? *Nothing, nothing, nothing!*

The cars ahead began to move; I jerked into gear and squeezed boldly into the faster lane.

Then I gave Mrs. Marlowe a big grin. "It won't be long now."

It would be so easy. After all, nothing on earth was going to keep me from getting Seth across the Mexican border. And what else could be achieved if I relied on my own nerve and inner convictions? Anything I wanted!

Mrs. Marlowe waited in the lobby. I ran down the corridors of the hotel to find Room 127. My whole body felt weak and feverish; the excitement sent my heart pounding harder and faster after every step. Then I stopped abruptly, panting and staring incredulously at the door, which actually said 127. Seth's door...127, yes 127...

I tapped lightly and the door flung open—no time to waste—Seth gazed at me for a second—then his arms found mine...

The door slammed shut as Seth fumbled against the barrier of my clothes. I ripped off my top and bra, leaning on the wall for support. The bed seemed miles away. Impatient to repeat that exquisite sensation of oneness, we found ourselves moaning together on the floor—climaxing within minutes. Again, in unison—and despite the odds.

A half-hour later Mrs. Marlowe found herself wandering in front of the stalls and shops of Tijuanna with none of the protection I'd originally promised. Seth and I, like two young lovebirds—were much too preoccupied to ward off the impolite and often lewd solicitations which bombarded her on every side: crippled beggars huddled against the walls, filthy children pushing paper flower-bunches against her arms, drunkards staggering and blocking her path, sweating men in tattered suits thrusting souvenirs in front of her nose. She managed to stagger the distance of two blocks, stopping and stubbornly tugging at my arm to get my attention.

"I don't see anything I want. I'm ready to go now!" she announced, having bought one packet of tortillas.

"Are you sure?" I asked, eyes still glued on Seth.

"Yes I'm sure."

"All right, I guess it's time to head home."

"I've got some liquor and blankets, a leather belt and a wooden donkey wearing a sombrero," Seth reminded me, "so I guess we have enough to show."

He leaned over and pulled me close, for yet another kiss.

Mrs. Marlowe led the way back to my car, Seth and I still arm in arm, straggling a few yards behind. Luckily the car sat just as we'd left it; thanking the parking attendant, I tipped him well. Seth threw his purchases next to him in the back seat, and, unable to procrastinate any longer, we headed for the border.

The customs drive-thru area was packed with cars—a traffic jam which provided one last opportunity for the Mexicans to sell their wares. Mrs. Marlowe rolled up her window.

"They *never* give up, do they?" she wailed.

"It's getting near our turn," I nervously announced.

"Don't worry," muttered Seth, rustling into a brown paper bag to retrieve an opened bottle of Tequila. "I'll just take a shot to fortify myself."

"Remember, don't say anything unless the guy asks you to. And if he does, use your best American accent."

"Yeah, if I'm your brother, I better sound like you," Seth drawled.

I laughed. Nervously. "Boy, that's pretty good! But really, Seth, just pretend you're passed out."

"No problem," drooled Seth.

"Okay, get ready, I'm moving up fast!"

I might as well have been hiding a kilo of cocaine in my car, the way my body tensed and nerves tingled. I cursed myself for choosing the right lane, having discovered too late that a harmless-looking female officer was checking the left lane. No such luck in my lane, of course: a rugged, scowling, monster of a male (the epitome of every American TV tough-guy cop) loomed closer and closer, fists clenching his clipboard as if flexing for his next arrest. As I stopped the car and lowered my window, I noticed my own frigid-eyed cold terror mirrored in his sunglasses.

"So how long have you been in Mexico?"

"Just for the day—shopping in Tijuanna."

"And you are all American?"

"Yes."

"And who are the other passengers?"

"My mother and my brother."

The officer turned to Mrs. Marlowe. "And what are you declaring?"

"We've got two bottles of Vodka, two bottles of Tequila, three blankets, and a wooden statue," rattled Mrs. Marlowe. "As you can see here in the back seat."

"Do you want to check the trunk?" I suggested, hoping to move the officer's attention away from the back seat. Although Seth lay quite motionless, a magnificent specimen of a man oblivious in sleep.

"Can you wake him up?" the officer asked me. "Everyone in the car must be alert—so they can answer questions, if need be."

"Oh, I'm sorry. I didn't realize and I'm afraid he is awfully drunk," I stammered. "I don't know if he'll wake up, in that condition…"

The officer looked at me as if I didn't quite fit the picture. Not of a woman simply wishing to avoid the unpleasant task of waking a drunk. I knew we were in trouble now—by the way his head cocked to one side, and he persisted to stare, with growing interest, at Seth's impassive face. Or perhaps he was merely listening to the strain of noisy grunts coming from Seth's mouth, which hardly passed as snores.

"Wake him up." The officer moved aside so I could open my door and get out of the car.

I complied. Without another word I stood next to the officer and leaned over to shake Seth to his senses in the back seat. For a few seconds I silently prayed, and just as I placed my hand on his shoulder, I noticed the Tequila bottle sitting on his lap.

The bottle was half-empty!

"Seth, bro! Wake up!"

Seth grunted, then suddenly opened his eyes. Before I had time to wonder what might happen next, Seth lunged forward. With a terrified look he pushed me aside and vomited, the lumpy green spew landing in a disgusting pool in front of the officer's shiny black boots.

Fortunately the man had managed to jump out of range in the nick of time. "All right—THAT'S IT! Get him out of here!"

I complied. Jumping back into the car, with Seth's retching head still hanging in misery out the window, we sped across the border toward the freeway.

CHAPTER 20

The Pie Contest

Seth's next camera assignment was in Paris. He had to be there in eight days. I was terribly disappointed when I found out, but nevertheless we had to be grateful for every minute of time we did have together. Besides, the inevitable moment of doom—yet another goodbye—would be tempered by a lifetime of hope. The first step was explaining my newly conceived plan to Seth.

We were sitting on the couch in my apartment, waiting for our pizza to be delivered—when I told him.

"Move to England? Are you serious?" Seth asked.

"Yes, I'm dead serious," I answered. "I've always loved England, so why not? There's nothing really keeping me here. I only moved to San Diego because I had to get away from Paul—and International Marine had the job connection."

"So what about your job?"

"I'm not doing quite the same thing here. I wouldn't mind leaving. The West Coast charter business is basically brokering for small daysailers and catamarans. Pretty boring, really. All right as a temporary thing—but that's all."

"And you think you can be a charter broker in England?"

"Sure, why not? There are lots of Marinas and Yacht Rentals in England too."

"Your dad won't be very pleased."

"I don't care. It's my life. Anyway, he's happily doing his thing in the Philippines. He doesn't even know about my divorce—yet."

"But you haven't been in England long enough to really know what it's like. What if you gave up everything here, only to find out life in the UK isn't for you? Maybe you're being too hasty, acting on a misguided whim."

"No—this isn't a whim. It's a special feeling that I've always had about Britain. And why can't I go live there if I want to?"

"Lauren, you know I'd love it. It's not that I haven't wished—but I don't know—it also worries me when I think of the risks involved. If it didn't work out like you imagined, the whole thing could end up a disaster."

"Of course the main reason I want to do it is because you're there," I confessed. "But that's not the only reason. After I went to London and saw you again, I've felt so—" I hesitated, searching for the right words. "—So different. I mean, excited. I've got all this energy bottled up inside. I want to grow even more, to do things, to act."

Seth smiled. "Good."

"I'm following my instincts. And those instincts are telling me right now, to head for England."

Seth's smile still failed to disguise a slight flicker of misgiving. I could see it swirling around the edges of his eyes as well: a dark spot, a lingering trepidation. But why?

"Don't you *want* me to come to England?" I asked, beginning to feel awkward about my assumptions.

"Of course I do! Christ, I'm in love with you. Maybe too much. Maybe it bothers me that you're the one making all the sacrifices," Seth explained. "And for what? If it's for me, well, how do you really know if I'm worth it?"

"Jesus!"

"I'm just trying to warn you. As a fellow romantic, you know…"

"I know! But aren't you curious, Seth? To find out what love requited feels like? Or would you rather stay bitter and defensive—over something that happened over seven years ago?" I blushed. I hadn't meant to bring up that subject again.

"I don't think you've finished yet," muttered Seth. "By all means, go on."

But I shook my head. I could feel my heart pounding like mad. I knew what that meant. I was getting too deep.

Seth reached for my hand. He leaned over, touching his face to mine. The warm tingle of his cheek caressing my ear made me sigh.

"Love addict," Seth whispered. "Tell me."

"Let's have some whiskey," I answered. "Then I'll tell you."

I got up to get the bottle, as well as two glasses and two chairs to sit out on the little balcony. Joining me outside, Seth poured the whiskey and we sipped it in between kisses; watching the sun disappear over the tops of the palm trees just visible over the roofs beyond. Beyond that, an orange horizon disappeared into a faint blue belt of ocean.

"Nice sunset," I muttered. "Isn't it? Tomorrow we'll watch it from the beach. I do like San Diego, but it's awfully crowded and built up."

"Not quite the same as sunset in Ridware, Staffordshire," mumbled Seth.

"An entirely different feeling."

"And I miss that feeling."

"But this *is* a nice spot," Seth added, reaching for more whiskey. "Yet I guess we'll have to admit, no beach here is quite like a beach you'd find..." he grinned defiantly back, "...in Cornwall."

"That's what I'm trying to tell you!" I exclaimed. "I feel like I'd be settling for less, if I *didn't* risk it. Risk leaving my home and moving to England, that is."

I paused, collecting my thoughts. Then I took a deep breath. "You see, I have this theory now. I call it the challenge of the Pie Contest. It's a kind of analogy for human beings shutting themselves off from expressing love."

Seth raised his glass—assurance he was still listening. "You English majors like your analogies, don't you?"

"That's right. And I've been thinking about it all day. It's like a Pie Contest."

"A pie contest?"

"Well, you have your maps and sharp stones—I have my pie contest," I replied. "It's part of the same thing, you know? Because in choosing love we are also choosing pain. So it goes, we would sometimes rather accept *any* other kind of pain, because we think it won't hurt as much. And just like a Pie-Eating Contest, we have different types of contestants."

"I'd personally rather have some pizza..."

"Stop joking and let me finish. Where was I? Contestants. Right—first, you—and every contestant—must face the dilemma of having to bite off more than you can chew. And once you go as far as the first gobble, all that sweet gooey fruit goes down your throat—smack into your stomach—and you know you'll feel sick and in pain afterwards. So if you choose to take the first bite, and enter the contest, it's hard to back out. You don't want to look like a fool to the audience, and there'll no guarantee after all of it—that you'll even come close to winning."

"I'll agree to that," said Seth.

"Or, you might be the super-cautious contestant who won't even consider entering the Pie Contest in the first place. Then again, you might be the contestant who ventures one or two mouthfuls and then spits it all out—the kind who quits half-way, before having to face indigestion and failure."

"And what happens if you choose to enter and go all the way?" Seth was getting impatient for the answer.

"If you see yourself as basically against the odds—and you are—then the pain will be all you're left with when it's over. Besides, you might even question the person who did win—as to whether or not the prize was worth it."

I paused, waiting for Seth to say something. Did he get the point about the last contestant?

"So you think going all the way is the only admirable course of action?" he asked. "That ironically—we envy the fools who have the courage to try, and are disdainful towards those who think they are keeping face by staying out?"

"You got it," I said. "Now do you see why our story is so fantastic? Here I am, given one more opportunity to enter the Pie Contest. And it's the same Pie that confronted me all those years ago when I came to Lichfield and met you! But this time I've learned something new—for *you* aren't really the prize. You're the by-product: the actual prize is the *feeling* involved, the ability to open up your heart. All the way."

"I'm not the prize?"

"Isn't that what's bothering you? No, you're not the prize. Now let me finish!"

"Go on."

"Well…seven years ago, facing the same odds, I gave myself all sorts of excuses for not entering the Contest. So, many things have happened since then. I sampled all the other kinds of pain instead."

"Like what?"

"The pain of settling for less, pretending the 'real' me doesn't exist," I said. "Or living a life full of lame excuses. That kind of suffering is actually more painful—in the end—than the gorging of pies. I had to find out why, for myself. It's true. All those other substitute-pains are a dead kind of pain. They're lifeless—utterly insincere and untrue to really living. Of course I could fall back on the old excuse that I'll never win. I could end up in England sitting with a bloated stomach full of nausea, wondering why I had been so foolish to have eaten all those pies."

"You've made your point," Seth interrupted. "And I suppose I'm the poor sod who's too cautious to give it a go?"

"Maybe you dived in head-first the first time and forgot to collect your booby prize."

"Probably," he muttered, leaning over to grab me. "Tortured to distraction by the most fantastic pair of boobies known to man…"

Chuckling to himself, he forgot all about the pizza. And the analogy quickly melted under a barrage of backlog kisses, just as sweet and luscious.

As any banana cream pie.

❦   ❦   ❦

That dreadful goodbye, now imminent in the air as we sat together at the airport, was at least offset by a definite means to reunite. No full stop. Instead, I stubbornly insisted I'd move to England as soon as possible.

"I will find a way," I kept telling Seth. Though the tears still stung. "I'm not going to endure this ever again."

"If only there was something I could do to help," he groaned, squeezing my hand and gazing at me—nevertheless—as if it would be for the last time.

"In the meanwhile, I'll write and try not to call too often," I whispered, my voice cracking. "Because we'll go broke calling each other all the time. I'll be thinking of you constantly…I'll probably pick up the phone every day, start to dial, then hang up—because it's crazy—too expensive just to say hello."

"Just do it!" Seth insisted.

"I couldn't."

"Wait…yes you can, because what you just said just gave me an idea. When you feel like saying hello, go ahead and dial—but let it ring just once and hang up. Then repeat the one ring again. If I'm home, I'll know it's you and I'll ring once back. That way we can talk to each other without paying for the call."

"That's a good idea. We can use it like a code, whenever we're missing each other."

"And you can save your money," Seth added with a grin, "toward that one-way plane ticket to England."

"I won't let go," I promised.

"Good."

"You better catch that plane, then."

"Bye, matey."

"Bye for now."

"See ya…"

Despite the growing optimism, I watched Seth walk out of sight as if I'd never see the likes of him again. It felt as if I'd just been thrown in the middle of another freezing gale. While Seth, turning back for a final glimpse, witnessed what was left: a scarecrow.

Rooted to the spot, my rigid arms—suspended like sticks and furiously wafting in the air—imitated a cheerful wave.

❀   ❀   ❀

The months passed. I sent letters and résumés to every Marina in Great Britain, having instantly located the names and addresses in *Reed's Nautical Almanac.* Replies were forthcoming, and several yachting firms surrounding Greater London were anxious to interview me. I flew back to Newport in November to finalize the divorce, promptly cashing in the settlement money to purchase a transatlantic ticket. Then I traveled on to London the following day.

It all seemed so easy; Seth accompanied me on numerous interview sessions scattered within a 120-mile radius of London; British yacht brokers appeared genuinely intrigued and enthusiastic—actually welcoming an American colleague! Even the Charter Company of the highest reputation in London offered me a position.

I flew back to San Diego full of arrogance and reeking of success, hardly able to contain my excitement. Then, suddenly, the bubble burst. Having already booked a one-way fare to London in December and arranged for a mover to ship my belongings overseas—a letter arrived from my new employers.

The letter stated they would, unfortunately and with much regret, be forced to withdraw the offer. After the interview, the appropriate steps were taken to obtain a work permit from the Home Office. The permit was denied. Sadly enough international yachting qualifications are not, after all, specialized enough to warrant permission to hire an American.

Well, so it wasn't going to be quite so easy.

I tried another plan. I paid an immigration lawyer to investigate all possible means of obtaining a work permit. The lawyer concluded that unless I either married a British citizen, or managed to join a U.S. company which had subsidiaries in Britain, my chances of working in Britain legally were virtually exhausted.

So I called a few companies who had subsidiaries in Britain. They offered nothing but discouraging information. Was I willing to work for a bank, or a large manufacturer, and then wait years in line for the few vacancies that became available overseas?

I couldn't wait.

What option was left? Only one.

I would not give up. I called Seth and point blank asked him to marry me. Already anticipating his surprise, I had not anticipated this: he hesitated.

He hesitated. I staggered back against the wall, clutching the phone, astonished and ashamed.

There was a long silence during which the phone buzzed and crackled along its three thousand mile cable, as I clung to the receiver in a state of shock.

"Lauren," Seth implored, "Please understand. It's just seems all wrong. Why should the bloody government dictate when we get married? Please give me a chance to explain."

"What's there to explain?" I stammered. "That you'd rather stay single and see me once or twice every year?"

"But you're suddenly pressuring me with marriage to solve everything," he exclaimed. "Why can't we wait a bit and see what happens?"

I laughed. Bitterly. "Oh, I see, you've loved me for over half a decade, and finally, now that I admit I love you, it's time to back out."

"I do love you—goddamnit Lauren—but why is marriage the only answer?" Seth insisted, equally upset. "And you're jumping to conclusions. That's not fair."

"It sounds to me like cold feet. A lover is a lover but a wife is something else. I thought you trusted our love." I paused, then blurted into the phone, "If you remember, Seth, I've just wrenched myself out of one marriage. True, a marriage can stifle your personal freedom. But I'm positive *our* relationship," I went on, "even in marriage—would never, ever threaten that."

"You see, you are jumping to conclusions," Seth interjected. "I'm not saying we *won't* get married. I just resent the way fascist red tape dictates what we do."

"There isn't any other way," I said flatly. "You'll have to take my word for it, or better yet, contact my lawyer. He'll tell you."

"Don't get mad."

"It seems so simple to me," I replied. "Either you want us to be together in real life or you don't. Your excuse sounds pretty lame. It reminds me of that twinge, as you once called it. The twinge you had with Jenny. Even with me—you're feeling a twinge! There's no use pretending…"

Another horrendous silence.

I couldn't believe what was happening. I felt like a little girl all over again, who'd just discovered there wasn't a Santa Claus.

"Lauren, forget the twinge."

"No. All I'm asking is for you to trust in our love for each other," I pleaded. "Why all of a sudden does it scare you?"

"I'm not sure." Seth's answer.

"So where does that get us?"

"To be honest, I just can't know anything this minute," he muttered.

"I love you," I said, "and the bitter irony of it is, I'll gladly get out of your life the minute I start feeling you don't want me around."

I hung up. Nothing seemed sensible except to let him go. All the arguments on earth wouldn't change what was already doomed to failure by that annoying twinge.

❦   ❦   ❦

The final twist of the unexpected occurred just after Christmas, when I received news of Paul. Apparently he'd been sleeping with his head waitress. The waitress, Wendy, had announced a week ago that she was pregnant by him, and to everyone's surprise Paul insisted she keep the baby. Wendy was living with Paul and spreading the rumor around town that marriage was on the agenda.

I immediately phoned Sandra to verify the story.

"I can't believe it either," said Sandra, "but it's all true. Paul's thrilled by the prospect of being a father. Conveniently for him, he's also got someone to look after the house for him while he's gone."

"Gone where?" I asked.

"Didn't you know? He's starting another Greek restaurant—somewhere in Long Island. He's already there—indefinitely—hiring staff and supervising the renovations! They say he's going to sell his house in Newport and move to Long Island, just before the baby's due."

"Well that news—and promising for me. Maybe it's all right for me to come back…"

"I'm sure it's safe now," Sandra replied. "We all miss you, and I bet you'd get your old job back."

Sandra was right: my old boss at International Marine instantly offered to take me back. He said he'd even provide a place to live—his own estate's gatehouse cottage, which just happened to be vacant. How could I refuse?

Next to England, I'd rather be living in Newport than anywhere else. At least I'd have the distraction of my old job and familiar clients to help me cope with the loneliness.

I wrote Seth a brief note to let him know I'd be moving back to Newport. Our marriage disagreement had caused a serious and stubborn standoff: a stasis of mutual annoyance. Seth had meekly suggested a break, time to think things over. I'd agreed.

A breathing space. No calls, no letters for a while—just the code.

"Fine," I said to him, "but I personally don't understand what any more time will accomplish."

So, for the most part, I spent most of my time and energy on booking a record number of charters that year in Newport.

CHAPTER 21

The Code

Some memories exist like an explosion of light; an exposure transfixed by a magical lens. Such pictures are developed indelibly in your mind—just as if someone branded your thoughts to a piece of film, which (over and over) splices to the moments transfixed. Splicing stops time.

And I know time stops because I can still feel it: silent morning-mist rising to freckled out-stretched arms, warm cow-breath vaporizing in the barn, gravel crunching underfoot and the vat a gushing tide. Seth's ghostly grin still licks the milk-white foam; the laughing tail of a dog wags on; a hand covering mine won't ever let go.

I've waited many years for that look, that picture—to betray itself.

But I suppose Seth will always be sharply focused in my mind, splicing to expose the light, dissolving years into obscurity; transgressing the fading, transitory boundaries of Time; flashing in cruel bursts and taunting me to come back, once again, to Lichfield.

And now, sitting here in the pub, I've been thinking our whole story is a tribute more to pleasure, rather than pain. Perhaps I might admit as much to a taxi driver some day—tossing that coin. Though I could still avoid the subject altogether, speaking with a British accent. Then would we even get to that opening question, "So, love, where are you from?"

The fact is, having started with the train ride in 1979, I found myself in 1990 right back where I started, in Newport, Rhode Island. Still madly in love with Seth.

Back *then* it felt as if I was stuck—trapped—to those memories, to the moments when time stopped. I wanted to move on and change, like the seasons: letting it all go, retreating and hibernating, triumphantly emerging again with the freshness of new splendor. But all the self-reprimand and willful self-preservation in the world wasn't going to get rid of my true stasis. All I really accomplished was a kind of surface-sham existence in pretence of time's passing.

During the winter, I sat in my cottage in Newport, neither snug nor warm. I had the trees outside—they seemed like knowing friends—bare, skinny skeletons with bleak and barren arms, silent and lonely. In twilight, their black branches pierced the orange horizon in network patterns of endurance. Somber, irrevocable, I crept—shivering—through winter.

During the spring, I sat in my cottage with the windows open. The birds sang; the trees outside were a brilliant green, glutted with leaves. Leaves that danced to the ocean breeze in contented nods. But I was stuck in winter, unable to share their joy. I watched the land sprout and bloom at my doorstep, but I couldn't go out. Listless, forlorn, unfertile, I slept—oblivious—through spring.

By summer, I sat in my cottage as if nothing had changed. I survived because I still performed my usual duties: making good money at work, spending some time with my friends. So only the trees outside my window knew how I sat inside my cottage, simply *waiting*. And feeling like time had stopped. Of course I was hoping that Seth might prove—once and for all—that love was a linear journey leading to a definite answer.

For until I knew the answer, my only salvation lay, like a secret drug addiction, within the closed walls of the cottage. My only escape was hiding inside an object. Behind the ring of a bell. A feeling of well being, of hope, of joy. I was an addict and my drug—my crutch—was the Code.

On a good day I might come home from work in the evening and be sitting by the window, reading. The phone would ring, then stop. Jumping up, I'd race to grab the receiver, heart pounding. Wait. Wait. Second ring: stop. Yes! I'd furiously dial and ring once in return, hand wistfully lowering the receiver. And for a few minutes, high as a kite, I'd wallow in bliss.

But this 'high' would always subside, and I'd have to wait for the next fix—retreating back to my gloomy book by the window.

The animated trees of summer, no longer sympathetic, began to taunt through the window: "Is our friend going to sit here in this hide-away all year long, like a hollow-headed scarecrow propped up against a telephone?"

No, I couldn't keep it up. I was even beginning to hate having the Code. I resented his 'wait, everything will work out' method of keeping me hooked. How many more wasted months must pass? And as soon as I was almost convinced he'd never decide—he'd ring the code—just in the nick of time, to keep me going...nowhere.

Inevitably I began to see the Code as something evil. After all, it wasn't healthy. It became more like a coward's substitute for a life together that would never really happen.

It had to end in autumn, when the leaves outside wilted into dry, broken flakes and the charter boats had all gone south. Shaking like a twig in a chilly wind, I vowed to give up the Code: I promised myself I'd be cured. Though I still had to prove it.

As the bell clinks, so the fool thinks, and the phone rang. Once. It rang once. I listened: so long without a fix! And now it was ringing. Having vowed, I began to sob. It rang again, once, twice, five times. It rang as if it just didn't believe I wasn't at home.

All those rings! I wavered; guilt weakened my resolve. How could I ever intentionally hurt Seth again?

I held out for two hours. But I was certain it was Seth.

So? said a little voice. *If he has something to say, he'll ring again.*

But this was different. It wasn't the Code, I kept thinking.

No?

Maybe not!

And then I just couldn't stand it. I had to find out. I dialed once, then again: no answer. But wasn't it five o'clock in the morning his time by now? He was probably asleep; of course, that could be why he didn't answer. So I dialed again, and this time I broke the code, letting it ring, and ring, until it seemed like a hundred rings before I finally hung up.

My mind raced, my body grew rigid with fear. He was either not at home—sleeping with another woman—or he had another woman there in bed with him so he couldn't answer the phone. How could he be somewhere else at this telltale hour, when I was sure he'd rung just a few hours earlier?

Suddenly I knew; I was certain Seth just couldn't love me the way I loved him. It had all been a terrible waste: Lauren's Law.

Lauren's Law! Suddenly that dreaded fear exploded in my brain, blasting apart my psyche and scattering it across the room in fragmented hell-bound moans of chaos and despair.

Blackness. Nothingness. I screamed.

Pacing the room, sobbing, begging and pleading with the phone to answer, dialing, dialing, ringing to the stabbing silence of no answer, sinking lower and faster into the burning void, praying and groveling to be saved.

He wasn't going to answer. Not now, not ever.

The anguish was excruciating. My umbilical cord—my link to Life—was severed. Crashing down, down, into the blackness, I realized everything I'd said about the Pie Contest was a lie. I couldn't exist without Seth.

Yet when dawn slowly filtered through the faded hues still clinging to the trees, I sat on the couch—ravished and beaten, but intact.

And I was amazed. Time no longer stopped.

What had happened? I could only remember crying all through the night. And through such anguish, I'd experienced the reality of my fear. I faced the fact of Seth's death, as it were. He was no longer 'there' for me.

And yet I didn't lose my mind.

I didn't, after all, self-destruct. The night ended and the dawn arrived; that dreadful anxiety—once unleashed—had simply consumed itself, culminating into a strange and peaceful calm.

Then I understood. If memories in love bring light, then fears are an explosion of darkness; an exposure threatened by a diabolical lens—a picture *undeveloped* indelibly to your soul. Just as if someone condemned your heart to fear death: the moment when All Time ends.

Sitting on the couch, I felt surprisingly clear-headed. *This* is what survives, I was thinking. Then it hit me. When time ends, the original picture disappears; but the vision-maker, the camera, would continue on. Yes! A specter of love, or fear, must travel *with* Time—the kind of Time that doesn't stop—the molting, changing cycles of Life's time: endings, but not death.

Would he ever code again? It didn't matter. I'd out-lived my fear; I'd broken the code. I already knew that my love would go on—with or without him.

🍁   🍁   🍁

The following Saturday I picked up the phone and dialed a local number.

"Hello Sandra, it's Lauren."

"Lauren? Well how are you? This is a surprise."

"I know, and I'm sorry I've been such a stick-in-the mud this summer. But I'm feeling adventurous again—what about tonight? Are you going out?"

"Is the Pope Catholic? Of course I am! Actually though, I promised Carl I'd go to that new club on the waterfront where his band's playing tonight."

"That's all right. If there's live music, I'd love to join you."

"I'll pick you up around nine. Well, this should be fun. I'm so glad you called—it's been ages. How are you, anyway? Is everything all right?"

"I'm fine," I replied. "I should be feeling really miserable but actually I'm feeling fine! See you around nine then?"

"You got it," said Sandra.

CHAPTER 22

The Return

The irony of it.

Finally crack the code and by then it hardly matters. The process takes years; the final battle is won regardless; the war is suddenly over.

Or, as they say, a watched pot never boils. And I'd simply stopped watching. Or getting back to my favorite: as the fool thinks, so the bell clinks. I guess I simply stopped listening.

So I'd been out most evenings. I wasn't aware of how many times the phone rang once—or not at all. But my triumph was short-lived because strangely enough Seth felt compelled to ring me at work.

"International Marine. Lauren speaking."

"Hello Lauren, it's me."

"Oh, hi Seth. This is a nice surprise."

"Is it? I can tell already by the sound of your voice—you know why I've called."

"Do I?"

"Well, it's been over three weeks. You haven't answered the code. I was really worried."

"I haven't been home much."

"You've been going out a lot then?"

"Yes!"

"Are you seeing someone?"

"Oh Seth, let's cut this out! How can you ask me such irrelevant questions?"

"I deserve it, I know. The least you can do is be honest and tell me."

"If I was going out with a guy—even sleeping with him—what does it matter?" I answered. "You know I'll always love you best. I'm just getting on with
my life now—I'm not waiting around while you decide what you want to do
with yours."

"I'm sure now. I want you to marry me!"

"Do you?"

"Well, yes. Yes I do."

"I'm hearing you say that—like a defeated warrior. One who failed to slay a
certain twinge."

"Fuck the twinge. I don't understand it any more than you do!" Seth was
adamant. "I've been miserable—I want to marry you."

"No, wait a minute. Seth, I'm sorry. I can't do it like this."

"Great…I'm finally asking and you still aren't satisfied."

"But Seth, you've got to believe! Isn't that what's really bothering you? Isn't
your twinge this little niggling doubt, that our love won't last once we're finally
together?"

It doesn't matter."

"Yes it does," I insisted. "You've got to *believe*. But you don't really believe,
do you? You'd rather not risk putting our love to the test—just in case."

"And if you're right?"

"Then *nothing* on earth—not me, not you, not fate—will change what happens. Not if you've already subconsciously made up your mind not to believe
or even go as far as putting it to the test."

"Okay Lauren, but tell me—what makes *you* so sure?"

I hesitated for a minute, wondering what did make me so sure. But deep
down, I knew that most of Seth's misgivings were about me. Yes me, moving to
another country and giving up everything to live with him, cold turkey. He was
thinking of me. *My happiness.* Because if it didn't work out, he didn't have as
much to lose.

"Seth, haven't you always tried to tell me how some things endure?"

"Yes…"

"Remember that first sunset? Our kiss by the River Blythe? Sandymouth?
Remember the pitcher of milk? But that's all we've got to go on—just hints.
We'll never get anything more. Yet if you see these hints, feel them, and dare to
believe them—you have it!"

"You sound so different," he replied. "It's not what you're saying, but the
way you're saying it. Like the pressure's lifted. Has something happened?"

"Sort of," I answered.

"Maybe you should come over here—we'll go back to our river and church…"

"When?"

"Now! Or as soon as you can."

"Actually it's not a bad idea," I muttered. "Right back to where it all started."

❦   ❦   ❦

The journey ended in the darkness of night, but we didn't wait. We were too impatient to get down to the river. The winter wind was blowing fiercely; the trees stood adamantly rigid, trailing in a chiseled line the faint boundaries of earth and sky. We could see the way, for the path was illuminated by the milky sheen of moonlight—bathing the landscape in pliable shadows and lucent space.

The fields seemed to know: drawing in deep breaths of silent wisdom, listening after us.

"I've applied for a job with BBC at Pebble Mill, in Birmingham," Seth confessed. "If I get it…" he smiled and reached for my hand, as we scrambled furtively down the path.

I said nothing, but wondered at the possibilities: switching from sea to canal, from sailing yachts to narrow boats; dislodging rocks and stones which echoed noisily as I tumbled underfoot.

The hoot of an owl could be heard, and the rustle of sheep turning to move away as we neared the river. Then the path opened out, spilling onto the expanse of open pasture and winding ribbon of water. Breathless and transfixed, Seth and I found ourselves back, hand in hand, at the edge of the River Blythe.

The moonlight splashed twinkling currents of light across the surface; the reeds standing like a silent army reached at the banks, spikes and swords pointing up, ready to bridge the gap or disappear into the depths the current's caressing thrust.

As always.

Seth squeezed my hand, pulling me toward a clearing in the distance, where the cropped grass beckoned and the river flowed and gurgled past a bend of dense, unknown forms. Our laughter was whisked away into non-entity by the wind. Why were we both suddenly laughing? I thought. Was it because a place like this, so incredibly simple, still exists?

We reached the clearing, surrounded by a column of trees; the wind instantly subsided. The next moment seemed hushed—unexpected. Seth turned to face me, his eyes filled with vibrant, moon-wolf lust. For a few seconds he stood rigid and indomitable in the dark, with the look of a Roman about to cross the Rhine. Our eyes interlocked; fused in mutual homage.

Was it the moon's reflection, or did I see something crossing his face? I suddenly realized what it was: *he believed.*

I nodded, heart racing. Yes, this was it: the timeless caress of an ancient river; holding the damp, mysterious glow in the palm of Seth's hand. The warmth of feeling, of thirsty lips, of moist cheeks brushing mine...

Seth succumbed. I was only vaguely aware of the wet grass, mud and sand seeping into my hair and limbs; my jeans falling away and the cold air wafting between our naked bodies as we made ourselves one. Mad with haste, writhing in fury, our lust—like two spiraling demons envying God—dissolved in the night.

Even so...rising higher and higher like the river, until our relentless motion broke loose in a cascading flow of swirling jets, diminishing—gradually—toward a smooth fluid journey; creeping gently through unseen crevices in the clay and rock.

I opened my eyes. How long had we been lying there? I hadn't a clue.

"Lauren," Seth whispered. "I'll always be hungry, I'll always want to roam."

"I know."

Still lying on top of me, he said nothing more. Finally the cold permeated our skin, and reluctantly we rose and left our place in the clearing.

"Look," Seth exclaimed, stopping in his tracks. "We left a sign."

He pointed at two large holes gouged in the mud by his hiking boots.

I blushed. The indentations were rather disconcerting in size and deepness—but they told a simple tale.

I knew the fields would still be listening when we returned; the moon would still be shining; the river still flowing; the graves at St. Michaels sitting on the hill, keeping watch. I hugged Seth, knowing our paths had merged: we had really just begun.

"If that's a sign," I said, "Tell me, cousin. What does it say?"

Seth turned, cupped his hands in front of his mouth and shouted out the answer so all the Midlands might hear: "Long live the Riverfolk!" A yell so loud it disturbed the sheep, who baahed in instant chorus.

Long live the Riverfolk. While the rolling, wind-swept clouds of Ridware seemed to carry his voice high across the hills, past Wales and over the Atlantic...

To every wayward shore.

❦   ❦   ❦

Last call.

Nope, I won't have another. Besides, I'm thinking, two pints is enough. Chester and Elizabeth might worry if I take too long. Best just to ring for a cab.

There's no reason not to leave the story with a happy ending. What fool chooses to dwell on a loved-one's demise? Latch on to a lightning bolt and the ride may be bliss, but all too short. Perhaps I suspected something would happen all along.

Lauren's Law will always have its day. Seth's bones may turn to worms and dust, but I'm living proof that the case for love isn't made up. The jury may be hung, but Seth survives.

He died on his motorcycle, just two months after I'd returned to Newport. We'd made plans to marry in April as soon as the Home Office approved the application. Now working for the BBC at Pebble Mill, he was home—right in Lichfield—looking for the perfect place out in the country for us to live. And there sat his bike, itching to be used again. But on one particular Saturday morning a woman pulled out in front, so fast he had no time to stop. She didn't see him coming, of course.

And I have only one thing to say.

Fuck Lauren's Law.

I still come to Lichfield every year, in September, to visit his grave. And probably one day, with hair as white as chalk, I'll discover a young lady sitting on a bench that's always been my spot, with a nice view of the spires on my Cathedral.

"Excuse me," I'll mutter, pointing my trusty cane. "Would you awfully mind?

Epilogue

The Dream

You'd think—at night—I'd dream about Seth, but the strange thing is, I often dream about Henry. It's a recurring dream and we both always end up on Hunger Hill. It's one of those dreams where you actually know you're dreaming while you're having it—but that's all right. In dreams, everything makes sense.

....It always begins in Aunt Bea's parlor. I'm sitting with Henry.

"Please listen, Uncle Henry," I keep saying in the dream, "Because I need to know if you've ever heard Seth's story of Hunger Hill."

It's a struggle to remember all the details, even though I've thought about it over and over—that whole made-up tale of Seth's about the Celtic sacrifice on Hunger Hill. After all, I never did get an answer as to why the young girl was left all alone to face the Romans.

I get to the end: "This Celtic girl said nobody loved her, so she might as well carry on," I explain to Henry.

Henry doesn't look impressed. He frowns and pretends he doesn't know what I'm talking about. But he obviously knows—I can tell by the twinkle in his eye.

"So come on, what's the point?" I moan. "Seth must have meant something by it."

"It's so simple!" Henry suddenly exclaims, losing his patience and bending closer to whisper in my ear. "Don't you know who she is? That poor girl who thought nobody loved her enough to save her from the Romans?"

"She isn't supposed to be me, is she?"

Henry slowly raises his finger. "Awwhhgg!"

I laugh, for Henry talks in the dream. He's as lucid as they come. But I'm glad he still chooses not to spoil the moment. He wants *me* to say it.

And I can't wait to give the answer.

"Wait...no....She's not just me...she's all of us!" I exclaim, suddenly figuring it out.

Delighted, Henry gives me a big hug.

"I suppose she never considered the possibility that she was spared *precisely* because she was loved so much," I add. "In fact, loved more than she could ever imagine."

Henry grins.

"Like Seth loves me."

The next minute we both find ourselves sitting on the grass, right there on Hunger Hill. I look over at Henry, who has suddenly turned younger. His hair, a pumpkin orange, is braided in strands and twined with crow feathers. Purple-black freckles cover his face. And his eyes, an iridescent silver-green, scan the sky like a hawk.

I grin. Henry has turned into a Celtic king.

Gazing at me with his preying eyes, he raises a claw-like finger. "Awwwggh! Do you wish I had told you?"

"You could have said something to me back then," I insist. "I knew you wanted to."

"I could have," Henry replies. "But at that age, you youngsters *never listen*."

0-595-29881-8